WE ARE THE CRISIS

A NOVEL

CADWELL TURNBULL

BLACK STONE PUBLISHING

Printed in the United States of America

First edition: 2023
ISBN 978-1-9826-0375-5
Fiction / Fantasy / General

Version 1

Blackstone Publishing
31 Mistletoe Rd.
Ashland, OR 97520

www.BlackstonePublishing.com

PACK MAGIC

RIDLEY GIBSON, LAINA CALVARY, AND REBECCA VÁZQUEZ
OUTSIDE BOSTON

MARCH 13, 2026
TWO YEARS AND FOUR MONTHS
AFTER THE BOSTON MASSACRE

Start with the wolves.

They leave the city at midnight, under the cover of darkness. Sleep is not a thing they worry about; they can ride their wolves until the morning, borrow energy from their strange well of magic. What they are worried about is the eyes on them, particularly the ones they can't see—the ones in the shadows, looking on at their break in routine. If it were before, they might have thought a straight, predictable life would protect them. But they know that's not true, not anymore. Whether they decide to act or not, the world will eat them anyway.

They wait until they're hours outside the city before they stop. Rebecca and Laina go inside to peruse the shelves of the small gas station convenience store. Ridley stands outside, looking at the highway, the cars speeding by as streaking lights. His senses are keener now. He can hear not just the cars but also the scurrying of small creatures in the surrounding woods. The scent of gasoline fills Ridley's nose, someone fueling up at one of the service stations. A van is parked in one of the parking spaces a few feet from where Ridley is standing.

The night sky is a comforting black. Ridley thinks comforting because all the light pollution keeps the darker places far off in the inky shadows of the surrounding forest. But Ridley can also see better in the dark now. He has become one of the creatures at home in the liminal space between comforting black and true darkness. The things that can eat him are deeper in that true dark.

The van's driver-side door opens, and someone drops down to the curb. Ridley can only hear this person. He can't see them, not yet. And only now does he realize the van's windshield is tinted so black he cannot see inside.

The person comes around the van and walks sweetly up to Ridley.

"You got a lighter?"

The person's voice is smooth and high—a silky treble that shudders just a bit at its edges.

Ridley shakes his head.

"I figured since you were standing here . . . How old are you?"

Ridley gives his age.

"A young person like you probably doesn't smoke, right? You probably eat edibles? Or you vape. Vaping isn't smoking—not that it won't kill you just the same, right?" The person extends a hand. "I'm Mason. You probably want my pronouns, right? She/her."

Ridley is alarmed at the way she is using "right" at the end of her sentences without being the least bit concerned whether she is right about what she's saying. Ridley did want her pronouns but still hates the presumption. He is also alarmed by the use of "young person." She looks Ridley's age. All smooth skin and fat in the face that makes Ridley think she's in her thirties at most.

He looks back through the window. Laina is at the cashier, pulling a bag of what has to be junk food off the counter. She has one of those terrible hot dogs in her mouth, and it occurs to Ridley that he wants one as well.

"Your name?" Mason asks again.

He returns to her. "Ridley. He/him."

"Ah," she says. "I'm glad you told me your pronouns. Does your friend in there have a lighter?"

"My wife," Ridley says. "No, she doesn't smoke either."

"Shame," Mason says, with a look that makes the statement completely ambiguous. "Well." She sighs. "Serves me right for not keeping a lighter with me."

Mason's hair is cut short. Large eyes, set in a pale face. She barely blinks, is barely blinking, even as her expressions change.

A sound comes from the back of the van. Ridley thinks it might have been a growl.

Mason smirks. "Looks like the princess is up. Feeding time." She does something with her hand. A salute? Another thing that aggravates Ridley beyond reason. Even her gesture of goodbye feels mocking, the whole conversation a joke at Ridley's expense. The door to the convenience store opens. Laina hands him a hot dog. "I ate mine already," she says, and Ridley knows why she says it. She knew he wanted one even before he did.

Ridley gives her a kiss on the cheek in gratitude.

"Who was that?" Laina asks.

Ridley shrugs. "Someone asking for a lighter."

Laina laughs. "Sounds like something from an old movie."

She's right. Sort of. Ridley never gets asked this by strangers. Not for a long time. But when he was younger, he did hang out with the sort of people who asked for lighters. Sometimes he forgets how different their experiences were, his and Laina's. He expects her to have been around people who asked for things like lighters, who stood outside bars or clubs getting high before going in. But he knows why he might think that. Because she grew up in a rough neighborhood and he grew up well-off in a nice neighborhood, everyone bored out of their mind. He feels a shock of shame for stereotyping her, and then he considers his history and how much of his experience was in rebellion to his safe, sheltered upbringing. Ridley didn't want to admit how much of his experience was to prove that he could exist within another context—a context that wasn't his life as a "spoiled rich kid." Not how he saw himself but how he thought others might see him. Laina had better reasons to rebel from her own circumstances: rebellion out of necessity.

Rebecca finally comes out of the convenience store, and they all squeeze back into their little Honda Fit.

Ridley finishes his hot dog before pulling out of the parking spot. He looks at the van again as he turns toward the road. It hasn't moved. He keeps checking the rearview as the gas station and tinted van shrink into the distance.

Rebecca and Laina notice Ridley's behavior, but neither remarks on it. They both assume this response, this habitual checking, is a fear response—a reasonable one since they are acting outside their normal pattern. They've been good little monsters for *years*, the only evidence of their new agenda being the footage of Lincoln's death, rereleased and now openly accepted among most people as real. That and the conference room on the bottom floor of Anarres Books, locked when they're not in it, the place where they keep the evidence of their ongoing attempts to understand this new and strange world.

After another hour on the freeway, Ridley stops looking in the rearview mirror, and they all feel a collective relief, a release of tension. For now, they have evaded their own fear, and there is no indication they should be afraid.

Ridley is playing Carly Rae Jepsen loud and singing along. Rebecca doesn't particularly like Jepsen, but constant exposure has awakened in her a Stockholm-like joy when she hears the eighties-inspired bubble-gum poppiness that is the singer's signature vibe.

Laina is moving her head to the music as well. Rebecca can see them both in the front seat, and briefly she feels like the child again, a third party intruding on a relationship long established. Happily, Jepsen is soon replaced with a Rihanna song—one of Rebecca's contributions. Rebecca is singing along now too, but this is not unexpected. Rihanna unites everyone—a favorite of all four of us.

At 3:00 a.m., they switch, and Laina drives for three hours. Rebecca falls asleep, and Laina puts on a more chill playlist: instrumentals and folk music. She is wide awake.

Laina spares a glance at Ridley. He is looking out the side window. His posture indicates that he is awake as well.

"What are you thinking about?" she asks.

"I'm just wondering how many monsters are out there."

Laina thinks on it. They've been wondering that for a while, and she suspects there's a thought under that thought.

There is.

"In this scenario, are you worried about the monsters, or the humans?" Again, that purely reductive distinction. They all three are monsters *and* humans.

"Both," Ridley says. "But I'm wondering if it might be useful for both sides to know—really *know*—how many. Or would that just lead to one or the other side being wiped out faster?"

"The humans will remain," Laina says. "I know, at the very least, that there are not enough of us."

"No, not enough of us at all."

That's the trick, Laina thinks. She imagines the history of monsters as a type of ongoing guerrilla warfare. There's an advantage in the haziness of the shadow world. It could be hundreds of monsters, or thousands, or millions. A useful degree of uncertainty. And now, with the world as it is, they need that murkiness even more.

A few years ago, Laina wouldn't have considered herself a part of the murk. But her brother was, and now she is too.

None of this gets to the heart of Ridley's questioning. The true heart is a sort of infinite regression. How many monsters? Where did they come from? The world of monsters exists beneath the human world. What is the world beneath that? Or the world above? The heart of the question is the fear of infinite unknowns, descending forever, turtles all the way down. Places to hide and places hidden. The universe has legs.

It is reminiscent of Laina's black sea, the thing she considered when Lincoln's death filled her with the nihilism of despair. Now, years later, Ridley is considering a near sister to that idea. It is the existential question haunting the whole world: Can anything be trusted ever again?

After another couple of hours, sunlight spills into the window of their little car. Laina is beginning to feel groggy, so they stop, and Rebecca completes the journey. She doesn't like driving, but she will do it now since there is only a few hours' worth to go. They make the turn down the dirt road at 10:30 a.m. Rebecca has never been to this part of Pennsylvania. Once, in college, she went to a conference in Pittsburgh, but that was a city. This is the backwoods of Pittsburgh. Sure, she grew up in a sort of backwoods, but Rebecca doesn't trust other people's.

They pull up to the house and are greeted by dogs' frantic barking. A woman in her nightgown comes out on the porch.

"You're here," she says, a just-woke-up rasp to her voice. "Well, come on in," she says and walks back inside, leaving the screen door open. The barking dogs stare at them until a whistle from inside the house pulls them away.

When they enter, they can hear the rattle of kibble being poured into dog bowls, then the excited scrape of the bowls being dragged across the kitchen linoleum.

"Have a seat in the parlor there. I'll be right out."

They oblige. Of the three, Rebecca is the most nervous. Laina puts a hand on her knee, gives her a kiss on the cheek to calm her nerves.

The woman—her name is Agatha—comes into the parlor from the kitchen and bends to sit in her comfortable chair. No one chose to sit there. Normally, this decision might come out of a sixth sense that all humans have, an understanding of a new context through dozens of subtle contextual cues. But in this case, the sense is smell. Agatha's scent has accumulated in that chair over many years—a clear marking of preference that the guests' wolf senses can pick up on.

When she sits, she lets out a groan that is all old age and bad knees.

"The dogs will come back out," she says. "But don't you worry. They'll be well behaved now that they've eaten."

They nod together; the pack magic has strengthened between them. There is no leader, no alpha of this pack—only well-established roles among the people and their wolves: a maternal role, a protective one, and a comforter, corresponding with the personality types of these three people.

They've managed introductions by the time the dogs come into the parlor, and Agatha asks if someone would open the door and let them outside. Ridley volunteers. The two German shepherds run out into the yard and immediately find familiar spots to do their business.

"Connor used to clean up the backyard, but now I go out there occasionally and do what I can. Sorry about the smell."

"It's fine," Laina says, although—for her wolf most of all—it isn't.

"Can you tell us what happened?" Ridley asks.

"Well, it is like I already told you on the phone. He packed a bag and left."

"Yes," Rebecca says, jumping in. "But did you notice anything? People hanging around. Did he seem frightened?"

Agatha shakes her head. "You know, if I noticed anything, it was from Connor. But not because he was frightened. No, nothing like that. He would run off sometimes at night, you know, and he'd come back with a strange look in his eyes. The dogs loved him, but they were sometimes afraid of him too." She shakes her head again. "No people hanging around. Just my Connor."

"Agatha," Ridley starts, leaving some space to prepare himself and the others—and Agatha—for what he's about to ask, "do you believe in monsters?"

Agatha laughs—a short, dry laugh that passes quickly through her body. "Well, there's not much use for believing around these parts. People leave me well enough alone, though Connor's parents have been asking me to come live with them. I don't like living in town, you know. All the noises, smells, and people. Good Lord. But I suppose I'll have to take them up on it now that Connor's run off to God knows where. The house is the problem. And my dogs—I don't want to give them up. My kids don't want anything to do with this place. I was going to leave it to Connor, you know. I hope that boy's okay."

Ridley rephrases the question: "Did you ever talk about monsters with Connor?"

"Sure. He mentioned it from time to time. It was strange, you know? He'd just bring it up in the middle of meals. News and some such. I just thought he was interested in that stuff. I entertained him, nodded along as he talked about werewolves." She laughs again, longer this time.

Ridley looks at Laina and Rebecca, and they both look back. It's a quick look, but Agatha notices. An expression of her own, brief but distinct. She's thinking, *They are like him.* She is thinking, *They're not scary at all. Just like my Connor.* But the mask slips back on.

"Well, can you help me find him?" she asks.

"We can try," Ridley says, but even as he says the words, he knows he has no idea where to look.

They had all sat together, planning this out. This trip and this conversation. And in their minds, they imagined that some clue would present itself during the conversation to help them track down another clue, and then another. They had watched crime dramas where this exact thing would happen, and they hoped the reality would produce the same result. Something clear and concrete that would send them down a path to increased revelations. But to just disappear? Here one day and gone the next? Did he run? Was he abducted? But who would abduct a werewolf? Of course, they knew the answer to that, even if they didn't know any names.

Rebecca asks another question. "Did he talk to anyone while he was here? On the phone, I mean?"

"Well, yes, some of his friends from Boston. Might've been you, I imagine."

Rebecca frowns. It might've been. Another dead end.

Laina asks, "Did you see anyone around the property that night? Hear anything?"

"I'm a deep sleeper," Agatha says. A fleeting crease of the brow. "Well, come to think of it . . ."

They lean in.

"The dogs were barking that night, but I didn't get up to see why. They sometimes get to barking if they hear things outside. Deer, foxes, raccoons—you know, that sort of thing."

Their collective deflation is palpable.

"Might need to get those dogs back inside before they get themselves into trouble," she says, looking at Ridley.

He gets up and opens the screen door, and the dogs surge in. They're friendly. One of them comes close and sniffs Ridley's hand. The dog steps back, whining. The other one growls in warning.

"I don't know what's gotten into 'em," Agatha says, appalled. But her eyes tell a different story.

"We should go," Laina says. "Thank you for your hospitality."

Agatha stands. "Tell me if you find something, okay? His parents and I have been worried. It feels like the old days again, when he used to get himself in all sorts of trouble."

Rebecca is the only one who fully understands what she means. All the previous members of her pack were homeless at some point in their lives, by necessity or choice—a self-imposed exile for the guilt and shame they felt over their addictions. Connor and Rebecca were like that. He got his life back together, like all the other members of her pack. Two are dead now. Three disappeared. A surge of grief passes through her.

"We'll do our best to find him," Rebecca says, and she means it, though she has no idea what she'll be able to do. In a normal world, she might stand a better chance. But not in this new world, where people can just disappear without a trace. Where a man made of smoke can just take someone away, or ants can form portals in solid earth.

Agatha watches them leave. On the front porch, Rebecca sniffs the air. She doesn't say anything until they get to the car and shut themselves in.

"He's been hunting for miles in each direction," she says. "No strange scents."

"I didn't pick up anything either," says Laina.

"We head back?" Ridley asks. The question is mostly for Rebecca.

Rebecca weighs it carefully. There is nothing here for them to find. Frustrated, she stomps her feet down hard enough for the sound to reverberate through the car.

No one tries to control Rebecca's anger. Laina and Ridley just sit in the unsteady silence.

Finally, Rebecca says, "We go home."

It'll be at least a nine-hour drive back. And so they point their car toward Boston and begin the journey.

That first hour is quiet, the music low, the tension high.

They all are thinking of different things, but each mind eventually circles back to the same theme. This is the reality now, a half-seen world within an impenetrable fog. There's no control here, no figuring everything out. Dead ends everywhere, at the end of all paths, long or short.

Eventually, Rebecca says, "We need to find more monsters ourselves. That is the only way forward."

"That is dangerous," Ridley says and has always been saying.

"I'm telling you," Rebecca says, "we're not the only ones who are lost. We can't go any further in any direction if we don't have guides—or aren't willing to be ones ourselves."

"How are we going to find them?" Laina this time.

"We put ourselves out there. Call them to us by showing them who we are."

"We'll be dead inside a week," Ridley says.

"We're dead anyway. Eventually. They already know who we are, Ridley."

"There are rules of engagement here," Ridley says. "I'm not opposed to looking for other monsters—"

"You were two seconds ago."

"—*in theory*. But we should do it carefully. We make ourselves a lightning rod, who knows what we'll attract."

"We're getting nowhere. We have no leads and zero options for getting any. I'm tired of sitting on my hands."

Laina is watching them both, helpless. Every once in a while, it gets like this, and she has to be the intermediary. It isn't so bad yet. It might blow over.

It has been years like this for them. Knowing what they know, what they don't know, bottomless. Life continues.

Rebecca has been secretly talking to people online for a while, but what she is saying now goes beyond that. Meeting monsters in the real world. Monsters she doesn't know, from origins she doesn't understand.

They've had a bookstore to run and bills to pay and their own relationship to manage, Rebecca moving in permanently, becoming a pack.

If they were being honest, this step was always on the horizon. Laina knows this. They're at the cliff's edge, and now they must jump.

"Hypothetically, if there is some sort of secret way monsters signal each other, what could it be?" Laina asks Rebecca.

Ridley frowns at the question and says nothing.

"Well, saying you're a monster wouldn't be enough," Rebecca says, getting to the heart of the question. "And . . ." Rebecca trails off.

"What?" Ridley says.

"From what I can tell, there aren't a lot of monsters like us. I keep getting the sense that . . ." Rebecca finally says what she has been thinking for a long time, what she has been reluctant to admit to herself. "We're accidents."

Silence.

Rebecca continues. "I think whatever network there is for establishing connections across monster communities requires vouching from within the network. We have no one to vouch for us."

"So how do we attract them without sacrificing whatever anonymity we still have?" Ridley asks.

"The monster solidarity movement is likely filled with monsters," Rebecca says. "We have to plug into it."

They all shudder, Rebecca included.

"It is time," Rebecca says.

"Where do we start?" Laina asks.

"The cooperative network," Rebecca answers. "Two things have been happening lately: an upsurge in monster solidarity and more co-ops. I can't imagine it's a coincidence."

Ridley can feel Rebecca's attention on him. He doesn't acknowledge it.

As the sun is setting, they stop for the second time to get gas. Again, Ridley is outside, this time at the pump as Rebecca and Laina go inside for more snacks. There is a palpable difference in everyone's demeanor. What was once a mix of apprehension and excitement is now dejection and melancholy.

Every part of this has been different from what they expected. That early resolve in the hospital room has given way, over many years, to a collision with a difficult reality. But what did they expect—that creatures who were smart enough to remain hidden for thousands of years would somehow be easy to find?

According to Rebecca, there had been monsters at the march. A fox shifter and a snake shifter, at the very least. A few witches. Where did they come from?

There's the snap of the gas pump shutting off. Ridley pulls out the nozzle, places it back on its hook, and that's when he sees the van again, idling in the parking lot, the engine still running. Ridley is slow to move, as if any strong response will make the van more real than it already is. He considers the possibilities. They saw the van on the way to Agatha's. Is it possible it was on its way to a similar location, and they just happened to catch each other on their way back to the city?

Ridley tries to look through the back windows, but they're just as dark as the windshield.

Rebecca and Laina come out of the gas station, and suddenly a woman is there. She approaches quickly and says something to them. Rebecca doesn't seem uneasy at all, but Laina is tense the whole time.

The brief exchange ends, and the woman shrugs before going into the store. Laina and Rebecca make their way to the car.

"What happened?" Ridley asks. "What did she say?"

Rebecca reads the alarm on Laina's and Ridley's faces.

"She asked us for a light," Laina says.

They all climb into the car and hit the freeway.

"What the fuck?" Ridley says.

Laina explains to Rebecca that this was the same woman who talked to Ridley before, standing in front of that other gas station. Rebecca nods, determined to do what is necessary. This is it. This is what they've been waiting for years to meet, and for years it didn't come. It is here now.

They look back as they barrel down the highway, well over the speed limit. They are all looking for a certain shape of headlights—one that could match the old van with the tinted windows. None of them paid much attention, not even Ridley, so they're not entirely sure what they're looking for.

A car speeds past them—some muscle car that'll likely get pulled over by the cops somewhere down this stretch of highway. Out of self-preservation, they slow down to just a few miles above the speed limit. A safe speed in step with the cars around them. If it's escape they're looking for, then they must accomplish it by subtler arts.

"She was very pale," Ridley is saying. This statement doesn't carry enough meaning for Rebecca, but Laina understands. He is asking, *What kind of monster is very pale?*

"A vampire?" Laina asks, evaluating the words. "Are those even real?"

Minutes stretch into a half hour and then an hour, and the tension in everyone's shoulders eases, but only enough for them to carry on a conversation.

"Was she following us the last time?" Rebecca asks.

"No," Ridley says. He doesn't see the confusion on her face, though he is wearing a similar expression.

Laina verbalizes it. "How did she find us again?"

"She must be tracking us another way," Ridley says. Obvious enough, but in *what* way? That part, the important part, is not something any of them can answer.

They settle into the middle lane of the freeway, letting the car ahead determine their speed. They had planned to stop and grab dinner, but should they stop? Maybe it's safer to continue—drive all the way back to Boston.

"I'm hungry," Laina says. "Maybe if we pull off now they'll pass us."

Ridley is hesitant, but Rebecca agrees. A brief debate ensues, which Ridley loses, and they pull off the freeway and find a diner.

It's full dark now, a fog lying over the landscape, heavy and watchful. They note the scene—perfect for a horror movie. In such a scenario, lit from the outside, inside would be dark and deserted. Or the diner would be crowded on the inside, and then, late into the meal, they'd notice that everyone's clothes aren't right. And then they'd see all the little injuries: gunshot or stab wounds, or the red marks of hanging nooses, and the ghosts would start laughing at them.

A bell jangles when they enter, and nothing is amiss. The diner is not full at all. Just a few people at tables, already eating their meals. A couple of families—mom, dad, kids. A boy looks up at them as they enter, and they all meet his eyes. This alarms the boy, and he ducks back into the booth, startling his sister. She looks but quickly loses interest.

All this in seconds; then a waitress passes and tells them to sit wherever they like. They do, near the door and up against a window so they can look out at the parking lot.

They all order steaks, rare, and take their pick of the sides available. Fries for Rebecca. Roasted vegetables for Laina. Mashed potatoes for Ridley.

Music pipes from the speakers—soul classics that are loud enough to hear but not to sing along with. The lights in the diner are dim enough to be cozy, not seedy. Enough atmosphere to relax them before the food arrives.

"Straight shot to Boston," Ridley says. "Just a few more hours."

Rebecca has other things on her mind. "What about that one organization: New Era? What do you know about them?"

Ridley sighs, resigning himself. "Not much. It's an open-value network."

Rebecca blinks.

"A loose coalition of co-ops, collectives, activist organizations, and influential individuals. They have a network fund they use to do projects for the collective good. Actually"—Ridley's voice pitches up an octave—"they have a food delivery program, free for low-income members, that has been getting a lot of attention lately. They're trying to expand the service beyond Greater Boston, which could be really exciting if they produce a good model for scaling—"

"Okay, but when did they start?"

Ridley shrugs. "I started hearing about them after the Emergence."

"We have a candidate, then. Do they attend the Federation meetings?"

"Sometimes . . . Rebecca, I just don't think it's a good idea. What about those forums you've been investigating?"

Rebecca rolls her eyes. "Would *you* confess on an internet forum that you're a monster?"

Ridley doesn't have to answer. His frown says everything.

Satisfied, Rebecca says, "We have to create our own network. In real life."

Laina isn't completely invested in the conversation. She is thinking about the woman, the odd grin on her face when she asked for a light. This isn't just some creepy human curious about what they are; this is the underworld coming up to meet them. But she can feel the vibe. They are distracting themselves with this other conversation. So Laina goes along with things.

Rebecca again: "All I'm saying is, most of those monsters at the protest must've gotten curious just like me and Sarah were. And then the massacre sent them back into hiding. We have to figure out a way to ignite their curiosity again."

"But why would they be *curious*?" Ridley says. "Look what happened last time."

"I know. But mobilization takes risk. Someone has to take that on. Someone has to lead the monsters back out of the shadows."

Ridley goes quiet. It isn't as if they hadn't gone through this before. They've rethreaded this same conversation several times and have come to the same conclusions. It is symbolic of a frustration they all feel. Their world, even after the protest, is one of mist and shadows. A monster group could be anything from real to a lure to nothing at all. A phone call could be anything. Even the monsters they could confirm—the invisible woman, for example—seem more phantom than real, their motives inscrutable. They are angry and trying to spur one another into doing something reckless, doing something that would make them feel less helpless. They are grasping at control.

Ridley glances out the window. They can't even tell if they are being hunted or not, or what is hunting them, or whether they stand a chance against it. Imagine being that vulnerable, all the time, for the rest of their lives! Terrified that anything at all could turn sharp and cut them. The thought infuriates Ridley.

Rebecca lets out a huff of exasperation. "Fine. Ignore me, then. I'm going to the bathroom."

When she leaves the booth, Laina asks, "Well, what will we do?"

Ridley doesn't have to guess what she's talking about. "As long as she doesn't threaten us directly, we should be fine until we're home. We stay in public places. Drive the freeway, avoid secluded roads. And hope we've somehow lost her."

"And if we haven't? What happens if she follows us home?"

"There's only one other option. Fight her. And lose. But on the off chance we do survive, it'll be worth the risk."

Another silence that lasts until Rebecca slips back into the booth. "So, what are we going to do about this vampire?" she asks.

"Run if we can. Fight if we need to," Ridley says. "But away from people."

They've been practicing for this—what they would do if a threat appeared. They've gone to the woods regularly to prepare their wolves. It may not be enough, but it'll have to do.

They finish their meal with their eyes on the parking lot. Then they pay the check and carefully, quietly leave the diner.

There's nothing to worry about, not at first. But then Ridley sees the van, parked on the side of the road a few yards away. He doesn't have time to warn the rest. They see the real threat before he does: the woman, standing in the wooded area beyond the diner's parking lot, a large doglike creature tethered by a leash beside her. She whistles, and Ridley finally locks eyes with her. Despite the darkness, he can see her clearly—the strange smile on her lips. There's a moment of stillness from everyone. Ridley, Rebecca, and Laina are tensed, ready. Rebecca most of all. Something about the creature has stirred a memory.

"We have to run," Rebecca says.

As if on cue, the woman snaps the leash free.

They take to the forest. It is too late now to pretend this isn't what it is. They are being hunted. Running, they tear off their clothes, throwing them aside as they clear branches and brambles. The forest is dark, but even in human form their eyes are adjusting quickly. Rebecca is naked first. She's been a wolf longer, has learned to undress quickly. She flings herself into the change, feels that dangerous annihilation as it takes hold of each part of her—the descent into the matter of herself, and back out again, paws landing in wet leaves and carrying her forward without stopping. Ridley and Laina are only a little behind in their own werewolf forms. Laina stumbles, unsteady in the change, but finds footing. Ridley lets up next to Rebecca, then runs ahead. He is so good at this already. It reminds Rebecca of Sarah. She tries not to think of Sarah too much.

The woman has kept on them, her footsteps falling with terrifying speed. They do not look back. The other thing chasing them makes no sound, though Rebecca can smell the sick coming off it in waves.

Ridley reaches the clearing first, turning as he clears the trees. He is backpedaling now, keeping his eyes on the tree line and growling low with threat. Rebecca turns as well, recognizing they will not outrun whatever is following them.

Laina arrives last, the thing behind her swiping at her legs. She stumbles and rolls, and Ridley sprints back and puts himself between her and the pursuing creature. In the moonlight, Rebecca can see it fully now. A wolf. But not like one of them. This one is long and slender, with ears that point straight up. Mangy, with patches of its spotted-tan fur missing from its head and shoulders. Her heart pounds in her ears.

The years have not been kind to the thing that changed Rebecca. Back then, the creature was healthy, or nearly so, strong in the change and as formidable as it was terrifying. This version of it, of him, is not so intimidating. He has thinned out, and the wildness in his eyes has been replaced with something confused, just as likely to bite the woman as to bite them. The woman, though, is in good health. Ridley remembers her name: Mason.

Mason—pale, with short, spiked hair—stretches as if she were getting ready for a workout. She calls the creature to her, and it obeys.

"At first I just wanted to talk," Mason says. "But all this running around has worked me up." She looks to the animal. "Papa, you ready?"

The wolf growls again, halfhearted, but its front legs crouch.

Now in their wolf form, none of them can speak, but they ready themselves for what will be their first fight with other monsters.

The woman lets go of the chain, and the wolf—or the thing that is like a wolf and isn't—leaps forward. Ridley doesn't hesitate; he meets him in the air, colliding and falling with the wolf on top. The wolf goes straight for Ridley's neck, but Ridley rolls free, getting back up on all fours. Rebecca circles, coming at the wolf from the side. For a moment, the wolf shifts his attention to Rebecca, and Ridley takes advantage of the lapse, diving back into the fray. They both attack the creature at the same time, Rebecca clawing at the wolf's stomach, Ridley matching teeth for teeth and taking bites in turn.

Laina has been sitting back from the fight. As in a game of double Dutch, she edges closer, waiting for just the right moment. She sees the wolf is getting frustrated, and readies for an attack. But suddenly, the fight shifts again. The wolf bats Ridley away with one paw, Ridley stumbling back. Dizzy, he struggles to find footing. The wolf is on Rebecca next. As she tries to edge away, he bites down on her neck. He pulls her to him, lifts her, and throws her several feet. She lands hard, too disoriented to see the wolf approaching again. Ridley rushes up on the wolf's left flank, jumps, and lands on the wolf's back. The wolf tries to shake him off but doesn't slow as he charges for Rebecca. She crouches low, teeth bared. The wolf persists, a seemingly unstoppable force.

But suddenly, there is Laina, bigger than before, coming in from the wolf's side. At that moment, she and the wolf appear almost equal in size. Laina rams headfirst into the wolf, and with Ridley on him, the force of Laina's collision knocks the creature off his path. Taking advantage, Rebecca lunges for the wolf. They are all on him now, biting at his legs, his neck, his face. He growls in anger at first but is soon overwhelmed. Within moments, he is quiet except for ragged breaths.

None of them see Mason approach until she grabs Rebecca by the scruff of the neck and flings her into the tree line. There is a loud crack as she collides with an old oak tree and slumps to the forest floor, unconscious.

Ridley registers when Rebecca is tossed into the woods, the distance she flies startling him into stillness. Ridley shifts his attention from the wounded wolf, who is now on his side, breathing slowly. Not dead, which is good—Ridley doesn't want its death on his conscience. He is doing this because he has to, not because he wants to kill anyone.

Looking at Mason from his wolf form, Ridley more fully understands what she is and gets the sense that she abandoned any pretense of humanity a long time ago. Her eyes shine with bloodlust, and her alabaster skin glows in the moonlight. He knows to be afraid. He also knows that letting in fear will kill him faster if he lets it stop him from fighting back.

Laina abandons the wolf as well. She takes one glance at Mason, then Ridley. And then she dashes for the tree line.

"Uh-oh," Mason says, grinning at Ridley. "Looks like it's just the two of us."

Ridley growls, circling in on her. Her eyes follow him as he moves, and then she turns her head to track him. He doesn't see her turning, but somehow he is always in her line of sight. He can't get behind her. She watches Ridley calmly, a slow smile emerging on her face. It is unnerving, this mix of slow and fast motions. He knows that once she decides to attack, it will be quick. And if he is too slow . . .

Mason takes a step. "I'm going to have to kill you now."

Ridley braces himself.

He is the first to see it. And then Mason, as the shadow

passes over her. She looks up and sees . . . Laina, airborne, arcing down to meet her. Ridley seizes the moment to rush in for the attack. Both of them are on the vampire woman at once. The combined impact of both werewolves knocks her to the ground. They are getting lucky, Ridley thinks, even as all this is happening. But the vampire also underestimated them. They've been going out some nights, learning how to collaborate with their wolf, with one another's wolves, to increase their individual power and the pack's power at will. Ridley is decent at it, able to grow in strength quickly. But Laina is better than he is, because she knows how to control when she uses her power, saves it up, releases it when needed. Though Laina is anxious about fighting and has less of the bloodlust than Ridley or Rebecca, she is stronger and more strategic than either of them.

Mason is fighting them, but with two wolves on her she can't regain the advantage. And they don't waste this opportunity. Laina opens her mouth wide and bites down on Mason's head while Ridley goes for the feet. The vampire is pulled taut between the wolves. She lets out a frustrated yell, muffled in Laina's mouth. Ridley pulls hard on her legs as Laina plants her paws into the soft earth for leverage. With all her effort, she pulls back. There is a terrible tearing, the start of a scream falling into a trembling gurgle, and then the woman's body, once taut between them, goes limp, slumping to the ground in front of Ridley.

Laina is facing Ridley, and the sight is gruesome enough that Ridley almost looks away. But he doesn't. He doesn't want to scar Laina in this moment for what she has had to do. Laina opens her jaws, lets the vampire's head fall from her mouth onto the dewy grass.

The wolf creature still isn't moving, but he is watching them with vague interest, panting.

Laina steps back from the head and begins her change. In a moment, she is naked and huddled in on herself, staring at what she has done, what they have done together.

In the tree line, Rebecca begins to stir. Ridley has a strange awareness of her through the magic that connects them. He has no idea if this is something every wolf has with the one who created them, but he has the connection to both Rebecca and Laina.

Ridley lets the change take him over as well, and he is back, naked in the meadow, and feeling a bit of the night chill. He is a little self-conscious, without his clothes in a place like this. His body, in human form, is a very intimate part of himself, and in this setting it feels out of place, exposed.

Ridley keeps his attention on Laina. She is beautiful in the moonlight but looks as uncomfortable as he does. Their clothes are somewhere in the woods. To retrieve them, they must go back the way they came. It doesn't seem as though anyone will come through here at night, but it still makes Ridley uncomfortable to think about it. A bad time to worry about being naked, and yet it will always matter for him because he is trans.

"You should go check on Rebecca," Ridley says. "I'll watch these two."

Laina gives him a questioning look. *Are you sure?* she is saying with her eyes.

Ridley nods.

The wolf lifts its head and follows Laina as she walks to the tree line. Ridley keeps his attention on the wolf, the vampire's head in his peripheral vision.

He asks the wolf, "Do you have a human form you can change back to so we can talk?"

The wolf shakes his head, humanlike. The action sends a chill up Ridley's spine—to know there is something human, or at least with human-level intelligence, behind those eyes. Somehow Ridley knows there is a person there, but the person can't shift. Some form of magic is preventing him from changing back.

"How long?" Ridley asks. "Years? Do you even remember how long it's been since you were human?"

The wolf's head shakes again, frustrated. Ridley can sense this too.

Laina and Rebecca return to the meadow together, Rebecca now in human form.

"You okay?" Ridley asks.

Rebecca rubs her neck. "I will be."

Rebecca, unlike Ridley and Laina, looks perfectly at ease being naked in a meadow with a dead vampire and a strange wolf that only minutes ago was trying to kill them. Well, that isn't exactly right. She looks comfortable being naked. She looks angry having had to fight for their lives. She's also a little unsteady on her feet, but with no other signs of damage.

"Why is that one still alive?" Rebecca asks, and the look she gives the wolf could peel flesh from bone.

"He's stuck like this," Ridley says. "He's been magicked somehow. I'm not sure he even completely understands what happened."

"He understands," Rebecca says. "He was the one who changed me."

Laina and Ridley both startle at this revelation. It means, Ridley realizes, that Rebecca did not share it with Laina before sharing it with him. Or perhaps she just remembered. But Ridley likes the first option, because it makes him feel good that she waited.

"So, he is our grandsire?" Laina asks. "Grand-changer? Father to our line? What words do wolves use for something like this?"

"No idea. Maybe if we were changed the normal way and not just attacked, I'd have a better answer."

Rebecca has said this before—that she suspects wolves before her were changed willingly, knew what they were getting into. Like what she did with Laina and Ridley. There was a way that the magic opened when she got their consent. The magic was ready to give them the change. What happened to Rebecca was not by her consent. And now, looking at this tired wolf, so strange in ways they still can't name, Ridley knows this wolf didn't give his consent either. The creature was out of his own control when he changed Rebecca. And—

Laina asks the question Ridley is considering: "Was he the same one that changed Lincoln?"

Rebecca nods. "I wasn't there, but it was the first in a string of attacks, of changes. This one matched Lincoln's description. And Connor's. And Sarah's. Toni too. Estra didn't get a good look."

Her former pack. Even that list is incomplete. During the protest on the freeway, there were nearly a dozen werewolves. Some of them were a part of Rebecca's larger circle—loner wolves to her more tight-knit group. But they were hers just the same. Potentially all victims of the creature now before them.

Two of the people she named are dead already. And the others too, if their disappearances are more than just them running away.

"So, what do we do with him?" Laina says. She gestures to the woman's head. "And her?"

Laina's expression is puzzled. Her feelings about this creature are complicated. It has caused so much harm, but it has made her who she now is, made them who they now are. A gift and a curse in equal measure. And it is sick and dying.

Ridley offers his own opinion. "The wolf we can take with us. I don't think we should just leave him here."

"And what if he decides he actually wants to kill us?"

"He needed to be commanded. I don't think he can attack us without someone telling him to."

"That is a big leap, Ridley. And a dangerous one." Rebecca still hasn't decided that the wolf shouldn't be killed. "He was alone when he attacked me."

"You *think* he was."

"And you think a dangerous werewolf has a magical muzzle? We're both going off what we think we know. But your idea still sounds foolish."

Laina steps up and leans down next to the wolf. She moves quickly or else began moving while they were arguing, and only now do Ridley and Rebecca notice. Both of them reach toward her, but it's too late to stop her. She isn't as volatile as Rebecca, but she is stubborn in her own way.

She touches the wolf on his head, and he just looks up at her, tired. He makes a small sound in his throat. Not a growl. It is more like a sigh—a sign of a deeper exhaustion that goes all the way to the core of him. Laina stands up, and Ridley and Rebecca relax just a little.

"We take him."

They look at Rebecca.

She bites her lip, turns her face away from them. "You both are going to get us killed."

That is as close to a yes as they are going to get.

"Sorry to interrupt."

They don't have to turn or shift their attention. The man who says the words is in their field of vision, and yet he wasn't in sight before the moment he spoke.

Ridley's eyes go wide in recognition. He grabs Rebecca, who is closer to him, and moves her farther away from the stranger. Laina reads the situation and follows.

Ridley is remembering his first rendezvous with this man. He remembers that this man—Melku called him Smoke—has the ability to turn to black dust and reappear at will wherever he wants. He also has the ability to do that to people he touches. Objects too? Is there a limit to what he can move with this strange power? Ridley still doesn't know what kind of monster he is. All he knows is that none of them would stand a chance against him. Melku barely managed to get the SEN Collective out of his grasp alive.

Smoke starts toward them. Rebecca tenses, readying herself for the change. Ridley puts out a hand to stop her.

"Good," Smoke says. "At least one of you got sense. Not trying to make this messier than it already is."

Smoke's Caribbean accent is carved into Ridley's memory. He is smiling again this time. The last time, Smoke was all smiles and taunts, but that was for Melku's benefit.

Smoke takes another step forward and picks up the woman's head. Has it been that close the entire time? The thought of it rolling toward them sends a chill through Ridley.

"Look what happen when you go out unsupervised," Smoke says. He makes a sound between his teeth.

He isn't talking to them. He is talking to the head. Ridley looks at it again. The mouth is open, the tongue hanging out between the parted lips and to one side. There isn't a lot of blood. The eyes are open too, looking up at Smoke's face. Were they like that before? Unnerved, Ridley stops watching the head.

Smoke unceremoniously tucks the head under his arm. He then goes for the body. They all watch him, everyone too stunned or frightened to speak. By this time, they all realize they expended a lot of energy almost dying. They aren't ready to try almost dying again.

Smoke turns the body to dust. Like a cloud of gnats, the dust follows him back to the wounded wolf. "Lawrence, you don't look too good. I'll give you some time with the witch when we get back."

The wolf creature makes a strangled sound.

"Don't be like that," Smoke says. "She gon' heal you up good. No funny business."

His tone ignites Rebecca's protective instinct. "Why don't you just let him go?" she asks, but her voice has some of that *I'm going to kill you* edge.

Ridley isn't sure if she could, but Smoke's expression gets serious. "Lawrence still has some use left in him. We'll let him go when we're finished."

"We?" Laina asks.

Smoke smiles. "If you don't know by now . . ." He puts his hand on the scruff of the wolf's back, and then they are all dust—Smoke, the wolf, and the body and head of the woman. And then the dust blinks out of existence.

Rebecca, Laina, and Ridley look at one another. They don't speak for a moment. What has happened is weird, but they've all seen a few weird things over the past few years. They are also unpacking in their heads the danger they've just been in, their adrenaline still burning out of them. They have survived the fight mostly out of luck. Again, a few things lined up there that could have gone very wrong. The werewolf's weak condition, for one. And the vampire—and, yes, Ridley is now convinced that's what she was—underestimating how strong they would be in their wolf forms.

This tells Ridley a few things, so he says the next part aloud. "They aren't always watching us. No way they'd be watching us all the time and not know we've been practicing and strengthening our wolf forms."

"I want to say that's a leap." Rebecca sighs. "But it's something I was hoping could be true. Maybe it is."

"*They* haven't been watching us." Laina looks at Rebecca. "Maybe. But the other ones probably have been."

Rebecca and Ridley know what she means by *the other ones*. They've gathered that there are at least two groups in the shadow underworld. Melku—one of the members of SEN, Ridley's grassroots collective that disbanded after the unfortunate incident in the barn—is a part of this other group (if there really are only two). And the sight mage, Cassandra, who was with Melku. And the invisible woman. That group has protected them more than once, also threatened their lives more than once. So, a little better than this other group, the one that hasn't been tracking them as closely as they thought.

"But why now?" Rebecca is asking. "Why follow us? Why attack us?"

Ridley is still considering this part. If she had shown up after they went to Connor's grandmother's house, Ridley would have assumed that looking for Connor had tipped them off. But she was on them before they'd gone.

"The other pack members," Ridley says, sitting in the unfinished question for a while longer. He still isn't sure. He is getting tired of not being sure about anything. At the same time, he is also getting angry at getting used to it.

"I'm cold," Laina says.

And at the exact moment, Rebecca asks, "Do you think they were trying to grab us?"

"I don't think so?" Goddamn it, Ridley couldn't even make that statement without a question at the end. "That man said she wasn't supposed to engage. Or at least, he implied it. They were watching us. Maybe started recently?"

Up until this point, Laina was mostly hugging herself. Her blood always ran cold, and that bit had crossed over, amplified even, becoming so much a part of her personality (needing extra clothes for all occasions) that even the change didn't take it from her. But a thought has occurred to her, and she forgets the cold. "They don't know where the missing pack went either?"

It is another question, but under it is good speculation.

"So either the disappearances are unrelated, and we should be relieved . . ." Ridley trails off again.

"Or there's something else happening on top of everything," Rebecca says.

Laina has had enough and starts off to the tree line. "Let's think it over on the drive," she yells back. "I'm getting my clothes."

Ridley and Rebecca glance at each other again. Rebecca shrugs and follows Laina. "Thank whatever divine presence created us that our noses are still fairly good in human form. It's going to take some magic to find our clothes in the dark."

Ridley lingers a while longer. There is the smell of blood in the clearing. And musk. He smelled it when they were fighting the wolf too. The creature is not being taken care of. And they allowed him to be put back into captivity. Because they were afraid. But also, in part, because they didn't want the responsibility.

Ridley starts walking, knowing his clothes will be the closest to the clearing. He thinks about how quickly they are all moving on after what just happened. A frightening thought: they were all getting used to this.

They argue more on the drive. Connor is either safe or in trouble or is soon to be in trouble and is on the run from it. It could be the bad group or the not-so-bad group or another group entirely. They could be in danger or maybe not in danger.

"Please," Laina says, "let's just put a pin in it for now." She is in the back seat this time, curled up. She's always had the hardest time bouncing back after the change. The exhaustion was all over her face when they reemerged from the woods. She has spent most of the drive with her eyes closed.

She doesn't say anything else, so Ridley and Rebecca think she has fallen back asleep. But they know, at the very least, that she wants them to shut up.

"Thank you," she says at last. "We need to get comfortable with what we don't know."

She is right. And yet Ridley and Rebecca can't let it go. It is a scab they can't stop picking at in their minds. Ridley decides he'll reach out to Melku. He still has their email, even if the collective has disbanded. He also has Melku's number from group text chains, but everyone else in the group has changed their number. Not for the first time, he feels a pang of sadness for what they've all lost. Not just their work but their sense of security in the universe, even if it was false.

At the very least, he can see if there is more that Melku can tell him about how the monster world works.

"Why didn't you ask before?"

Ridley looks at me through the rearview mirror with a half-dazed expression. The car and the world around it have stopped.

"Because I'm afraid of Melku."

If Ridley had asked himself this question, he would have used a lot more rationalizations. But with me, he cannot lie, even to himself. This power is the one that frightens me the most, for how easily it can get to the heart of other people, their most primal motivations.

It is always fear. Sometimes it also contains a bit of love.

Before he calls Melku, Ridley lets two days pass. Life takes over for a while. He comanages the bookstore while working through the anxiety of their near-death experience. Mostly, he is just letting himself feel like a human and not a monster. He knows the line between isn't so simple, has never been simple. But the fear of himself lingers. What he did out in those woods—what he could do if pushed again—terrifies him.

He doesn't really want to email Melku. He thinks that once he makes the decision it will be easy, but when the day comes, because he has decided not to wait any longer, he still hesitates at his computer. He sends a test email to get his nerve up.

Do you still use this?

The email doesn't bounce back, so either Melku still uses it, or it hasn't been disconnected.

He spends the next few minutes drafting the right words,

though he doesn't think it will matter. He thinks Melku will ignore him no matter what he says. But he doesn't want to blow it just on the off chance that something he says might make the difference.

He decides on as much information as he can offer. Maybe it's enough for an exchange, assuming Melku doesn't already know everything.

Melku,

It's been a while since we've talked. I hope you're okay. I've been in touch with some of the other SEN members. Venda could use some reaching out to.

Not the reason for the email. I assume this is secure. I hope so.

Rebecca's former pack members have been going missing. We went out to investigate a disappearance and were followed by what I believe to be a vampire and a strange werewolf. The werewolf was in bad shape. We killed the vampire. But that man from the barn showed up and took the body and the werewolf away.

We really need to know what's going on. Our lives are in danger. We don't think they know about the disappearances (this other group, I mean), but we're unsure if you do. It would ease our minds if you told us what you know. Is there a third, more dangerous group out there?

Ridley

He doesn't have to wait long. Melku responds within the hour:

167 Winter Street, Apartment 7B.

Come now.

The address is their apartment building.

Melku has an apartment in *their* building, just six floors above them—almost in the exact spot, if the floor patterns are the same. And they had no idea. Is it anger Ridley feels? He isn't sure. A little fear, but alarmingly less than he thinks he should be feeling. To be alarmed at not being afraid enough—what a thing! Will he someday not even feel alarm? Would something else replace it?

He goes to put on his shoes and meets Laina in the living room. She reads the worry on his face and turns the volume down on the television.

Ridley considers lying. For a second, he *really* considers it. Laina sees that too.

"Look, I don't want you to worry," he says.

"We don't do that anymore, remember? Protect each other from feelings."

"Okay, then." He sighs, slips on one of his sneakers. "I emailed Melku at their SEN email address. They want to see me. Upstairs in apartment seven-B."

He lets Laina process the implications. She isn't as afraid as he thinks she should be either. She stands up. "Give me a minute."

"You can't come with me. That wasn't part of the arrangement. I'll get more out of Melku if there's no surprises."

He expects Laina to argue. She folds her arms. "Be careful. I'll be here when you get back."

Upstairs, he tries the doorknob instead of knocking, and his hunch is confirmed when the door opens.

Melku is standing in the center of an empty living room. Ridley steps in, closing the door behind him. His footsteps echo.

After he shuts the door, Melku says, "Don't leave the city again. It isn't safe right now."

"We have to travel for work. I have family down south."

"Not those trips. I mean you can't go looking for answers about disappearances."

"You called me up here to order me around?"

"Part of why I called you up here."

"And the other part?"

"I would hope we could be friends again. Someday."

"Is this how you treat friends? Surveil them and then call them up to your empty apartment in their building because they did something they didn't know was trouble, because you neglected to tell them?"

"This werewolf—what did it look like?" Melku asks carefully.

Ridley observes Melku. "I'll tell you when you tell me what is going on."

"Okay." Melku takes in a slow breath, releases. "I am a part of a secret society called the Order of Asha."

Ridley stares. "I'm going back to my apartment."

"You already had a suspicion of what this is. I'm trying to treat you like you can handle it."

"Come on, Melku. I know when someone's trying to manipulate me."

"The other secret society is the Order of the Zsouvox."

Ridley laughs.

Melku doesn't. "The Order of the Zsouvox has split into two factions. One, the Cult of the Zsouvox, is in ascendancy. The Order of Asha and the Order of the Zsouvox have been around for several millennia, preceding the ancient Egyptian magic schools. The head of the Cult of the Zsouvox right now is a vampire designated as Twenty-Nine. The former leader was killed. They're in a civil war that is lasting longer than we thought. That doesn't matter. What matters is that all of what you're seeing now is the spillover of something that has been building for a long time. Before my time, though I'm older than I look. But other things are also happening. We're in a transition between ages."

"I don't know what any of that means."

"The wolf—what did it look like?"

"That's not enough information."

"Listen, friend. What I've given you more than pays for what you're about to give me, even if you don't know what it means. Thousands of people have spent their lives trying to learn a fraction of what I just told you."

Ridley glares at Melku. "It had pale spots on its back. It was . . . lanky. Long, slender limbs. Brown fur, I think. It was dirty, so it appeared black in places. It looked like a werewolf, but it was all mixed up with something else. It was sick, and I could tell it hadn't been in its human form for a long time, years maybe. I could feel him smelling my magic. Rebecca has a little of the ability, but it wasn't passed to us, or so I thought. Last night was the first time I could feel someone else's magic reaching out to mine."

Melku takes all the information in soberly. "Thank you. That's very helpful."

"So what about this conflict? Should we just sit back as it happens?"

"What else are you going to do? You won't be able to run from it. Or hide. If you wait, you might be able to ride it out. Be smart and don't run off on your own. I'll let you know what I can find out."

"Will you?"

"The Black Hand is mobilizing in the city. Keep your eye on that for now."

A portal opens up behind Melku—a circle of those same mechanical ants, linked head to tail on the living-room wall. Melku steps back through it.

"This goes for you too. Don't go wandering around right now. It's dangerous."

"Who are you talking to?" Ridley asks.

The portal closes and Melku is gone, and then it is only Ridley and me in the apartment. He looks around, paranoid. But I am an absence, so his mind pushes me from his thoughts.

When Ridley returns to his apartment, Laina is still on the couch.

She turns down the volume again on *The Great British Bake Off.*

"How did it go?" Laina asks.

Ridley tells her everything he remembers, even the parts he doesn't really understand.

At the end of the conversation, she huffs. "So Melku had to bargain for information, and to avoid giving you anything really useful they just told you a bunch of big secrets you couldn't understand."

"It was that or nothing."

"So, they were interested in the wolf," she says.

Ridley nods.

In the background of their conversation, bakers are rushing about in those decisive moments before the hosts shout, "Time!"—their anxieties and brushes with catastrophe reduced to a final dash and quick camera cuts. Laina likes the show, but this season it is really more about one of the contestants, who has interested her. It is the young woman's sense of smell. She sniffs her bakes, puts her nose up near the glass of the oven to tell when something is done. Laina has seen Ridley do this when he bakes bread.

"Secret societies," Laina says, staring at the muted television. "To hear it said aloud though."

"Yeah. Fucking crazy."

One of the contestants has dropped a sheet of macaroons and is freaking all the way out. With the volume down, it looks exaggerated, like one of those silent films.

"You remember that podcast you used to listen to?" Laina asks. "About that woman?"

"Karuna Flood. When Melku said 'societies,' I didn't make the connection right away. But now that you mention her . . ."

"She used to study secret societies, didn't she?"

Ridley pauses. "And then she disappeared."

"I'm tired of crumbs," Laina says.

"Well, eventually there'll be more than crumbs to keep us up at night." Ridley isn't sure he believes Melku's promise.

He is remembering Melku's speech about information, how Melku's access to it, and everyone else's ignorance of it, protects everyone. That Melku was different from the Melku upstairs. They weren't sure of that anymore. Which means Melku is hoarding information for another reason.

"I think they know where the missing pack members are," Ridley says.

"Why do you think so?"

"A sense. Monsters are going into hiding."

"Shouldn't *we*?"

Ridley can tell from Laina's expression that if he says yes, they'll pack immediately. But he shakes his head. "As far as I can tell, we're safe for now. If we stop looking into things."

"You might be able to stop," Laina says. "And I'd be fine with it myself. But you won't be able to stop Rebecca from looking into things. These were her people."

"I know," Ridley says. "But if we can convince her to stay in the city . . ."

Laina laughs.

"We have to try to convince her there is nowhere to run to."

Laina has a faraway expression. "There's always somewhere to run."

The Black Hand is an anti-monster extremist group that developed after the Boston Massacre, which was only one of four such mass shootings that took place throughout the country. The Boston Massacre was the largest of the four and so held the nondescript name that represented them all. There was another reason the Boston Massacre became the most infamous of the mass shootings: the perpetrators were all missing a hand. Documentaries still talked about it—how they never found the connection between those missing hands and what happened that day. With no easy answers, the mystery had lost significance over the years.

Except in some circles. Conspiracy theorists had no compunctions when drawing outlandish conclusions. The identities of the shooters told a certain story. Many of them were wealthy or were academics. Lewis Canter was a long-form journalist who had written several books. John Norell was a professor of psychology. What sort of menace would cause these people to do something so terrible? What would cause them to amputate their own hands?

It was important to conspiracy theorists to draw a distinction between these people's wealth and the wealth of the truly rich. Ron Harris, for instance, had two homes, but they were modest. His salary was a little over a quarter million. So, upper middle class? Lower upper class, at best. The "hardworking" rich. Not part of the real club. Merely drawn in by the truly wealthy and powerful as scapegoats. Most theories got incoherent after that.

The Black Hand didn't really care about the why. They latched on to the possibility that monsters could be killed. They scoured those massacre stories for other gory details. How many confirmed monsters dead? How many humans killed by monsters "defending themselves"? Sarah's face was emblazoned on T-shirts, posters, shooting-range targets. They didn't care who the people were who had missing hands, though some Black Hand did believe those people were somehow encouraged to do this—but *who* encouraged them varied depending on the faction spinning the tale. Radical patriots or the anonymous founders of the Black Hand, or the rich—sure, whatever, they'd get theirs in time. The wealthy and powerful must have known that these monsters from myth and legend existed.

The first appearance of the Black Hand came from streaming sites. Gangs of people with a black glove on their dominant hand, jeering faces at rallies, saying things like "We must remain" and "Darkness must be answered with burning."

Years before, there were random acts of violence by frightened and angry individuals. Surely no consolation for those lost in that time or for their families. But these shouts of violence were different. The violence was organizing.

From those early videos, there were news profiles, articles on the strange supremacist movement. Some of those articles, even the ones on credible websites, had an edge to them, a subtle ambivalence, a quiet agnosticism on whether these extremists were a problem at all. They were just frustrated, scared, angry. Nothing to worry about. And anyway, who could blame them for wanting to protect themselves? The world had changed. Countermeasures were needed.

But then the lynch mobs began. In rural areas, where the communities were small, where law enforcement was your neighbor who sometimes showed up to barbecues. Where everyone talked about how strange it was that Doree and her family had arrived in town right after the Emergence. And how, just as they arrived, animals started to go missing. Frank's cat down the road, which swelled in the imagination to become several pets. The family never came to cookouts, were never seen at the grocery store or the post office. What did they eat?

That sort of paranoia grows wings, descends on every corner of a small community—at the watering holes, the grocery stores, the post offices, the bars, the edges of those cookouts. First as whispers. And those absent, unable to hear the whispers, get noticed.

Some of the men of the town began watching streaming videos, began to entertain certain ideas. Harmless gatherings in the woods at night, the attendees wearing a black glove on their dominant hand. They chant the Black Hand's clarion call: *To the horde, all are welcome.* Weeks later, someone's house goes up in flames. Isn't it tragic how no one made it outside? And then that graffito on a wall of the local high school's gymnasium: *Darkness must be met with burning.*

It would be easy to ignore if it were just one place. But soon the cities have their share of disappearances, bodies found in parks, bomb threats to monster-friendly organizations, random acts of vandalism.

Even before Melku's warning, Ridley regularly imagined mobs of people thousands deep, pouring over the landscape, setting fire to houses in the dead of night. And so he takes to heart the task of keeping an eye on Black Hand activity in Boston. He starts by looking up hashtags on social media. They have a well-known hashtag, #TheCulling, which the social media sites keep from trending but don't do much else to prevent. And it is pretty obvious what the hashtag means. #TheCulling or #TheGreatCulling or #BostonMassacre brings up posts from anonymous accounts, people with few followers and animated avatars or nondescript images instead of actual faces. Or anonymous avatars with tens of thousands of followers. Terrifying that there are so many anonymous talking heads for this organization.

Ridley finds some chatter about a gathering happening at the Boston Common. Lots of comments and retweets. It is a week away in the late afternoon. He sets a reminder on his phone, though he can't imagine himself forgetting the date and time. He'll take the subway down to Park Street and have a look.

The day of the rally, as Ridley stays home, Laina and Rebecca go to work. The store is quiet—no sign of the disturbance of a few years ago, right after Laina leaked the video of Lincoln's death for the second time. That time, she caught the interest of local and national news. As soon as Lincoln was identified, everyone wanted to talk to known members of his family.

How does someone recover a sense of normality after a thing like that? Inch by inch, one day at a time. Early on, there were bomb threats, strange people coming into the store to confront her or anyone else they could talk to, but that dwindled. They even experienced a dip in regulars for a time, but the loyal community members returned as the world got used to accepting their new monster reality. Laina wasn't even a minor celebrity. After the second leak, self-professed monsters came out in droves. Witches, warlocks, shifters, even a heavily made-up YouTube personality who claimed she was a vampire. After public displays of monstrosity became a federal crime—in the wake of the police officers' deaths during the Boston Massacre—no one dared present their monster side in public. It provided a lot of cover for charlatans, and better cover for people tangentially related to confirmed monsters.

The werewolves on the freeway remained anonymous, the unedited video never appearing again. But it wasn't exactly a secret that the bookstore supported monsters. No, they weren't foolish enough to stick it on flyers, but the bookstore carried monster-themed fiction and nonfiction prominently and hosted the authors for book events. Many of the nonfiction authors were capitalizing on the new market, but sometimes after hours, they'd strike up a conversation with a fiction author about potential monster family members—all long dead, of course. It wasn't a thing anyone talked about outright.

Stories of monsters being abducted from their homes spread on social media. None of these stories were confirmed— the media doing its best not to fan conspiracy theories by investigating them—but real or not, just the plausibility of such an action in a post-monster world was enough to frighten anyone away from revealing their monster side in public.

If there was such a thing as normal, the bookstore managed it by not doing anything particularly controversial. They kept pace with the culture and bought themselves a modicum of safety.

Other bookstores did these events too. It was clear people wanted to read monster books, so capitalism made space for it.

Overall, things aren't much better than before, when no one talked about it. They still don't, but if the conversation comes up, it is impossible to tell where the believers or nonbelievers will come from. When a nonbeliever speaks, no one argues, but it isn't a conversation that develops further when people are sober. Human trafficking doesn't come up in mixed company. Nor do casualties of war. At gatherings, most people don't glee-fully discuss the actions of a serial killer. The topic of monsters has become that sort of conversation. Sordid, unsettling—the kind of talk that sends people away, jumping at shadows. How does someone keep sane in this new world? They walk home at night in groups; they leave the disturbing stuff to the media; they don't conjure human darkness into their living rooms.

To the marginalized, a response like this isn't surprising. People are comfortable denying the existence of things that frighten them, and when they can't, they're perfectly fine not talking about them.

It is under this shade that Laina, Ridley, and Rebecca can be werewolves and go to work every day. The desire for normality is strong even in unusual times.

As Laina takes her place at the help desk, Madeline greets her. And then: "Someone came by looking for you."

And just like that, the ease shatters. "A reporter?"

"No, didn't look like a reporter. An older man." Madeline stares at Laina, uncomfortable.

"A Black man?"

Madeline nods.

Laina feels an icy chill. This could be worse than a reporter. "Did he give a name?"

"No. But he said he'd come by again today or tomorrow."

Laina tries to hide her concern.

"Are you worried?"

"No, no. Thanks for the heads-up." When Madeline leaves, Laina tries to call Ridley. His phone goes straight to voicemail.

Downstairs, Rebecca is unboxing books. Just now she is having the urge to check her phone. This is one of her worst habits, this constant checking. It doesn't matter if something is happening or nothing is happening—the urge is there, a *knock-knock-knock* on the lizard part of her brain. When she can't resist anymore, she pulls her phone from her pocket and sees the text from her mother.

You should stop by the house.

Why?

I think we should talk about
it in person.

Rebecca texts back.

Okay, love you Mom.

Love you too Becca.

Her mother, out there in that house all by herself. Unprotected. Rebecca has considered going out there to live, but the commute would kill her. And she doesn't want to leave Laina and Ridley by themselves. She has also considered getting her mother a house in the city—something her mother will certainly decline as soon as she asks. Her mother is fiercely independent in her old age. But is it right to call it old age? Her mother will probably look exactly the way she does now for decades to come. Rebecca has been searching for her own signs of aging in the mirror in the mornings, but what has she found? One gray hair growing out from the top of her head. It arrived two years ago, with no other signs. Her skin remains unblemished.

Rebecca's mother also has no further signs of aging. And since her mother has started taking care of herself better, Rebecca has even noticed a de-aging effect—something that can't just be in her head.

But the reason her mother wants to talk to her isn't about moving or age. It has to be about Manny.

So much has changed since that time before. Rebecca and her mother have found some measure of peace within their relationship. She is still angry at Rebecca from time to time. Grateful sometimes too, and that particular feeling is becoming more frequent. Her mother was a hoarder, and Rebecca spent months cleaning up the house, yelling to her from various rooms that she was throwing away this and that. Boxes of newspapers and magazines mostly. Bits and bobs from objects and electronics that had long since gone away—orphans of earlier eras. An entire shelf's worth of VHS tapes that Rebecca had discovered in a stack of boxes in the basement. Movies she remembered from childhood that she'd probably watched a hundred times before DVDs replaced their collection (years later than in most families). A VHS cover of *Andre*, the tape itself lost to time. Rebecca watched that movie about a pet seal in a small town countless times, still knows entire scenes by heart.

What do they talk about during those weekend visits? (Sometimes Wednesdays too, when she has the day off from the bookstore.) Dad occasionally, though those conversations are fleeting. Mostly, they talk about Manny. Her mother knows so much that Rebecca has missed about his life. Rebecca and Manny have become estranged since their father died (truthfully, since before he died). Well, *estranged* isn't the right word. They talk at family events, whenever those come up. And she can ask him questions that he dutifully answers in the fewest words he can get away with. They plan and pool money for birthday, Mother's Day, and Christmas gifts for Mom every year. He even stopped by the bookstore to get Rebecca's employee discount on a graphic novel about mice. But they don't hang out. And she can tell he resents her by the way he looks at her sometimes.

Every once in a while, he says things outright.

"You weren't here when Dad was sick," he said once, "so I don't know why you're all of a sudden so interested in Mom's welfare. She was having a hard time then, and you didn't bother to show up."

It was at least twenty minutes after she'd mentioned clearing out the basement and garage. Mom had asked him to do it, but Rebecca had stepped in because she had more time off from work. But Rebecca didn't ask Manny if he wanted her to offer, and he must have resented her not asking. It felt as if their relationship was running on some kind of fucked-up autopilot of obligatory interactions and passive-aggressive resentments. Maybe it would have felt better if the resentment didn't seem so one-sided.

There's still time, Rebecca tells herself. She'll go by her mother's tomorrow and see what's wrong. And she'll figure out how to fix things with Manny, just as she figured out how to fix things with her mom.

In the afternoon, Ridley gets off at Park Street, passing from the hot heaviness of the subway into the crisp air above. The day is overcast and rainy, late winter edging into spring. The weather reminds Ridley of the day of the march. He has dreamed often about the march—that moment when he pushed the shooter and tried to run. The running, the sidewalk expanding ahead of him forever, the hot stab of the bullet entering him.

He is sweating under his coat and thinks it might be a bit of nerves. Sometimes it's hard to sort these things—where his mind really is, what relationship his mind has to his body. It has gotten worse since the barn, since the shooting and the change. There is more noise between his conscious self moving through the world and this "underself" processing what is happening to him. Nothing in his life has solid lines.

He figured the Black Hand would be congregating near the bandstand in the center of the park. And he is right, though he didn't need to spend time worrying. It is obvious where people are headed, where the crowd is growing, and there is chanting and someone has a microphone hooked up to a speaker. He is still too far away to hear what the person is saying. But as he makes his way toward the bandstand, mixing with the swell of people moving toward the voices and chants, he can make out snippets of what is being said.

The grass on the Common is the brown of late winter, though some of the color is coming back in. The cobblestones along the bricked path are slick from the afternoon rain. The people around him aren't all headed to this rally, but many are, while others are drawn by the commotion. He sees more counterprotesters than members of the Black Hand. Decent people holding up picket signs. An older woman has "Solidarity with Monsters" written with different-colored markers. Her sign stands out, though it feels a little upbeat for the business she is here to face.

What Ridley is hearing from the bandstand: ". . . my life, the lives of my children. Could you imagine it? I'd lost my brother, and now people were calling my phone, threatening me? Someone erased all my text conversations with the last people to see him alive. His so-called family of troublemakers all went silent. I couldn't get anyone to tell me anything."

Ridley recognizes the voice. Once, when Nick hosted the SEN Collective, Ruth had come by the house and spent the day with them, asking questions about "her brother's hobby." She was a young mother then. Her first daughter was only seven months old, sleeping in the stroller next to her as she asked them about the difference between worker and producer co-ops. She was rolling the baby stroller back and forth absently as they answered her questions.

Nick took the lead on the answer: "Producer co-ops form their relationship around purchasing common resources, not selling. Worker cooperatives organize around shared work, where the benefits are also shared. Basically, seller and buyer."

Nick wasn't always the easiest person to talk to. Sometimes his directness edged on hostility. But in that moment, seeing the smile on his face, Ridley could see how he was made, the deeper context of who he was. Seeing how his face lit up talking to his little sister, learning later that they both had struggled when they were kids—barely enough to eat, a father wasting away under the weight of his unfulfilled life and turning that dissatisfaction on his children—Ridley finally understood Nick's needing to create that tough, abrasive exterior. Nick had to grow up fast. But it was that struggle that made him love co-ops. The idea that people could, through cooperation, bring themselves out of poverty. Though he still subsisted on working-class wages, his work at the cooperative was taking a turn toward something better.

In that memory, Nick was sitting in the living room, an unlit cigarette in his hand. He was about to go outside when the conversation caught him. Ridley remembers the curl of Nick's fingers around that cigarette, and the mirrored memory of the way his fingers curved in just the same way when nothing remained of him but that hand. Ridley heard again the wet thump of Nick's severed limb as it hit the barn's floor, the bits of dirt sticking to Nick's skin, the spurt of blood from the open wound.

And then Ridley was somewhere else entirely, falling down, down, two spiraling eyes of space dust below him, looking up into him, through him. The SEN Collective had disbanded since the attack at the barn, everyone going mostly silent. Ridley isn't in regular touch with everyone, but he does talk to Venda every week. She is struggling with insomnia, waking up at night to the slightest noise. She has taken to helicopter parenting, working from home, always keeping her son in sight. Her hair is falling out, and lately she's started having facial spasms from the stress. Wiley went completely dark after what happened, but before that, she was the most out of sorts: insomnia, but also bouts of severe depression and intense anxiety. She's been on several medications.

Ridley hasn't told any of them that he is now a werewolf.

The wolf, just then, nudges him to alertness. There is a pause from the stage. He sees when she sees him, observes the exact moment Ruth's expression turns to surprise. Then to anger.

The crowd isn't large. The counterprotesters had stopped at the periphery. They didn't want to have anything to do with the Black Hand, didn't want to be confused with them. Ridley should have done the same, but he had put his hoodie up and slipped into the crowd. Pulled toward the sound of Ruth's voice, he was so distracted seeing her up there that he didn't consider the danger. He wasn't out as a monster to most people, and the last time he was here Ridley had been human. He didn't exactly *forget* he had undergone the change, but it wasn't on the surface of his mind. Ridley was new enough to it that sometimes he misplaced the knowledge of his wolf among all the other parts of who he was. The wolf belonged to his underself.

Ridley hopes the crowd will give him some cover. They might still miss him. But the hoodie is drawing their attention— most of them are bold enough not to cover themselves up—and then there's the way Ridley is looking at Ruth.

Someone grabs him by the shoulder.

After the change, Ridley complained a lot about the heightened senses the wolf gave him even when he was in human form. Rebecca said it was normal to be frustrated with the enhanced smell and hearing. But Ridley didn't complain about the greater strength and speed, or how his knees didn't bother him anymore, and he could dash up a flight of stairs the way he had when he was a teenager. Actually, the way he had when he was, well, never. He threw around boxes of books like boxes of breakfast cereal. The truth is, the enhanced physicality made him entirely different. Not part of him, but the whole of him. Every fiber of him has been changed.

Usually, he suppresses this new gift, but in this moment, with a swarm of hostile people around him, instinct takes over. Ridley pushes the first person off him, and the man crashes into three Black Hand. The crowd around him steps back for a moment. Their shock doesn't last, quickly turning to rage. Several charge in on him.

Again, on instinct, Ridley leaps into the air, clearing the heads of the encroaching mob. When his feet hit the ground again in a patch of grass several feet from them, he sprints away.

He is still running as he flees the Common. Some Black Hand pursue him, but there are too many of them, which makes it difficult for them to weave through crowds the way he can. He crosses the street during a green light, taking advantage of a brief gap in the traffic. Once he gets a few blocks away, he slows and then circles back to take the subway at Downtown Crossing. Ridley doesn't see anyone overtly looking for him, but at Park Street he has to hide as a group of Black Hand enter his subway car.

They don't recognize him and don't seem to be looking, so he tries to blend in. Ridley keeps his ear tuned to their conversation.

"They're getting bold. To just show up at our gatherings."

"Next time, we should let them get comfortable. We can follow them to their hiding places."

The Black Hand consists mostly of men, which isn't a

surprise. There are not many Black or Brown members of the Black Hand either. But they've been doing a better job of recruiting women lately. Is "better job" the appropriate way to phrase it? Ridley considers this for a moment. One of the three Black Hand on the subway car is a woman. And they found Ruth. Or Ruth found them.

He can't help but feel responsible for that last bit. He wasn't a werewolf then, and he was just as scared as she was. But his fear had bought his silence, and he hadn't reached out. Truth be told, he is still afraid of what might happen. All the SEN Collective members are.

"You were at that protest," someone says, too close to him. It isn't a question. Ridley looks up to a woman holding on to one of the handrails and frowning down at him. She isn't a part of the group that entered and isn't wearing a black glove, so Ridley didn't notice her there.

Unconsciously, he glances at the Black Hand members.

"Don't worry," the woman says. "I was one of the counter-protesters."

This makes Ridley *more* suspicious.

She laughs nervously. "I know—easy for me to say. Hard for you to believe. Dangerous times. Dangerous world." She laughs again.

It seems to be how she soothes her discomfort in a new social situation. Anxiety is something Ridley understands. He makes space for her beside him on the seat.

"Amethyst."

"Rich," Ridley says. "Amethyst is a great name. Are you local?"

She gives a sheepish smile. "Local enough. I heard about the rally and made the drive into Quincy."

Not particularly local. And headed in the wrong direction. "Did you know this train is outbound to Alewife?"

"Is it?" She looks around, which won't do much good in a moving train underground.

"If you get off at Charles, you can just go over to the other side. You've only added to your commute by fifteen minutes or so."

"Thank you."

At Charles, she doesn't get up. "You know any good restaurants in Cambridge?"

Ridley hesitates a beat too long.

"Never mind. Sorry. I was just thinking of grabbing some food before making the ride back."

"Sounds wise," Ridley says. "There's a really good Korean restaurant. I was going to go home and make Shin Ramyun. This'll be better."

Her face brightens. "I don't want to put you out."

"You're not. I just need to call my wife and tell her I'll be back a little later."

Her expression doesn't change, which crosses one thing off the list. Ridley checks his phone and isn't surprised to find it dead.

"You ever met a monster?" Ridley asks. It is the sort of thing he really shouldn't have asked. But she already knows something very intimate about him.

"My mother," she says, "or so I've been told. She left us when I was little. I've been looking . . ." She stops herself, glances away to hide some deep and true emotion.

"I'm sorry to hear that. Do you know what she was?"

"I don't. I only overheard a little of the conversation." She turns away from him.

"I'm sorry for prying. It's just . . . not a lot of people know what I am."

"Were you born that way?"

"No," Ridley says before he considers lying. He laughs. "Long story."

"You're brave attending a rally like that."

"I'm stupid. I hope no one caught me on camera."

"I'm sure it will be okay."

Amethyst doesn't know that Ridley knew the person speaking, and likely Ruth will identify him to the Hand, if not to everyone. He smiles, though, accepting her wishful thinking. She smiles back. She is attractive, but in an unremarkable sort of way. A face that would disappear into a crowd, and you wouldn't be able to bring it to memory a moment later. Ridley has the thought and then feels bad for thinking it. He supposes he isn't particularly memorable either.

They get off at Kendall Square and walk to the Korean restaurant. Ridley has fried rice, and she has something closer to the ramen he would have had if he'd gone home.

Over the meal, they talk about their backgrounds. Ridley has to be vague about certain areas and avoid others entirely. He doesn't mention Rebecca or Lincoln. He does mention Laina. He avoids details about his work, but he talks a bit about his activism. He is especially careful about the SEN Collective, avoids the incident at the barn. Amethyst is the type not to press where the lines are being drawn. If she follows up with a question and he redirects, she moves on to another point of conversation.

She discloses more: where she went to school, what she did once she was finished, what she is doing now—which is a disappointment to herself and her father, who put her through university. Details about her mother.

"You had Korean food before?" he asks.

"A couple of times. I've always had a good experience; just not around people who reach for Korean first."

"You should suggest it, then. There's another spot near Harvard, a Korean fried chicken place that's pretty good."

"What made you go down to the rally?" she asks. The direct shift in the conversation catches Ridley off guard. There is an expression on her face that wasn't there before, and it doesn't seem at home with his image of her. It's gone in an instant. Ridley takes in the observation quietly.

"I wanted to see this movement growing in my city," he says. "I wanted to understand up close."

"Like I said, brave." She smiles.

Ridley pretends to look at his phone. "I should be off. My wife is expecting me."

"Okay," she says. "It was nice meeting you."

They pay their bills and part ways. Ridley doesn't leave an opening to exchange numbers.

When Ridley enters the house, Laina's eyes meet his. She turns down the volume on the TV. "You went down to the protest."

Ridley takes off his shoes but continues standing by the door, wordless.

"I saw the news. But I already knew there was a Black Hand rally downtown. I thought, *He's smart; he wouldn't go down there.* I thought, *He wouldn't do anything dangerous without talking to me first.* Turns out you're a fool, and you had the audacity to keep it from me."

"Babe."

"There's video," she says. "*Video*, Ridley. My heart was in my throat the entire time."

"Was my face visible?"

"Fortunately, no—not for lack of you trying to get yourself killed."

"I didn't know," Ridley starts. "I tried to be careful." He

hesitates again. He *didn't* try to be careful. He stood in a crowd of Black Hand with only a hoodie for concealment. He is lucky the event happened so fast, and no one got the right angle on him. "Ruth was there."

Laina accepts the change in subject. "She's with the Black Hand?"

"Onstage. Talking about Nick. I . . . lost myself for a moment."

"She saw you."

"That's how it started."

There is a moment when Laina's concern for Ridley almost overcomes her anger at him. But then: "You went down to the Common? The *Common*, Ridley."

Ridley moves from the front door, sits on the couch next to her.

"I'm sorry," he says.

"You're okay," Laina says. "That's the important thing, I guess."

She is angry. Nothing will turn it around. But she's trying anyway. He'll ruin this too. "Melku told me to keep an eye on the organization."

Her eyes go wide. "They told you this when?" Her mind catches up before he can answer, and Ridley sees the flash of fresh anger.

"It slipped my mind."

"Melku telling you to keep an eye on a human-supremacist group in Boston that has been known to kill monsters just . . . slipped your mind?"

Ridley says nothing. Is it true? He's actually not sure. Could the slip have been deliberate, a subconscious decision to leave that bit of information out?

Laina shuts off the television. "We talked about this. You don't shut me out. When you're in trouble, you tell me. If shit is going down, I'm there. None of us going off on our own."

"I know."

"And that slipped your mind too?"

"Laina—"

"The rest of that sentence better be the truth."

"I'm not . . ." he stops. *Lying?* It's worse if he isn't.

Footfalls announce Rebecca before she appears at the entrance to the hallway, her hair wet from the shower.

"Hey," she says, looking at Ridley. "Good to see you in one piece. You really should keep your phone charged."

"Don't make this worse, Bec."

"No way I could make this worse." She grins at Ridley. The only thing missing is a bag of popcorn.

Laina gets up from the couch. "I'm going to shower. You done in there, Becca?"

"Yeah," she says. She glances at Ridley with something like remorse. "We hungry? I could make cheesy noodles."

Laina edges past her. "I'm okay, but thanks."

"I don't suppose *you* want some cheesy noodles."

Ridley shakes his head. He gets up and goes to his room. It isn't just his; he shares the room with Laina on nights she stays with him. A few times a week, she stays in the room she shares with Rebecca. It's an arrangement they've managed to make work.

Laina will be staying with Rebecca tonight. Unless she wants to talk through her anger. But they've agreed that sometimes it's better to let things settle before they have the healing conversation. Ridley doesn't like going to bed with hurt feelings between them, but he messed up big with this one. She is afraid, and angry that he has made her feel that way. And the video. Ridley tries to imagine her sitting there watching him on a screen, unable to do anything but witness what might happen. The image in his mind makes his stomach clench.

Ridley's phone has to charge a bit before he can turn it on. Nine missed calls. And a series of texts that get angrier as they go on. This is all his fault, of course. If only he had charged his phone before leaving the house. He has taken to walking around with portable chargers instead of buying a new phone—something Laina often begs him to do. These conversations are lighthearted, resigned even. No way is he buying a new phone until the old one is dead without the possibility of resurrection. Now he feels foolish. Why has he been so stubbornly frugal?

Ridley sends her a text back:

> I really am sorry. Can we talk in
> the morning?

Fifteen minutes later, in the dark, his phone lights up.

> Yes. I'm okay really. I'm glad you're
> safe. See you in the morning.

Terse is Laina's normal style of texting, so it's impossible to tell whether her polite yet distant-seeming response is still anger, just the normal state of things, or his own guilt playing things up. He settles on the third option.

It is still an hour before any of them would typically go to bed. He turns on a podcast and waits for sleep to hit.

The night lumbers on, Ridley asleep and then awake and then asleep again. In the other room, Laina has fallen into sleep as well. Hers is deep, caught in a recurring dream. Those seconds of running right before the shooter fires his weapon, trying desperately to reach Ridley and unable to. The way his arms go wide as the bullet hits his shoulder, the stumble and then the sprawl. Repeatedly this happens—a terrible loop, Laina stuck in sap. And the shadow of an earlier dream, Ridley's body peeling, turning inside out from the gunshot wound, revealing muscle and bone, the wound devouring the reality around it.

Another hour passes in the waking world. Ridley awake again to the sound of someone entering his room. He peers through the dark, expecting to see Laina's silhouette, but the shadow that enters is slimmer.

The person slips into the bed with him.

"She's murmuring in her sleep," Rebecca says.

Ridley feels a twinge of guilt mixed in with the newness of the situation. Rebecca has never been in his bed before, not even with Laina present.

She lifts the covers and gets under them as naturally as if she had done it a hundred times. She nestles close to him.

"I understand something about you," Rebecca whispers. "You're like me, in a way. But more like Sarah."

Ridley hasn't heard that name in a while. But like Lincoln, Sarah is present in every conversation, coloring all their fears and anxieties. Ridley doesn't speak. He waits for Rebecca to explain herself.

She doesn't for a while. Instead, she puts a hand on his shoulder. "Is that okay?"

He wonders for a moment if she means to seduce him. But there has been no hint of this from her before. Something else, then? "It's fine."

"You're affectionate with Laina. I've been wondering if you'd ever transfer that affection to me. We fight often enough. Why not an occasional hug?"

"I didn't know you wanted hugs from me." She is dancing around something. And she won't say it unless he engages. "Okay. What is it about me that reminds you of yourself and Sarah?"

"You want to protect people against their will."

He is fully awake now. He has the feeling like he is trying to move a metal ball down a tiny maze, but with his mind. "Laina was trying to protect me, too, in the beginning of all this. I didn't know who sent the video until almost a year after she'd gotten it."

"She didn't do that to protect you."

"What are you really trying to say?" Ridley says, a little louder than he wanted to.

Rebecca doesn't raise her voice. "You're like me because your first instinct is to hide things from other people. To protect them. I used to do that all the time when I was an addict. Let me finish. I used to do that to protect people from who I was. And then, after the change, I did it to protect the pack. Always worrying over what I thought they could manage. I knew Lincoln was struggling, and I didn't tell Sarah. It was a mistake. I understood immediately why you'd go off and check out the Black Hand on your own. I even understand how it might not have occurred to you to do otherwise. We're the same in that way."

"And Sarah?"

"Sarah had the same definition of *her people* that you do. Justice with a big *J*. I just wanted to protect my family, but Sarah wanted to protect everyone."

Ridley didn't really know Sarah, but when they disagreed, it was because they were on opposite sides of the argument about protecting everyone. He was scared then. Now, if she were still alive, he could see a version of that conversation where they would have been on the same side.

"It's a shame we don't talk like this more often," Ridley says.

"This is my pillow talk. You'll have to pay me in cuddles."

Ridley considers the proposal. He's romantic, even if he is rarely sexual. But until this moment he failed to imagine this level of intimacy with Rebecca. Now he can.

"I've been thinking. Maybe you're right." Ridley hopes he doesn't have to elaborate.

"Well, I need to check hell to see if they're ice-skating down there. Get it? Because—"

"Please stop."

Rebecca laughs.

"You staying?" he asks.

They've both been told separately by Laina that she'd be okay with this very scenario, but this will be the first time it has happened. Only way to know for sure is to play it out. Rebecca rolls to rest on her back, but she keeps her body close to Ridley's.

"Okay?"

"Okay," he says.

An hour later, Laina opens her eyes. The house is filled with the quiet of late night, of sleep. She walks out to the living room.

"It's you," Laina says.

"You're getting good at that," says the invisible woman.

This other woman has a nice voice, she thinks, not for the first time. Now that Laina isn't terrified, now that she knows not to be afraid, she finds the woman's arrival comforting.

"Someone else I know has the ability to sense monsters," the voice says. "Well, she smells them. Is that what you do?"

This isn't the first time Laina has heard her mention other people, her own life.

"Not what I do," Laina says. "Or maybe I do. I don't know." It's the wolf that does it, Laina is sure. She has gotten so strong. The wolf, not her human self.

Laina is only a passenger.

The next day, Rebecca is outside her mother's house, restless.

The world is subtly different after the Emergence—the name that most people settled into after the Fracture. But it is *less* subtly different after the anniversary massacres. Three more violent incidents came in the days immediately after the massacre, when protests were at their heaviest—outrage fueling outrage, hordes of people spilling onto streets and shouting, no good way to tell which side they were on.

Several books have come out after the massacres—books of essays, research books, books of interviews, all claiming to know and understand the shadow world. The world of monsters. The wolves (Rebecca mostly) read these books or skimmed them or read reviews of them, searching for the truth, for other monsters like themselves. Most of the books are obviously bullshit—fabulist stories that don't match Rebecca's experience at all. But there are a smaller number that slip into a nebulous space.

What does she know, anyway? She is a werewolf, but not all the books are about werewolves. She did read books about witch covens. She has never met a witch, though she knows they are out there. The shooters, the police officers who showed up at her door with lists of names—they had clearly been touched by magic. The books cover many things but don't fill in the blanks that Rebecca needs filled.

She haunts the message boards, and much of what she finds there could be thrown out with the books. But she has found a few small forums and Reddit channels that feel closer to something real. And she can see, with some of the members in those groups, that they are feeling each other out—coded language that is either taken up or not, leading to deeper and deeper initiations. A nonmonster haunting the sites the way she does might learn some of these codes if they are persistent, if they don't burn their alias asking stupid questions. But eventually, she stumbles across places where you just have to know things, have to be able to describe what it feels like to shift. If monsters are on these sites—and Rebecca is now sure she has found a few of them—they won't confirm or deny a particular experience. Or tell her what it's like to live with an animal inside you that is sometimes outside you.

But Rebecca can guess who the real monsters are, based on who they keep talking to, who passes through all the rings of initiation to a kind of friendship. Eventually, conversations leave the boards and become direct messages. Rebecca has had her share of those conversations, which have all unfortunately been dead ends—idiots with terrible theories to peddle, people slipping into insanity, propositions for sex. (Could she verify that she is in fact a woman and is she hot, and no worries if you're into women; I'm a woman too.)

It is one of these latter messages that makes Rebecca put her phone away.

Seconds later, she has the urge to look at her phone again. In rebellion, she places it back in the car's cupholder. And then picks it up again when she realizes this is the only thing between her and the house—a barrier.

Rebecca checks her phone messages. Nothing.

Only six minutes have passed, the clock on her phone shifting from 7:54 a.m. to 8:00 a.m. They look so different, these numbers, despite the small difference between them. She gets out of the car.

She is let into a clean house. Gone are the random collections of stuff her mother kept around before the change.

"Have a seat in the living room. I'll bring us some tea."

Gone is that terrible resentment she used to hear in her mother's voice.

The living room is very clean, and her mother's humming fills the house. Rebecca saw this change as it was happening—her mother slowly clearing things away, "starting new." Could the hoarding have been a symptom of the fear of mortality? She wondered back then and is wondering about it now. Eventually, in a world where monsters had equality and didn't have to hide, there would be scientific studies about them—their shifting, their regeneration, the psychological effects of being a monster. Whether Rebecca's mother stopped hoarding because she was no longer afraid to die.

Her mother returns with two cups, a smile on her face.

"You look good," she says. "I guess those two really are good for you."

Before, her mother wouldn't even have acknowledged Ridley

as her other partner. She is getting better or, at least, feigning understanding. First step to the real thing.

Rebecca is too anxious to be discreet. "What's wrong?"

"I'm fine. Promise. But your brother."

Rebecca lets out a huff. "Of course. What did he say?"

"You both need to fix things. He told me you haven't talked in six months."

"Was he here?" Rebecca asks. She sniffs the air, trying to catch his scent, and does.

"A couple of days ago," her mother confirms.

"You could've bothered me about talking to Manny over the phone. Please tell me there's something else."

Her mother's expression is sober. "He knows."

Rebecca sits up. "You mean, you told him."

"He figured it out himself. Look at me."

"Okay, sure. But what else?"

"He found one of my kills in the freezer."

"What? Mom, we talked about this!"

"I didn't know he was coming, obviously. It's my house. If I want to put a rabbit in my freezer to keep, I'll do it."

Rebecca doesn't argue. There's no use. "So how are you doing otherwise?" she asks.

Rebecca, in her car again, phone in her hand. She should call him, tell him everything from her side. He'll understand, knowing how Dad died, knowing their mother would have died, too, without her intervention. But she has abandoned those justifications for herself and can't go back to pretending that what she did was right. She has made her mom a monster, and her mother has forgiven her. A mercy and, by all appearances, true without reservation. But Manny won't forgive Rebecca. There's too much between them that needs mending first.

She should call him anyway. Reconnect first. Then take the blows when the time comes.

She opens her text messages and scrolls until she finds him. Their last conversation, months ago:

> Can we meet up? It's been a while.

He never responded. She tries a variation of the same text. This time his reply comes immediately.

> I'm busy this week. I'll let you know.

While Rebecca is on her way back into town, Laina and Ridley leave the house together. They walk down the morning streets, the sunlight soft on their eyes, the heat of it gentle on their skin. They are only another ten minutes from the bookstore. They walk in silence, the fight from last night keeping them shut off in their own internal worlds.

It is Ridley who eventually disturbs the quiet. Though it is metaphor, *a stone dropped into still water* is the best way to describe how it shifts the tension between them. If tension can be an unmoving state, his words disturb it.

He says, "I am sorry I made you worry." When she doesn't speak, he continues. "I've been trying to figure out why I did it. The best I can come up with is that night in the barn. The strange woman."

Laina knows who he means because they've talked about that night several times. A dozen times. Two dozen? She has lost count. But she knows his "strange woman" because she has one too. Remembers the difference between them.

Ridley continues. "She was directing Melku that night, and I think Melku was directing me."

"And you couldn't tell me—"

"Because you'd stop me, and I might let you."

"And what would be wrong with that?"

"If you stopped me, I was worried something worse might happen. If a person is being guided toward something, they're also being guided away from something else."

"How do you know you weren't being guided *away* from safety?"

"I don't. But, and I'm not sure this'll make sense, inaction was scaring me more than action. Inaction meant I wouldn't be looking at the thing that was coming for me. So I decided to look."

A few minutes of silence as Laina processes his answer. And it does make sense. She does understand. Not for the first time, she considers the name of the human-supremacist group, remembers the dizziness she felt when she heard it for the first time, as if she'd been caught by the legs and pulled down. Pulled *in*? The Black Hand . . .

"I get it," she says. They are turning a corner, the bookstore in view. She isn't any less angry—the emotion replacing all the worry and fear. But she understands, which is a mending of a sort, or the beginning of one.

Not an eventful first hour at the bookstore. Second hour, the same. Around eleven it happens. Laina is looking down as someone approaches. She's done the motion a dozen times. Reflexively, she glances up, smiles at the man standing there. But then her smile falters, its impression fading gradually.

"I thought a lot about how I would come to see you. If this is the wrong way, I apologize. I wasn't sure you'd let me talk to you, and I needed to talk to you. At least once."

No other staff are here. A few patrons are perusing the shelves, but no one else is approaching. No distractions. No witnesses.

"Do you go out for lunch? There's a restaurant nearby we could go to."

Several, actually. But the thought of being alone with him makes her want to jump out of her skin. "In an hour, I'll be on break. Meet me outside."

To his credit, he doesn't linger. But Laina doesn't want to give him credit, earned or not, even for the smallest thing.

At noon, she steps away from the help desk, and Madeline replaces her. She makes a cursory glance around the store. Ridley isn't here. He is downstairs at this very moment, having a conversation with one of the patrons about the latest release from a veteran author whose work has shifted since the Emergence—her latest about a monster that torments a small lakeside town. Laina doesn't wait to catch Ridley or go looking for him. She leaves through the front door.

He's standing just outside, against the wall, and looks at her before she can control her facial expression. A frown crosses his face.

Laina points across the street where a small park—if it could even be called that—is tucked away, with benches under the cover of old maples. They make their way over, and the silence between them is the silence of two strangers.

He is eager to say something, but Laina is grateful he hasn't found the words yet.

No one is at the park—just the two of them, which is both

preferred and not preferred. Birdsong pierces the quiet. The concrete pebbled with small stones of different colors.

"I'm only in town for a few more days," he says.

Laina is stealing glances at the man's face. Yes, there is a semblance to her memory of him, but he also looks strange. Before her mother got rid of all his photographs, there was something to keep his physical image clear for her. After, he was a blurry image and then just an impression. Lincoln would make a facial expression, and she would see him in it. She would look in the mirror, and there would be a moment when she would find him there in some quirk of her face. The truth was, Lincoln looked more like their mother. She was the one who bore his likeness.

There is gray in his beard and what remains of his hair. More gray than black. And he has blemishes that have become permanent residents on his cheeks, below his eyes, on his nose. A mole on an eyelid. Razor burn darkening the skin on his neck. He is clean looking, shaved, and either taking care of himself or being taken care of by someone else. A wife?

"I want to know more about what happened to Lincoln," he says, and the earnestness in his expression is painful. How far removed is this current man from the one she knew, the one who pushed her away from him when she wanted to be picked up, just so he could watch the television unbothered. She didn't remember being pushed—her mother had told her about this. But she did remember his voice—so loud, always loud, booming through the house. The time she heard crashing furniture late one night, and the next day her mother was wearing a hoodie in the summer. How old was she when she knew what it meant, and she had decided what kind of man he was? The man in front of her was not the man she had decided on.

But the audacity. To ask her, a child he has abandoned, about another child he also abandoned, who died never having seen this degree of concern expressed over its welfare when it was alive.

"What do you want to know?" she finds herself saying, and her voice is sharp. He must hear the anger in it, even if she's trying to keep her face neutral.

"How did it happen? How did he become that thing?"

Laina shrugs—the habitual response. How would she know? "What does it matter how it happened? It happened."

He is taken aback by this. "Well, it matters as far as his soul is concerned. Did he choose it? Was he attacked?"

Laina is stuck on the word "soul." She's doing the math in her head, arriving at a plausible path for this miracle of a man in front of her, his open face, the deeply felt concern in his voice. For Lincoln's soul.

"He didn't choose anything," she tells him. "A werewolf attacked him, and he became one." He wouldn't know that they were estranged at the time, so he wouldn't ask how she knew about the attack. *He is a stranger,* she reminds herself. She sees the wedding band on his hand. Reflexively, Laina lifts her hand from her lap, but she aborts the action. She has no idea what she was about to do. Her face remains neutral through this.

"Was he going to church when he died?"

Laina feigns confusion.

"Was he saved, is what I mean."

"No," she says, failing to hide her amusement. "So, you've found God. Mom would be happy for you."

"Don't get smart."

There's some deep-down part of Laina that flinches when

he says this, shrinking in, and then surprise, followed by the overwhelming urge to fight back against her own unexpected betrayal. "It is too late to save Lincoln. You're too late. Go home."

"Is it too late for me and you?"

"Yes," she says. Laina lets the human slip just a little and reveals her wolf. She catches the moment he sees the wolf too. Now it's *his* turn to shrink away. "Go home," she repeats. "We don't have anything else to talk about."

On the way back down the side street, she sees two men standing at the corner, looking into the bookstore. She moves quickly but glances down at their hands.

They are both wearing black gloves, but only on one hand.

She feels a phantom sensation of fingers grasping her ankles from below.

THE BLACK EGG:
PART ONE

*What is magic? And if the universe has magic, what are its
laws? Where did it come from, and what is its purpose?*
—Richard Wallace, *The Fracture Effect Redux*

9

Marjorie Cameron grew up strange. Even at a young age, she had that mystical quality about her, this beautiful and horrifying closeness to the edges of reality. She would lie awake at night and imagine Death just outside her window, dragging his scythe behind him. In winter, the trees around her house looked like the skeletal fingers of colossi sprouting from the earth.

At school, she excelled in art and staring out windows. Boys thought she was cute, but they didn't linger; something about her scared them off. Girls thought she was odd, but she managed to keep acquaintances. Nothing particularly damaging happened to her at school. She endured no cruelties, had no rivals. She was that friend who danced in the orbits of many groups, coming in to see what was happening before moving on, a comet's tail streaming out behind her as she left the solar system. She would return, predictably—always—but people learned not to expect much from her beyond her regular appearances.

She also excelled in drama club. She sang beautifully. All these things came naturally to her. And at night, she would hear the scraping of the scythe too heavy for Death to lift as he stalked the yard around her house.

Cameron grows up without hardship. She joins the navy during the Second World War. And then, after a superior officer notices her beauty and her easy way around men, she becomes a special agent in the war effort, doing work she can never talk about. When the war is over, she takes a government job in DC, and just as when she was an agent, she is tight-lipped about what she actually does. It is during this time that a coworker introduces her to Jack Parsons, the rocket scientist who will become her husband.

They meet at an occult gathering at his residence (Cameron has long been interested in occultism), and they exchange a smile and a fleeting word. But they don't connect until the next time she appears at his house, pulled back into his orbit by the same friend who invited her the first time.

"I performed a ritual of summoning," he tells her when she arrives at his house. "I knew you'd come."

He's handsome, so Cameron entertains the strange comment, curious. "I'm pretty sure I brought myself," she says.

They sit in his living room, engaging in light flirtation and talking about his interests.

"I love science fiction, particularly the work of Robert Heinlein," he says. "Do you like science fiction?"

"Sure," Cameron says. She has already decided to sleep with him. She isn't delicate about such things.

Cameron asks him how he got into the occult—the real story, not the one where an angel or some higher being appears to him in his living room.

"The way most people do. The way you did, I'm sure. I met someone, and we had a great conversation. I learned some things, read some books on my own. And then I never stopped."

Jack is being presumptuous. Cameron didn't have to meet anyone to discover her own interest. She has a flash of memory, her alone in her bedroom, the sound of Death dragging his scythe outside her window.

He continues talking. He tells Cameron that he works as a rocket technician by day—part of a three-man team he co-founded to work on government contracts—and investigates occultism at night and on the weekends. No, he doesn't see any distinction between physics and metaphysics; they're both the same, really. The universe is still a magic trick even if you learn its laws.

He says, "If you're thinking of going deeper, I can guide you further down this rabbit hole. If you like."

It is a perfectly normal thing for a man like him to say. But Cameron has already lived a full life, worked in intelligence, left her little town, and guided herself down her own rabbit holes. She doesn't need his guidance.

"I would like that," she says. Her laugh starts false and turns real. "And while you *guide me*, I'll show you what I know. You might discover more yourself."

He laughs back. "Fair enough. I'd like that too."

Is it love? Cameron doesn't need it to be. She is interested and thinks she'll be interested for a while. Love starts as a decision.

Jack hosts several more gatherings at his house that Cameron is witness to, but one stands out more than the rest. This particular gathering takes place after Jack and Cameron have married. The year is 1946, and it is a larger affair—some of Jack's more open-minded work friends, physicists and engineers with an interest in metaphysical questions; Marjorie's artist friends with similar proclivities; occultists whose interests are more than recreational; a few Thelemites of note; and the great man Aleister Crowley himself, the father of the Thelema religion, arriving fashionably late with an expensive bottle of whiskey.

This is Cameron's first time seeing the man, and the last. He is short up close, but when he stands anywhere in the room, he towers over everyone. It is like an optical illusion. He grows with distance, and when he's near, people's attention pulls toward him.

On several occasions the night of the gathering, Cameron and Crowley are at close quarters, and the people near them become dizzy in their combined presence, split apart. Cameron, by all appearances, does not notice her similar power over people unless she's actively turning on her charm, but even her passive presence attracts people's attention. Crowley will be the man everyone remembers, as is often the case in this era. But Cameron will be a spot of fire in everyone's mind for the rest of their lives. If she appears bright in hindsight, imagine her brightness undimmed by the biases of men.

The early part of the night is filled with small talk—people moving around in search of good conversation, but eventually they find their little clusters and hover there as people come and go. Crowley draws a cluster to him, and more and more people, sensing the change in the air, join him. He isn't a particularly interesting conversationalist, Cameron notices. He talks very slowly, as if he must dig each word up out of a pile in the back of his mind. He is soft-spoken, with none of the showy charisma she's seen in handsomer men—Crowley isn't handsome. But he has something else: a certain daring. No one can tell where he will go next, and his stories, even when they're dull, have surprises waiting around bends.

Later in the night, as people tire and drift away, Jack and Cameron linger, along with a handful of other attendees. Everyone is tired. They've been listening for an hour to Crowley's recounting of a conversation with Churchill. But then he shifts in his chair and reminisces about his brief time in the Hermetic Order of the Golden Dawn.

"I got into too many arguments," Crowley says. "I wasn't stuffy enough, I figure—hadn't narrowed myself to one way of thinking." His tenure in the Hermetic Order was short-lived. According to Crowley, the group had been embroiled in heavy infighting for some time, forming factions around key personalities. It was the law of mass in action—with so many of the English intelligentsia in such a small space, fractures inevitably began to form. Crowley was certainly at the center of some of the drama. He had an infamous rivalry with Yeats that led to its own chasms: William and his cult of the mind, and Aleister and his cult of the dark arts. Crowley viewed Yeats as a talentless hack, and Yeats, determined to counter this critique with a more scathing one, called Crowley a liar and a fraud of the greatest magnitude.

As she listens, Cameron is struck by the high drama of it, all these great people in the same place. And decades later, in the hospital on the eve of her death, she will smile as she recounts this gathering, and this particular point in the night as Crowley is sharing gossip from his time in the infamous secret society.

"When looking at this history from a distance, it is easy to forget just how many famous and infamous people cross over within their lives," Cameron tells me on the night before she dies. "But once the dates are compared, the comings and goings of every life in every era, it isn't difficult to draw a straight line of connection with all these key figures, entering and leaving, meeting one famous so-and-so, who soon dies and is replaced by another such person who has known so-and-so and had risen to prominence, telling stories of such and such to famous artist Y, who goes on to meet revolutionary C, has an awkward interaction with famous artist W, and passes it on to infamous character Q, who starts a school of thought and art that will attract artists H, J, and V. From a particular vantage, this can, as some people have said, begin to look like a great play, with famous entrances and exits. But the playgoers are sometimes actors, and everyone eventually dies, keeling over in their seats or backstage, or right there onstage. A solid line of passing acquaintances, deep friendships, and vicious rivalries. You know what I mean. Right?"

I nod. I do know what she means—intimately.

On the night of the gathering, Crowley continues: "I left the group in a bad way. But I wouldn't have lingered, in any event. The Hermetic Order of the Golden Dawn had no real insights into the great mysteries. But one interesting thing *did* happen during my time there, the only one that I still carry with me—a glimpse at a particular great truth . . ."

Cameron, on the eve of her death: "He's done it again—caught us all around the bend. The sleep lifts from everyone's eyes. There is a collective leaning-in."

Crowley, the night of the gathering: "I met a poet. Incredibly famous for a certain time. I met him at one of the socialization parties. Not much different from the one we're at right now. I remember he had big eyes. No, more like he kept his eyes open wide, trying not to miss anything, or scared of everything. Everyone else at those parties was busy presenting a persona."

Cameron, on the eve of her death: "I thought then, *Aren't you?* And then I thought, *Was he?* Perhaps he was exactly this strange person we were glimpsing. I'd seen so many performances myself over the years, people presenting a certain idea of themselves. With Crowley, I could not make up my mind. He was—sorry, where was I? Oh . . . yes, he told us he went over to the poet, and—"

Crowley, the night of the gathering: "He startled when I began speaking to him. It took him a while to calm down. I got us both drinks from the bar and found a chair away from the noise. Preliminary discussion first. I asked him who he was. I hadn't seen him at one of these things before. I told him I had joined recently. I asked him about his work, and he recited some of his poetry. I usually don't have the taste for the kind of poetry that makes a poet a name, but I liked his. After the reading, the poet suddenly asked me if I wanted to hear a story. I told him I did."

And so do the party guests Crowley has now enraptured. They have been pulled through a kind of tunnel, time and space shrinking before them.

Crowley: "He said to me that when he was a younger man, he'd taken a lover—an older man, pale but still in good health. And one night, after they'd made love, the poet's head on this older man's chest, the man told the poet a story.

"'I've lived a long time,' the man said. 'But when I was young, I was part of a secret society. I had an occupation within that society, as an indoctrinator. It was through this occupation I learned how to perform transformation. First, get a child. Any child will do, but it must be incredibly young, preferably preverbal. Pay a peasant, or a woman ready to be rid of her sin, or—and this was my practice—develop relationships with several convents and orphanages. Take a suitably young child and lock it away.'

"The old man paused. The poet, expecting him to take a breath and gather himself, waited for him to do so. The old man did not breathe. In fact, his chest had been still the entire time the poet was lying there.

"This should've been a great concern, but the poet was hungry for more information. He said, 'Okay, lock the child away. What else? Why do this?'

"The old man smiled without parting his lips. He said, 'What I will tell you is a curse.'"

And on that night, long before Cameron's death, long before the party with Crowley—and further back still, on the night the poet lies in his lover's arms—there's a moment when the poet considers stepping back from whatever his lover is going to tell him. And he will remember for many years those final seconds on that precipice between who he is and who he will never be again. But the poet is young, far away from that terrified older version of himself, famous and damned, telling his story to Crowley.

So, on that night in his lover's arms, the poet says, "Tell me."

And the old man tells him everything.

Cameron, on the eve of her death, going pale from the memory: "And Crowley tells us everything. Everything the old man says, recounted to Crowley by the poet and recounted to us through Crowley. The whole terrible truth, like an evil game of telephone. We are told that the entire time the poet was talking to Crowley, the poet was terrified, looking everywhere, searching for eavesdroppers, for onlookers, for ghosts. We are all transfixed by this recounting, every eye on this man in failing health— we can tell just by looking—but Crowley's spirit is very alive, and it is the spirit we cling to. And through Crowley we see the poet's fear, but also the spell the poet was under, the spell we're all now under, glimpsing this deep secret. Only the secret is grotesque in every way. Something shifts in the room with us. The rest of the house is dark, except for a light in the foyer to guide the way out. And despite the light in the room, I can feel the darkness waiting just outside the light, and it feels deeper, like a shroud. I find myself praying that the lights don't go out. I pray that the darkness doesn't consume us."

Crowley, the night of the gathering: "Do that," Crowley says, ending the story, and it is unclear whether these are Crowley's words or the poet's. "Do that and you can make a monster."

"Did he try it?" a man in the back asks. Within months, this man will become close friends with Jack and Cameron, and they'll give him the nickname Ace.

Crowley says, "Of course he did."

"And have you?" Ace asks.

Crowley doesn't answer.

"So, you don't want to go to UVI?"

Gina is so much her father's daughter, with that same wan-derlust in her eyes. "I don't want to make the safe choice."

I am thinking, *At least it's school and not the military. At least it is books and not war.* "You have any ideas?"

She shrugs, but she does list a handful of schools. By the tone of her voice, I can tell she isn't excited about any of them.

And it is in that moment when the terrible idea comes to me, leaping from my mouth before I can even consider why I'm saying it.

Gina considers what I've said, and my heart is in my throat as I wait for her to gather the full weight of it.

"I worked at State. But there's Chapel Hill and Duke." *And you'll have family there,* I want to say but dare not.

Those eyes, so terribly sharp, taking me in. "Okay."

Mom has never actually spoken to Gina since she was a

child. For Mom, it is an active choice. But she's kept money in an account for Gina's college, which she doesn't know I know about. I can tell that her distance from her only grandchild is hurting her. (She hasn't been shy in expressing her disappointment that I haven't settled down yet.)

So I float the question on a phone call: "I've been talking to your granddaughter about college."

"Oh," Mom says, and tries to change the subject.

I let it happen that first time but bring it up again later in the conversation.

"She's thinking about colleges stateside," I say. "Told her there's some good ones in the Triangle."

"University of the Virgin Islands is a good school."

"It is, but she wants to see the world."

Something about my response sets her off. She changes the subject. "Your little sisters want you to come up for their birthday."

This time I don't let it go. "I'll bring Gina up to look at schools."

"Don't you dare."

"We'll get a room at a hotel. You won't have to see her." *Unless you want to come see her,* I leave unsaid.

I chew on the silence that follows, waiting.

"They said they don't want any books," she says.

"Oh, they'll get books. And they better read them this time."

"Call me to let me know when you're getting in. I'll get Daryl to come pick you up from the airport."

"I can get a rental from the airport to the hotel."

"You'll stay with me."

I don't need to ask about Gina. I also let that part stay unsaid.

We get a pair of cheap flights together. Economy because I'm still needing to scrounge enough dollars together to pay rent and utilities and keep paying off my student loans. But I can't imagine a version of myself that would ever go first class, even if I had the money. Gina stares jealously at the first-class passengers as we file past them, and as we sit down in our cramped seats, she says, "One day I'll sit up front." It's the first time in my life that I have considered "up front" when it comes to airplanes, or how seldom I ever see other Black people sitting there. Gina has always been like this, making me aware of the world around me in ways I wasn't before. At some point, without my realizing it, she has become my tether to this world.

On the plane, Gina is reading another of my stories on her phone. Soon the plane is ready to take off. The same trip I made, but in reverse: the short runway, the plane leaping along and releasing itself from the earth, just as the water comes into view. Takeoffs are the hardest, and I hold on to the armrests as the plane lurches up and up, my heart loud in my chest. I'm awake for the first fifteen minutes, asleep not long after the plane reaches cruising altitude.

Over the past few years, I've traveled a handful of times, mostly to see Mom and my little sisters, though I try to hang out with Tanya as well when I'm in town. When she has time to hang out with me.

When I wake up, Gina is staring out the window. I nudge her in the side, and she squirms.

"Stop it," she says, but a smile crosses her face.

"Are you finished?" I ask.

Her smile goes away. "He died," she says.

I nod.

"And the grandmother too."

"But you knew she would. She was old and sick."

"So much death," she says. "I wanted the grandmother to live."

"Everyone dies eventually." I observe her watching me, incredulous. "You know what I mean."

"Not in the story I just read," she says. "In the story, some people get to live forever."

"A lot of people had to die to get there," I say.

"I still wish I could see it," she says. "Visit that world."

For the hundredth time, I consider the harm I might be doing to Gina. It does something to you, this envy of other worlds. I can see the envy in Gina's eyes. She is older now, and I've watched it happen—the same sharpness but grown into itself. Wise and piercing at the same time. That same spacey awe her father had at his best. If there is anything I envy now, it is those intermittent years when other people got to see her grow. All that time I've missed. But then I think of Cory, all he's been denied: a life, seeing his daughter grow up, growing old.

There's nothing I can really say, so I let the conversation die.

Landings are better, although for a moment, this descent unbalances me—the added turbulence of passing through the cloud layer. The bounce of wheels against the tarmac.

Daryl doesn't pick us up from the airport. Mom does. There's an awkward moment when Gina says hello and leans in for a hug, and though Mom doesn't stop her, she doesn't meet Gina's eyes. The drive home is quiet and tense when I'm not filling the silence. I talk to each of them and pretend not to notice they aren't talking to each other.

At the house, Mom observes Gina from across the room. Gina pretends not to notice. I am there in the middle, watching them both when they're pretending not to watch each other. I turn on the TV to fill the space between all of us, flick through channels until I find a movie: *Lethal Weapon 4*, just a few minutes in.

"This is a good one," I say. "It has Jet Li in it."

Gina turns to me. "Who is Jet Li?"

"Stop it. You're making me feel ancient."

"You *are* ancient."

I laugh and look at Mom. The smile on her face turns to something complicated.

During a commercial break, Mom gets up and goes to the bathroom. When she comes out, she doesn't return to the living room.

Daryl comes home at 7:00 p.m. He is nothing but grunts and long sighs as he drops his bag, stuffed with who knows what, at the door. He steps on his right heel with his left foot, frees himself from his right shoe, and then does the other. Stuffs his socks into his worn Converses.

I watch him from the living room, wait for him to acknowledge us.

He doesn't look at us but says, "You both eat yet?"

"We were going to order some pizza," I say.

"Your mom okayed that?" he asks.

I see my folly. "No."

He yells to the back of the house, "You thinking about making food, Anne?"

The sound of Mom's first name makes Gina's eyes light up. "Anne," she says.

"Annabel," I say, which only sends her spinning further.

"What kind of name is that?" Gina whispers to me.

Had she not heard Mom's name before? In Gina's presence, I'd only said "your grandmother." Keren must have called her "Ms. Turner."

Mom doesn't answer Daryl. He looks to me. I shrug. "She been in there since midafternoon."

An expression crosses his face. I can't name it, but the contours of it are clear to me. He disappears down the hall, closes the door behind him. They're in there for thirty minutes. Gina watches the TV for another fifteen, then whispers, "I'm hungry."

They both emerge from that inner dark, everything made clear. Mom's eyes are puffy and red. Gina looks up, her lips pressed tight, too smart for her own good.

"I'm going out to get some food from Alice's. Caribbean spot down the road," Daryl says. "You both like chicken, right?"

We nod like obedient children.

"Mac and cheese, peas and rice, greens?"

We nod.

He does the door dance in reverse, his bag still resting against the wall.

Mom shuffles into the living room, sits in her chair. We continue watching the television.

"You going to check out Duke too?" she asks after a few minutes. She's looking at Gina.

"Yes, ma'am."

I manage to keep my expression neutral at the use of "ma'am."

"I'm your grandmother," Mom says.

"Yes, ma'am," Gina says. "Grandma."

Mom nods, satisfied. "I want to watch a movie. Something funny this time."

We surf the movie channels, settle on *Hitch*, even though it's halfway through. Dinner arrives as the credits roll.

Later that night, before Gina and I settle into our beds (the twin beds my younger sisters used to sleep in), Asha appears at the window. She could just have appeared in the room, I suspect, but she always arrives first outside, to give us the option of letting her in.

Gina unlocks the window, muscles it upward. There is a high-pitched screech as it moves along its seldom-used grooves. She repeats the action with the bug screen, and Asha slides by her. Barely a sound as she lands on the rug between our beds.

Sometimes Asha talks to us. Sometimes she just arrives, and we play with her—could *play* be the right word for it?—and we talk to her.

Asha looks at me, and I scoop her up, stroking her head. *This is a god,* I remind myself. I shake myself alert and remember Damsel's words years ago: *She is the god of everything you know.* I pause a moment to give these words the proper awe even though I never fully understood them. What, then, is the universe, and the contracts it issued? Is the universe Asha, or did Asha create the universe? All my time lurking in that other world, and I still don't know.

Gina drops down to sit on the floor. She puts her hand out and invites Asha to come to her. Asha stirs in my arms, and I release her. She folds herself into Gina's lap, and Gina resumes petting her in my place.

"Tell me," Gina says, "how many people do you visit like this?"

This is a test. Gina has asked this question before. Asha never answers her, though she does choose to answer other things, or ask us questions, or offer cryptic messages that I've come to expect from gods and the creatures that enter into contracts with them.

There's no telling when Asha will speak, or even whether she will at all, so I just settle into Gina's string of questions and statements.

Gina isn't careful with Asha at all—tells her about her day, the plane ride, the drive home, the awkwardness between herself and her grandmother. This is the first time I'm hearing about it, so I listen.

"She hates me," Gina says.

Still Asha doesn't answer.

"Or she can't make up her mind if she hates me."

She's mourning, I want to say. All this time, and she still mourns. I suppose I do too, in my own way, though I can go days without remembering that I've lost a brother. Did the visits in Gina's dreams help me? Does he now exist in some demi-monde I find comforting?

She is a mother. I hear the voice in my mind, so I know where it's coming from. I look down, and Asha is staring right back up at me. "Sometimes distance protects."

Gina shakes her head. "That's stupid. I have a cousin who lost her father, and her grandmother doesn't act like that."

Asha goes quiet again, and so does Gina.

"Have you visited other versions of your mother?" Gina asks.

There's a logic to the question—where it came from, where it's leading. "I have. But I try not to pry around in the heads of people I know. Even other versions of them."

"But you did with Dad," she says.

"I did."

We've never discussed this, so I don't know how she knows.

That is when I get the sense that someone is standing outside in the hall. I turn to look, just in time to see my mother
disappear back into the dark. Her expression is all worry and
confusion. And anger.

Cameron, on the eve of her death: "After the gathering, we all had to decide whether the story held any real truth. Crowley's interests, my husband's interests, all those silly people at the gathering—it all felt like play. And I was happy to play until the real thing came along."

But even though Cameron doesn't believe it, she feels a chill run up her spine. Something in it feels real.

Over the ensuing months after the gathering, Cameron returns to that story at the party, tonguing it like an ulcer on the inside of her mouth. She doesn't like Crowley, she has decided. She won't say this to her husband, who adores the man, or let it slip at a party where everyone is hanging on his every word. But this dislike is irrefutable.

He has dead eyes. Not unreadable eyes, or even evil eyes. No, they turn her stomach in a specific way. He is without concern for good or evil, which is worse than anything. Her senses tell her this, and she's learned to trust her senses. They've saved her life more than once. Her senses also tell her that the story isn't over.

The day Ace calls them to his house, he leads them into his living room. They haven't been to his house for a number of months. They talk there, but all the while he keeps looking over their shoulders. Cameron gets a strange feeling when she looks behind her. Later she'll realize he was looking at the door to his basement.

And then, several times on the next visit, Cameron thinks she hears something in the basement—a stirring. But as Ace gets drunk—they are all drinking from his collection of scotch— he becomes less self-conscious about his basement project, so Cameron stops paying attention as well.

Jack doesn't say anything until they leave. "What do you think he's doing down there?"

"Raising the dead," she jokes. But then she goes quiet, her voice taken right out of her. She sleeps fitfully that night.

The next time they visit, Ace has a lock on the basement door, a crude latch drilled into the wood, and a bandage around his forearm.

"What happened to you?" Jack asks. He watches Ace closely, obvious in his suspicions.

"An accident in my laboratory."

They've heard this talk before. Ace has a few ongoing projects in his laboratory, one of which is his own religion, partly inspired by Crowley's. He is also writing two novels and a book on the Hermetic Order.

None of those projects would result in an injury on his forearm.

Ace moves them once again to the living room, where they drink more of his scotch, and Jack argues with him about space travel. Cameron is not paying attention. She lets her thoughts carry her, and four times that night she finds herself looking at the basement door. Eventually, she looks over at Ace, sees that he knows she is interested. A smile briefly reveals teeth, and she imagines that his canines are sharp enough to draw blood.

Over the years, she'll come back to the house, and the door to his basement will grow more elaborate—three rows of sliding bolts, the frame reinforced with steel. She wishes she could say she hears something behind those doors, but there is a noticeable absence of sound near that basement. She knows how crazy this sounds, but there is no other way to describe it.

One night, they all get really drunk. It's raining outside, the wind a banshee screaming to be let in. They draw the windows, and Ace lights candles. It is an intimate setup. Cameron drapes herself over his sofa, propping herself up on one elbow. Every once in a while, she catches a lustful look from Ace. She entertains it. Jack hates it and loves it at the same time. He becomes wildly possessive, which she likes.

They've drained so much of Ace's alcohol, she reminds herself, for the fourth year running, that they've planned to get him the most expensive whiskey they can find—and can pay for.

For the next hour, they discuss high magic. And then it is too late, and they are too drunk to leave. The storm outside rages. It sounds like a stampede of little people running up the windows, which means the rain has turned to sleet.

"Strange," Jack says. "Sleet in California, at this time of year?"

"Stranger things are inside this house," Ace confesses.

Jack and Cameron both stop moving, as if they might startle

the deer in front of them. Ace lets out a laugh that blends with a crack of thunder.

It is all so gothic, Cameron thinks. She is grateful that the next words out of Ace's mouth don't mesh with those that preceded them. "I need to take a piss."

But then he returns with a set of keys and stands next to the basement door. He says nothing. Neither does Cameron or Jack, but they stand all the same.

It takes time to unbolt the door, and in that time, Cameron realizes she also needs to pee. But the door swings open, and Ace descends the stairs. First, Jack looks to Cameron, who is clearly frightened, but he smiles gleefully. Down they go. There is no dramatic hesitation. When they reach the bottom, a wall of brick is there to greet them. At the center is a door small enough that they must stoop through. Ace unlocks it— another set of bolts to free. Hunched over, he enters, and again they follow.

The room smells alive. Like mud, sweet and musky.

A child is chained to the wall. The child lifts its head, murmurs words Cameron doesn't hear.

"He's caught something," Ace says.

Cameron will remember the child's eyes in that moment for the rest of her life. Red. Not the red of sleep deprivation. Red entirely.

The child's skin might have been brown at some point, but now it is gray, like putty.

"I told him he was an incarnated god. The Faery Lord of the Inner Chamber. Eyes of the Eternal Blood," Ace scoffs. "Drivel."

At his words, the child looks up, a pained expression on his face. The red eyes turn wet and ooze. Cameron isn't sure those are tears. She isn't even sure the tormented thing in front of her can cry.

"The fiction took," he says. "For a time."

Jack isn't speaking, hasn't spoken since they entered, and Cameron honestly has forgotten he is there. She jumps when Jack says, "The fiction took?"

"I told him he could conjure flames from his hands. And one day he'll burn the world, cleanse it of its sins. His destiny was to remake humankind as his firelings. I got carried away," Ace admits. "But two years ago he began to conjure flames from the air. Truthfully, I'm a little relieved he got sick. I'd frightened myself thinking what he'd do if he reached maturity."

"Maturity," Cameron says. Her mind is empty, but it fills then with a question on a repeating loop. She asks it.

"Only one other time," Ace says. "I convinced that one she was a vampire and introduced her to daylight. Let the evidence burn away."

He says this without remorse, and Cameron notices those dead eyes, like Crowley's. His whole demeanor has changed, as if he's cleaved away a false skin.

"I'm ready to try it for real the next time."

At some point, Jack has sat on the floor. His mouth is open. He is trying to speak, but the same sickness has caught him that caught Cameron that night a year ago, when she said Ace was down here trying to raise the dead. Cameron remembers anew the coldness she felt when she said the words, as if something passed through her, slipped between her atoms.

The child starts coughing, trembling through each expulsion of sickness.

She asks the only other question.

Ace answers: "I stole him from a children's home. It works best when you get them young. Before they can speak."

Each admission is a knife twisting in her. Jack has turned all the way into himself. The interest has evaporated. Only fear and disgust remain.

The child coughs again.

"He'll probably die tonight," Ace says.

Cameron, on the eve of her death: "My whole life could pass me by, and the sight of that child would be enough to haunt me for a lifetime. But the night had further plans for all of us."

Cameron doesn't know how long she's been standing there in quiet observation of what Ace has done. Enough time for her to take in the implication of what lies before them. Magic can make monsters. Magic itself is monstrous. A lie received can be transmuted into fact. What is the world if that can be true? Where are its limits?

"What happened next?" I ask.

"Near the child, the wall shimmered. And a goddess stepped through. Made of starlight."

NEW ERA

DRAGON
MEDFORD, MASSACHUSETTS
EARTH 0539

AUGUST 12, 2026

When they pull into the BJ's parking lot, he goes in by himself. Dragon starts by grabbing items off the shelf that he knows from memory. He is pulling a bag of rice into the bottom of his cart when he sees a man looking at him. Dragon recognizes the look of curiosity. He makes himself strain a little more moving the bag of rice. Dragon is still skinny, though he is starting to gain some muscle. But he doesn't look like someone who can lift a bulk bag of rice so easily.

He puts two bottles of oil in the cart and again catches the man at the end of the aisle looking. He doesn't usually worry about being followed by someone from his old life. No one who knows him from that life would be in a place like BJ's. And the glamour that Damsel has put on him masks him well enough from anyone trying to sniff out his magic. But he does sometimes get a look from someone that makes him think they can somehow tell he's a monster.

Dragon can't be sure, but he thinks the man is looking at him like that.

Dragon gets eggs last—crates of them. Then he goes to check out, keeping his attention ahead. He can hear someone come up behind him in the line.

"That's a lot of food."

Dragon turns and quickly regrets it. Too late to pretend he didn't hear the man. "Yes, sir," he says. "We have a big family."

"A very big family," says the man. "You're a good kid to be doing this all by yourself. I've seen you in here before."

Dragon doesn't know what to say to this, so he just smiles and turns back around. The man ahead of him is starting to put his items on the belt. He has a lot of items.

"I started working when I was around your age," the man says. "Do you help pay for all this?"

"No, my mom gives me a card."

"Wow, your own card. And you never buy anything you're not supposed to?"

"No."

"You're a very good kid."

The man is wearing a T-shirt with the word *Burn* in flaming letters. His jeans are a little ragged, but in a way that suggests either that they are his favorite pair or that he bought them that way. Dragon still can't tell the difference.

He makes sure to look for a black glove, but the man isn't wearing one. The man's cart, however, is suspiciously empty.

Dragon tries to turn away, but the man starts talking to him again.

"How old are you?"

Dragon isn't sure how old he is, but he gives a plausible age to anyone who asks. "Thirteen." He might be twelve or fourteen, but he always chooses the one in the middle. Dragon doesn't know if it matters anyway. Maybe he is years older, and dragons age slower. But he is the only dragon he knows of.

"A good age," the man says, nodding. The man has a beard that has turned white and fairly good teeth. Dragon's teeth are fine, but they could be better. All those years underground. "How's school?" the man asks. "You getting good grades?"

Dragon doesn't know how to answer him. He is surprised by the question. The man's skin is brown, his hair low and curly. He has bulging eyes that make him look like he's trying to take in everything at once. It is unnerving how steadily he is watching Dragon.

"You must go to school, don't you?" he is asking.

"Leave the child alone," says a woman with a cartful of bulk items. She is behind the man, a little girl standing beside her. The look in the woman's eyes—something about the man has made her angry. She reminds Dragon of Sondra, and he suddenly feels a pang of missing her.

"I'm just talking to the kid," the man says. "I have one his age."

"Of course," she says, and the smile she gives doesn't reach her eyes. "You should focus on your own."

"You're being rude," the man says.

"You're being creepy."

"You better leave me alone, or I'll—"

"Stop it," Dragon says. The voice that comes out of him is fiercely protective. He has decided, sometime in the past few seconds, that he'll kill this man for this woman. He finds it a little strange that he wouldn't do it for himself.

The man turns to look at Dragon, sees his face, is surprised for a moment, then afraid, then angry. It is more than anger. Hatred. This man is not what the woman thinks he is. This man is dangerous. After Dragon is done buying his items, he'll stick around just to make sure the woman is safe.

As a result, he is a little late for his pickup.

"Trouble?" Alex asks—his driver for today's errand. She is looking at him as if she already knows the answer.

"Not really."

She scopes out the parking lot. "You're sure?"

"Yes."

She seems satisfied. "All right, let's get this stuff to where it needs to be and get you home."

Dragon doesn't have a home, but he smiles when he thinks of the Wallaces.

When Dragon enters the Wallaces' apartment, Mrs. Wallace is sitting on the couch, and Mr. Wallace is in the kitchen, the sounds and smells of food cooking on the stove.

Mrs. Wallace stands. She's done this before, standing when he comes in. Dragon sleeps on the couch. He wonders if she feels weird about using it when he's over. Dragon feels weird using it himself, taking up space in their modest apartment.

"Have you eaten?" Mrs. Wallace asks. "Patrick is making chicken stir-fry."

Dragon shakes his head no, but then he realizes the ambiguity of the question and the answer. She is asking him if he has eaten, but she wants to know if he wants to eat their food. He says, "I'd like some chicken stir-fry. Thank you."

"So polite," Mrs. Wallace says. She sits back down again. "I'm watching a show. Will you watch with me?"

Dragon comes over and sits next to her. On the television, two people are descending a long ladder into a dark underground tunnel. They have to leap down once they've reached the bottom of the ladder, and when they do, one by one, there's the splash of their feet landing in water. They trudge forward, flashlights pointed into the darkness ahead.

"Where are they going?" Dragon asks.

"Oh, they're investigating a crime," Mrs. Wallace says, "and they think the . . . uh, the *criminal* is down there."

Something about the way Mrs. Wallace says "criminal" bothers Dragon. "Why would the criminal be down there?"

Dragon keeps his attention on the television, but he can feel Mrs. Wallace's eyes on him.

"You know what, why don't we change the channel instead? I didn't know it was going to be so creepy."

"It's okay," Dragon says. "I can keep watching."

"No, no, don't worry. I like this show, but it's a rerun. I can catch it another time."

She changes the channel to a game show. Contestants compete for a chance at $10,000 by answering trivia questions. Dragon finds that he has no idea what the answers are to any of the questions.

Mrs. Wallace, for her part, calls out answers. More than not, she's right.

Dragon has the feeling again of not belonging. This world aboveground remains a mystery. At any moment, he is reminded of all that he has missed.

On a commercial break, Mrs. Wallace asks, "How are your studies?"

"They're fine," he says. "My tutor is nice."

"You should be in school," she says. "I'm sure you'd do well."

Dragon doesn't know what to say to this. He isn't in school, because he doesn't really exist. He has no birth certificate, no Social Security number, no name besides Dragon. He's explained this to Mrs. Wallace before, exactly the way it was explained to him.

"I know, I know. But I've been talking to people. There might be a way around your . . . problem. If you want." Mrs. Wallace is smiling at him knowingly. She has a nice smile. She is pale white, red freckles on her cheeks, dark-colored hair falling to her shoulders. Dragon's hair is curly and doesn't grow very fast. It loops in on itself. Dragon is also brown-skinned. He knows these things mean something, that he is of a different race from Mrs. Wallace's, that she is white, and he might be Black, though those pieces of information don't mean much to him. He has learned a lot since coming up from underground, but so much of what he has learned remains abstract. Dragon doesn't know how old the Wallaces are exactly. They seem young, about the same age as Sondra, younger than Karuna and Harry.

He thinks about being around other children his age. He imagines another version of himself, in a school, in classrooms, doing his work with students around him. He finds the thought both thrilling and terrifying.

"You don't have to answer now. Just think about it."

"Food's ready," says Mr. Wallace from the kitchen. The smell makes Dragon's mouth water.

Mr. Wallace comes out into the dining-room area with two plates and sets them down at the small table. The Wallaces' apartment isn't very big, but it's clean, and they have nice things. Dragon feels as though he is taking up a lot of space, but he also feels very comfortable.

Mr. Wallace comes back with two glasses of water.

"Come, let's eat," Mrs. Wallace says. They both go to the dining table, and Dragon sits down in front of the smaller plate. Mrs. Wallace reaches over and swaps his plate with hers. When he looks at her, she winks.

The chicken stir-fry looks amazing—peppers and onions and broccoli cooked together with chunks of white meat, darkened by a rich brown sauce. The white rice on his plate is steaming. Dragon looks at Mrs. Wallace.

"You go ahead," she says.

Dragon does as he's told.

Mr. Wallace comes and sits down at the table with his own plate.

The food is delicious, like on those special days underground after Dragon had done something terrible. He has some distance now from those meals, has eaten amazing food without having to darken his soul. Some nights, it is with the Wallaces. Mr. Wallace, Dragon has learned, is a chef. At the moment, Dragon sees Mr. Wallace watching him eat. He is quieter than Mrs. Wallace, not quick to smile, but Dragon has learned to read his face. He is pleased that Dragon likes the food.

"It's delicious," says Mrs. Wallace.

"I left it on the stove a little too long," he says. Mr. Wallace pushes a hand through his thinning hair. "Got distracted by my phone."

"Of course you did," Mrs. Wallace says.

"Don't start."

Dragon looks at both of them. Mrs. Wallace is smiling. Mr. Wallace looks annoyed, but he smirks mischievously when he catches Dragon watching him.

"Do you like it here?" he asks.

Dragon nods. After he's swallowed his food, he answers again: "Yes."

"Good."

"We were thinking that if you were okay with it, you could spend more nights here. As much as you'd like."

Dragon puts down his fork. He looks at both of them. "I don't want to . . ." He pauses to think. He wants to say that he doesn't want to bother them, but is that the right thing to say in this situation?

"It's fine if you don't want to," Mr. Wallace says.

"No," Dragon says quickly, and then, panicking, "yes, I just mean . . . don't you want to be alone? I don't want to . . ."

"You wouldn't be intruding."

Yes, that's the word. Dragon tries it out: "I don't want to intrude." Then he realizes that Mr. Wallace has already assured him. "If you're sure . . ."

"We're sure," Mrs. Wallace says. "We have lots of space."

Dragon smiles. "Thank you." He eats more of his food, trying to find more words. When nothing comes, he gives up and continues eating.

"And if you like staying with us, maybe—"

Mr. Wallace touches her on the shoulder. "One thing at a time," he says. He gives Dragon another subtle smile.

Dragon finishes the rest of his meal without speaking.

Later that night, lying on the couch, he hears talking from the bedroom. Sometimes Dragon can hear what they're saying, but he is too embarrassed to tell them. This time he hears Mrs. Wallace say, "I really do think he likes it here."

He doesn't hear anything after that. Whatever else they're

saying is too soft for him to make out. He wants to tell her that he does. They're nice. But he is also mistrustful of nice. Nice makes him worry. Sometimes nice is a weapon. What if he has to do something he doesn't want to do to keep them nice? Dragon has always felt used. By everyone he's ever known. But sometimes he looks at other people and sees that everyone is being used. Humans live off the using of other humans. It makes him feel better to know he's not so special. With that, he shakes the bad thoughts away. He likes the Wallaces. They haven't asked him to do anything. He's safe. He tells himself the last part several more times before he can sleep.

ALEXANDRA TRAPP
BOSTON, MASSACHUSETTS

After Alex drops off Dragon, she returns to the community center. She sends Tez a text message, and he comes downstairs, opens the passenger-side door, and sits with her.

"You got anything for me?" Tez asks.

"I'm still tracking the shifter from the anti-monster rally, but he hasn't been doing anything particularly interesting. Just his regular routine."

"Okay. And the Black Hand?"

"They've been busy. The several I've been looking into have started hosting meetups. In apartments, bookstores, the library. There's a group that meets on Wednesday nights at the Panera Bread downtown."

Tez takes all this in without comment or a change in expression. "Concerning, but not unexpected. We just have to keep growing our numbers. And looking out for one another."

"And we will."

"That boy you dropped home—what do you think about him?"

"Besides him being anxious all the time?"

"Besides that."

"He's definitely been abused. And I get the sense that he doesn't really understand the world as it is. Not the way a normal teenager would. I think he's been locked away for a long time. He is still learning how people work."

Tez nods. "Matches my gut feeling." He pauses to consider something. "I'd like you to keep an eye on him. Give him more rides. I think he might be something special."

"Okay. You need anything else, *boss*?"

"Yes," Tez says, side-eyeing her. "Could you drop me by Fred's house?"

"That's a new name. Where'd you pick that one up?"

"On the corner of none of your business."

"You're so corny," Alex says, laughing anyway. She turns on the car, pulls out of the parking space, and is on her way.

Tez punches in the address and puts his phone in the holder stuck to Alex's dash.

Alex spares glances at the phone, but she's been driving through the city long enough to know where she's going by memory. Roxbury is just a short drive away, made a little longer by late-rush traffic.

Tez retreats into himself, as usual on these drives. Alex doesn't press. She likes the silence too. It gives her time to think about her own concerns. It takes practice and confidence to become a driver who allows for quiet, doesn't try to fill it with useless talk. She is grateful for quiet passengers.

They get there within five minutes of Alex's projected

time—within a minute of the navigation's prediction. Robots win again.

She slows in front of the apartment building. Tez hops out, knocks twice on the hood of the car—his version of a goodbye. It reminds Alex of someone from an old movie. He does a slow jog onto the sidewalk and up the stairs, which also reminds Alex of a movie—a rom-com perhaps? He rings up and is let inside within seconds. Alex waits for him to go in, ignoring the car beeping behind her. Then she starts moving . . . slowly, out of spite.

She drives home in silence. When she gets there, she has to circle her street twice to get a parking spot. She lives in Somerville, which makes her vigilance over Ridley and his wolf pack an easier job than it would be otherwise. She parks between two cars, has to shimmy her way in, which means she'll have to shimmy her way out again—enough of an annoyance that she prays one of them is gone by the time she has to leave in the morning. Unlikely, but a girl can dream.

She takes the longer-than-she'd-like walk to the apartment building, climbs the stairs, and enters her apartment on the third floor.

A spare living room meets her. A couch, a thin square rug under the coffee table, on the stand a television she barely uses.

She sits on the couch and turns the TV on, then off again. The bedroom is just down the hall, but she's now realized how tired she is. She could sleep right here, right now. She kicks off her shoes and leans back.

As she lies there, sleepy and restless, her mind starts turning over the events of the day, sifting her memory for important details that may need more attention. It isn't a particularly disciplined attempt, so her mind wanders on still, past the day's events and into the yawning past.

When Alex was a girl, her mother was sick. An autoimmune disease that was taking her slowly. It might have been tragic if Alex had any real relationship with her mother, but she was always distant. Saving herself or saving Alex from the inevitable loss—Alex could never tell. Her mother didn't go outside. And her father traveled a lot, so it was often Alex all alone in the house with her mother hiding in her bedroom. Someone came by to drop off groceries and sometimes cook. But Alex learned to cook for herself out of an old recipe book they had in the house. She'd give the woman little slips of paper with the necessary ingredients. The woman never seemed to mind much. Alex amused her, but she was not interested in any deep relationship.

Alex vaguely knew what her father did for a living. He worked in government, though the specifics of his government work were unclear. "Low-level grunt," he would say. But then people would ask him about the house, which was big enough to raise a few questions, and her father would smile and say, "Low-level in a high office." As a kid, Alex thought he should have a better explanation for his work. His cover was suspiciously awful. But as she grew older and got involved in similar work, she began to understand the need for suspiciously awful covers. In the regular world, these were the sort of explanations that stopped conversations cold for most people, because they knew the underlying message. Her father did the sort of work he couldn't talk about.

It was better to respond this way than to open up room for conversation and more and more opportunities to slip up or be caught in a lie. Besides, a classified job didn't necessarily mean CIA, though for her father and herself, it absolutely did.

There are two versions of how Alex got into the same line of work as her father. Version one: She knew that line of work was possible, and after what happened with her mother, it was the only line of work that interested her. A means for someone clever to climb into or descend into, or unearth secrets from, hidden places—not the silly kind, but the sort of secrets that ran the world. The very gears of the intricate mechanism that was society. Lofty and imaginative, but then, Alex was always lofty and imaginative. She had read spy novels in high school and watched spy thrillers, rewatching and rereading anything that seemed even remotely accurate. She wanted to be a part of that world—back alleys, broken bones and bullets to the head, and deeper shadows still. She considered herself tough enough for the task. As it turned out, she was.

But later, much later, she realized the second version of the story was closer to the truth.

A man used to come by the house every once in a while, always at night. His name was Valter—like Walter but with an inexplicable *V* instead of a *W*—but Alex always called him Mister. Mister would come for dinner and stay after. When she was young, he'd play games with her. Board games, mostly—a favorite was Battleship—but puzzle games too. Word puzzles, math puzzles, and critical-thinking puzzles where you had to solve logic problems to advance. Those game boxes had only the titles of the games on them. No artwork or fun lettering. No colors. She liked one called Resurrector, though she couldn't find it anywhere as an adult. As she got older, he would come by and they'd talk, and he would read to her from philosophy books and ask her questions about the reading to keep her engaged. Alex liked the attention, so she went along like a prized student, even though she wasn't as disciplined in real school. Later still, Mister came by with gifts, and eventually she learned that he was the reason she got into a particular private high school for gifted young people.

She had overheard a conversation he had with her father once. Her mother was very sick by then, and her father was begging Mister to do something about it.

"She's a shell of herself," her father said.

Mister said, "What I can offer will not give you back the woman you love."

"Do it."

"You're not listening."

"Don't talk down to me. I've known you my entire life."

This part, Alex thought, was very strange. Mister and her father looked the same age.

The conversation went on. Alex got careless and let herself be seen at the doorway, and Mister called her to him.

He said something to her. She doesn't remember what it was. But afterward Alex had trouble remembering the specifics of the conversation.

A month later, her mother was in the basement.

TEZCAT, THE WANDERER
BOSTON, MASSACHUSETTS

They exchanged words at the end, but Tez has already forgotten them. Fred isn't going to be a long-term thing, but there's been nothing alarming so far, so he thinks he can probably ride out a relationship for a few more months. Tez has gotten good at knowing when he's reached that threshold with someone. Get out before the getting out has to be preceded by an awkward conversation.

What he likes about Fred is that he's a chronic bachelor in denial about how lonely and empty his life is. Like Tez, minus the denial part.

Tez doesn't spend the night at other people's apartments. He leaves when the fun is over, and then he walks the streets until he finds his way home. Sometimes he doesn't make it until the sun is rising over the city—that black of night turning to that sunrise orange and grayish blue of early morning. But Fred doesn't live very far—just a couple of hours on foot, less if Tez decides to sprint home, which he can easily do without winding himself. Absently, he wonders how long that will last, whether he'll eventually slip past his prime.

He doesn't sprint though. If he walks leisurely, he'll still arrive at his apartment in under two hours.

As Tez walks, he passes under a streetlight. There's something about that very moment, some smell in the air, that takes him back:

"I am prepared to die for this." Harlan was standing at the top of the stairs outside the courthouse. This was the day he was released from prison the second time. "Are you prepared to die for your freedom? Are you prepared to die for the peace our descendants might receive? If you are not prepared to die for it, you do not deserve to live within it."

Tez was there, leaning on a lamppost. He was way back, but he could pick up Harlan's words even over the screaming crowd. At the time, Tez didn't agree with him, even as he felt his heart moved by his words. Every person deserved to live in peace, whether or not they were willing to die for it. The dead do not acquire peace for their deaths. They are dead, in the dark, unable to enjoy even the peace they've given to others.

Death was death. It couldn't be prettied by words. And it was little comfort to those left behind after a life had been ground to dust. But Tez knew full well that he was a bitter asshole who had lived too long, past the natural window for the folly of youth or even the lesser folly of old age. He was outside this time.

"I am a revolutionary," Harlan said, and Tez felt a certain shame for not being able to say it with him. Tez stood quiet and watchful. Across the street, a cop car was idling. He knew it was a cop car, not because it declared itself with the colors of the Boston PD, but because of the tinted glass, the curl of smoke floating out from a cracked window. He knew it for a cop car the way a predator knows another predator. And he could feel in his bones what was to come, was always coming.

What Tez didn't know was that there would be a future where he'd be the one channeling old Harlan's voice, using his best memory of Harlan's charisma to lift the spirits of his own revolutionaries. What he didn't know was that he'd be a fool just the same.

And what he knew now, because of this, was that he didn't see that old struggle as his. He had the right color, but not the same heart. He was of something else, and that sense of otherness had kept him from folly. But when it's your head on the chopping block, or the heads of those you believe need to be protected, it changes you. Or, at least, it changed *him*. Now he was willing to consider dying.

When Tez comes back to himself, comes back to the present, he is looking up at his apartment building, the housing co-op where he lives. He punches in the access code, climbs a flight of stairs. Once inside his apartment, he strips off all his clothes. Standing there naked, the smell of Fred still on him, he considers a longer walk. He isn't tired, but he is hardly ever truly tired, hasn't been for a long time.

In the end, he decides to stay put. He leans into his change— gentle probing, like a rendezvous with a stranger. He finds that when he doesn't force it, when he leans in just so, the change comes the rest of the way. A meeting in the middle. His animal self and his human self, reaching slowly for each other in that middle dark.

Suddenly, Tez is on all fours, his black paws flexing against the wooden floorboards. He sees the scratches from before, exactly where his claws extend. He chuffs. He's made this change in exactly this spot several times.

He saunters over to the couch, edges between it and the scratched-up coffee table he should replace but won't. He is big enough to pull himself onto the sofa and curl up. Resting his head on his forepaws, he closes his eyes.

Finally, in this chosen form, he can sleep.

15

Dragon still remembers the darkness. He remembers the smell. Then, he didn't know it was human waste or monster waste or monster-human waste. He just knew it as background noise. The smell of the world. And knew the difference only once there was a difference. He remembers the sounds of sleep, distant and near, of the others. Angry shouts when someone came down to feed them. He remembers the feeling of being an animal, of need that was more important, more vital, than want. The feeling of living on base function. To eat, to shit, to want to eat, to want to shit. And having those things be greater things than wanting to be whole or wanting to want or having things to want. He remembers the sunroom where he felt almost human. He remembers the sadness of going back down into the dungeon, of loss, of despair. He remembers devouring and being the thing that devoured. He remembers love and not knowing it wasn't, the way Smoke stroked his head and said, "You're okay." Not as a question but as a command. And how badly he wanted to be okay, for Smoke's sake, and how that want makes him feel sick now, deep in his belly—something wanting *out out out*, though he cannot name the thing needing out, or where out is.

There were so many things he didn't understand about the outside world. The freedom people had and how they didn't seem to notice it. It was a thing they carried absently. To go anywhere. To have the resources to do anything. He hated them for that carelessness, even as he walked among them. Because he didn't know what it meant to be free, or what to do with freedom.

Dragon had stayed with Harry and Karuna because he thought he should, because it felt like earning a living, earning the right to live. He owed them what he could never repay, so he thought he deserved to be under their foot, to be used as they willed.

Karuna was kind. She never used Dragon, but Harry used him all the time. He would try not to, but then he'd stare at the stump of his right hand and remember what Dragon had done, and he couldn't help but be angry at him. He made Dragon do everything for him: Open doors. Clean his room. Make Harry food and clean up afterward. Karuna joined Dragon most times in the upkeep of their little cabin and chastised Harry whenever she saw him not carrying his weight. But it only made Harry more clever, whispering his demands and rebukes under his breath when Dragon was nearby. "And don't you tell Karuna I told you to do it."

Karuna still knew what Harry was doing. And eventually, she made some calls to some people in the city. She'd done some research on Boston's solidarity movement and had friends who worked in cooperatives and community organizations. She talked to them late at night when Harry was asleep. Harry wanted to call colleagues at the university, but Karuna had continued to block him. By the time Dragon left, Harry resented them both.

Karuna had learned about how the movement was changing. She'd been told about the radical pro-monster faction that was doing "interesting work around open-value networks and community funds." Her eyes sparkled when she said this, and Dragon knew those nightly conversations meant more to her than anything he could fathom. She had started practicing writing with her nondominant hand and had gotten a typewriter and paper to type down notes for a book she would write under a pseudonym.

"And that isn't dangerous?" Harry had asked. "You're on the phone all hours of the night and working on a manuscript, and somehow *I'm* the problem for wanting to reach out to my research colleagues?"

"Can you guarantee they'll keep quiet about it?" Karuna asked. "About you?"

"Yes, of course they will," he said, but he didn't sound like someone who trusted himself, and Karuna only smiled at him.

"You can reach out to close family or friends," she said.

She had said this before, and Harry only got angry at the suggestion. They both knew something about what she was saying that Dragon didn't.

Karuna told Dragon to go, that she had arranged for someone to pick him up at the nearby station, but he would have to get himself there.

"Do you know how to get there by yourself?"

Dragon said yes. He had told no one that he went out late at night, shifting into his halfling form with his wings too large for his body, and would take to the skies, high enough up that he wouldn't alarm anyone. But he'd seen the subway station several times on his flights.

Later Dragon called Damsel, whispering the incantation she'd told him to use. And she was there by that night, in her shroud, outside the cabin. He went out to meet her.

"Karuna is sending me to the city."

"That's nice," Damsel said, but she seemed only a little interested.

"I'll be gone for a while. I want to know if they'll be okay."

"You're asking if harm will come to them if you leave?"

"You said if I stayed with them, they'd—"

"I know, I know. That was then." She sighed, annoyed by something. Dragon didn't think it was him, or he was trying hard not to. "You are meant to go to the city. And they are meant to be alone for a time. Don't worry. You're on your path. You can go."

In the years since he first met Melku and they told him about his "path," Dragon had come to resent it a little: this important thing he was supposed to do, supposed to be. But it also made him feel safe from being too sad about not knowing his place in the world. There was a destiny for him, somewhere in the future. And he was going to meet it, so he could bear the sadness a little longer.

"Okay, I'll go."

"Good little Dragon," Damsel said.

Something about how she said it made him angry at her. He was feeling that more too: a big-big anger swelling inside him.

Ants were in a circle around Damsel's feet, and he saw them

only when they lit up. She fell through the ground, and the hole in the world quickly closed, the ants scattering.

Dragon wondered how many of these insects Melku possessed and how many places in the world they were located. Were they everywhere and just waiting to be used? Dragon tried to catch sight of one, but they were gone. He went back inside.

The next night, he was on his way to a new life.

Dragon wakes to a quiet apartment. Already the kind couple has slipped past him, somehow without waking him. He used to have a sharper awareness of the world around him. What has changed? He knows the answer but doesn't trust it. He feels almost safe and, at the same time, distrustful of that safety.

They left a plate of scrambled eggs, and near it a note:

You can toast some bread if you like.

There's butter as well on the kitchen counter, and Dragon does as the note suggests.

Dragon has slept a lot of places, but few like the Wallaces'. Most of the other places don't leave out scrambled eggs and pleasant notes with nice, even lettering. Dragon is thankful he has taken the time to learn to read, or he wouldn't be able to appreciate this small kindness.

Dragon eats his eggs and buttered toast. He takes a quick shower. Out the door in under thirty minutes. There's a key under the mat that Dragon uses to lock up. He knows now that leaving a key under a mat in a big city like this, even in an apartment building, might be asking for trouble. But the Wallaces do that only when Dragon leaves after they have left. They'll pick it up when they return from work. Dragon knows this because the key is never there when he arrives.

Dragon takes the subway to the community center, using the year pass that has been sponsored by New Era. He has to take the Red Line and then the Orange, but he's a little ahead of the crowded subway hours, so he manages to find a seat and sit comfortably while enjoying the screeching-clicking noises of the subway car crawling its way through dark tunnels into lit subway stations. Dragon doesn't know why he likes this so much. Perhaps it is the comforting feel of being underground. It took him a while to admit that he likes being cradled within the earth. Sometimes, when he is outside in the open air, he feels naked, vulnerable, as if a large creature might swoop down and take him away. The feeling of being watched from above. There's nothing particularly rational about the fear, and Dragon still isn't at a place in his awareness to untangle all of it. He just knows what he likes: an elemental desire to be in some dark hole somewhere, guarding himself. But what he likes even more is the freedom to leave at any moment—the choice to be out in the open even if he doesn't want to be.

He gets off at his stop and climbs the stairs into the open air, which is better than the bouquet of bodily excretions of human beings below. The smoke from car exhausts, but also the faint smell of trees, and the soft breeze, which also has its own scent. He pushes away the sudden nakedness, looks up to the sky to calm his nerves, and takes the short walk to the community center, mixing with the other pedestrians.

As he walks, Dragon listens to the way people talk. How they take up so much space with their words. It is weird. Back in the underground, no one talked unless they had something to say. Dragon had a cell neighbor, an older woman who'd been some kind of monster he didn't know. A dryad, one of the dead or dying monster types. She was one of the last of her kind. And they talked sometimes about the world outside.

"It is big," she said to Dragon often. It wasn't very clear what she meant by it, but Dragon thought she'd been trying not to overwhelm him. Or had been down there so long she'd lost the ability to give deeper information.

But as he walks, Dragon thinks, *The world is big.*

When Dragon arrives at the community center, he helps with sorting and packing things in containers. Items Dragon packs: rice, a lot of it; black beans and pinto beans and kidney beans (mostly dried, but cans too); ramen noodle packets; pasta; little crates of eggs (are they called crates, those papery-cardboardy ones?); and milk in little glass bottles (also clearly reused, some with the stickiest parts of the stickers still on them); ketchup and mustard and mayo and spices in small ziplock bags. Canned vegetables. Canned meats. Spam and corned beef and Vienna sausages and tuna and canned chicken. Corned-beef hash. No real meats—too hard to carry—but sometimes checks with *Meat Allowance* on them, or *Fresh Vegetables*—and *Milk* if they haven't packed milk because sometimes it is hard to keep so much milk refrigerated in the center's communal fridges, which have to be used for other things too, especially around the monthly food parties.

This time when Dragon leaves the center, he is on another route, dropping containers off out in Quincy and near UMass, at the far end of the Red Line.

He rings up to apartments. Sometimes he is allowed up and thanked with a bottle of water or a juice box. Other times, a tired-looking person comes down and retrieves the items with thanks before ascending back into the building's belly. Dragon welcomes every response like a student memorizing the exact phrasing from the textbook in preparation for a future test. All the variations of human interaction, all the subtle ways each person is different even if they're saying the same thing. The marvelous emergent qualities of humanity.

They're done by early afternoon. This driver, a man named Goose—Dragon accepts the name without a thought—tells him that he is a good worker, quiet and patient.

"You're not spoiled like a lot of kids I know. Do you go to school?"

Dragon shakes his head but tells Goose that he does have a tutor and is learning his lessons quickly.

"Smart too," he says. "Your parents must be proud."

Is it sadness that Dragon feels? He doesn't know enough to understand the sudden stab in his chest. His feeling of missing out is mixed up with his feeling of missing Smoke. A parent, and not.

"Be good, now," Goose says, and there's some sort of admonishment in it. A warning? Though it is good-natured enough not to raise Dragon's sense of unease. Nothing will happen if he isn't good, he tells himself. He is being told to be good for its own sake.

Dragon smiles with the full earnestness of a boy who wants to be his best self. "I will."

Inside the community center, he goes to the kitchen to do his homework.

He is working on his algebra when someone walks in. The tall, slender man looks at him before retrieving something from the fridge—a small cup of yogurt. He opens it and reaches for a spoon from the drying rack.

Dragon looks back down at his algebra. He knows who it is, though he doesn't think they've spoken more than a few times in passing since he came to the city.

"You want one?" Tez asks.

Dragon looks back up to see Tez with the open cup of yogurt. Does he want one? A little bit. "Is there more?" he asks.

"More than enough if you want one. They're mine anyway."

"Okay," Dragon says.

Tez retrieves another cup from the fridge and tosses it to Dragon. "People sometimes come in here to eat," he says.

"I'm sorry," Dragon says.

"Oh no, no, not saying you should be sorry. I was just wondering if it gets noisy. There's not a lot of space in here either." Tez smiles at Dragon, handing him a metal spoon. "You can come hang out in the conference room if you want."

"But you work there."

"Sure, but there's a couch and a big conference table if you need something to write on. People come in and out, but there's plenty of room."

Dragon nods. "Okay."

"Enjoy the yogurt."

When Tez is gone, Dragon opens up the banana-strawberry-flavored yogurt. He savors every spoonful. When he's done, he goes to the conference room.

As Dragon enters, Tez is there, behind the desk nearest the window. Afternoon light shines in through the open blinds, the noise from the street audible.

"Make yourself at home," Tez says.

Dragon nods, goes quietly to the couch, and sits on it. The

couch is far enough away that Dragon can disappear into the background if Tez chooses it.

Tez, for his part, doesn't allow Dragon so easy an exit. "How are you liking the routes?"

"They're nice," Dragon says, and means it.

"I am glad to hear that. It's a lot of work for a kid, especially having to talk to all those strange people."

"I've done the route before," Dragon says.

Tez smiles.

"Sometimes I do get nervous," Dragon admits.

"What makes you nervous?"

"Sometimes the people are sad or tired, or maybe a little angry. I just don't want to be in the way."

Tez nods slowly. Dragon listens to the noises from the street. Two people are walking. One says something indecipherable. The other laughs.

"They shouldn't be like that. Not with you."

"Oh no, they're usually fine to me. I just can tell when they're . . ." Dragon searches for the words.

"Acting?"

Dragon doesn't like the sound of it, but he says yes.

"People act all the time. To get by. To make other people feel more at ease. To protect themselves."

"Protect," Dragon repeats.

"Do you tell people when you're nervous?"

"No." Dragon considers how he might do this, tell people his feelings. It seems a weird thing to share emotions out of nowhere.

"Well, it probably doesn't cross your mind," Tez says. "But even if it did, you might keep that to yourself. When people feel vulnerable, they protect that feeling."

"Vulnerable," Dragon says. He likes the word, feels the rightness of it. "Like when I'm outside."

Tez furrows his brow. "That's an interesting comparison. You feel vulnerable outside?"

"There are people outside. A lot of them. I don't like crowds."

Dragon has communicated something to Tez that he understands. Tez says, "I feel like that too. I worry about crowds. And I worry *for* them. Depending on who is in the crowd."

Dragon chews on this for a moment. Understanding comes to him. "People get hurt sometimes in crowds." And sometimes they do the hurting. But Dragon has a sense that Tez is thinking about the hurt people, not the people doing the hurting.

"Yes, they do," Tez says. "You know, I thought you came across as very young. But you see a lot, don't you?"

Dragon doesn't see why "very young" is an insult. He *is* very young. "I want to see everything." A shiver runs through Dragon, as if he's said something very true about himself—a deeper, truer truth.

Tez seems similarly taken aback. "What an interesting person you are."

Dragon feels warm from the inside. He likes being called a person. He wants to return the compliment, but at the moment it is hard to speak.

"You got homework?" Tez asks.

Dragon nods.

"Go ahead and do it."

Dragon does the math sheet his tutor gave him and writes about his day in the journal he has to do for English. He avoids some of his vulnerable thoughts. Like a person, he protects them.

Dragon doesn't get a ride home this time. He has finished

his homework early enough to take the subway back to the Wallaces'. Most of the people offering up a place to stay for the night don't like when people stay over more than one night. There's another place Dragon can go that has a second bedroom and an open bed, but he likes the couch at the Wallaces', likes the food they sometimes prepare for him. And they said he can come over and stay anytime except on Fridays, when they host a driver on a long route outside the city.

This time Dragon hits the early subway rush—the people trying to beat the full rush at five. He has to stand and hold on to one of the rails. He makes his body loose so he can sway with each curve in the track. He imagines himself in the belly of a long metal dragon, and the thought isn't frightening. He is a dragon himself and can leave at any time. And it is nice to have another dragon to keep him company. In his mind, he talks to the metal dragon, asks if it likes crawling through the underground tunnels. He imagines an answer: *Yes, but sometimes I wish I could fly.*

I can fly, Dragon thinks. *I will take you in my belly someday.* Dragon would have to get bigger to do that.

Sometimes Dragon fantasizes about Smoke finding him. Dragon thinks about Smoke often. He remembers Smoke's little lessons. He would come down to the cell—*come down* isn't quite it; he would *appear* in Dragon's cell—and teach Dragon a new word every day. Dragon loved those little gifts. He wouldn't resent them until years later.

He misses Smoke and feels angry for missing him. He doesn't understand that part of himself that could miss Smoke while never wanting to go back. It is impossible to feel just one way about his life before. The fantasy terrifies him. But it is a fantasy, and so sometimes he would rub the top of his own head the way Smoke used to do and imagine Smoke saying, "You want to come back with me?"

Not there. Never *there*. But a home somewhere. Smoke would take him *home*.

Those were the happy fantasies. They were so unlike Smoke, so unlike how Dragon knew he would act. Most times, Smoke was looking sternly at him, with anger and disappointment. Why couldn't Smoke be like Karuna? Scary, yes. But kind. Dragon is angry at Smoke for being himself. He supposes he was also angry at Harry for being himself, but not like this. Not with this sense of being hurt, betrayed.

Dragon had one other fantasy. In it, he would turn into a dragon, his true self, and turn Smoke to dust with a quick release of flames. Those fantasies made Dragon feel sick.

Do other people understand their feelings? This is what he hates most about people: The sense he gets that they know themselves, know what they should be doing and being. The way everyone moves through the city as if they had someplace to be. Not just the place they are going. The place beyond that: A true destination. A life to live.

The stop arrives quickly, and Dragon gets off the train. He ascends into the open air again, searches the sky. And then he walks to the Wallaces' apartment. He rings up, but no one answers. So he waits for someone to go in—an older woman—and goes in behind her.

"Your parents in the building?"

Dragon considers this. He decides that he will pretend that the Wallaces are his parents. "Yes," he says. "The Wallaces."

The old woman looks him over. "Good on them for adopting an older child. Take care of those two."

Dragon nods. He can feel butterflies in his belly.

When he gets to the door, he knocks, but the Wallaces don't answer.

He tries again. Are they not home yet? Well, it would make sense. Dragon is a little early.

He stoops, checks under the mat, but notices that the door is slightly ajar. Something buzzes in the back of his mind, like bees. A woman is looking at him from inside a crowd of people snaking down a city street. She has wild eyes and a missing hand. A hurt person about to hurt people. Dragon's fault. No matter what, it will always be Dragon's fault.

He nudges the door open. The sharp smell of blood. Dragon isn't surprised. He already knows that the Wallaces have been punished for what he is, what he will always be. Dragon wants to save them, offer himself up instead. But it is already too late.

He doesn't want to see. He wants them to remain alive and whole in his head. Not dead, just gone, somewhere he can't reach. He steps back out into the hallway, closes the door and the death behind it, puts the key back under the mat.

He must be quiet as he cries so that no one hears him. He must be good.

16

"Jesus," Kwame says. "What a fucking way to go." Arms folded, he shakes his head, a single thick dreadlock falling over his face. Kwame is Tez's right-hand man, an early recruit to New Era, and an old guard in the co-op scene in the city. And if Alex's intel is correct, he's also a selkie.

"They were good people," Tez says. "And we've got to make sure their families are taken care of."

"Not much family," Kwame says. "On their application, they both said they were estranged from their relatives. Apparently, they came up in a small town near Austin, Texas, where they met, fell in love, and ran away together. Pat Wallace had a brother, though, who he still talked to. He'll likely get stuck with the bill."

"We'll cover it," Tez says. "Anonymously if we have to. But I also mean we need to find out who did this."

"Dragon," Kwame says, "you see anybody hanging around outside or . . . ?"

Dragon looks up.

"He's in shock," Alex says. "Probably not best to talk to him right now."

Dragon looks back down to his lap without saying a word.

"I'll figure it out," Tez says. "Don't worry."

Kwame again: "Who notified the police?"

"It doesn't matter," Tez says pointedly. "They should be on their way if they're not there already."

"Jesus," Kwame says. "What a way to go."

The Wallaces were stabbed fifteen times, with Pat Wallace taking the brunt of it. Whoever did it hadn't liked having to kill a woman, Alex guesses, but that didn't stop them. This was a message killing, the message being that supporters of monsters were to be punished.

Alex was sent to pick the boy up. Dragon had called the center, asked to speak to Tez, and Tez had called her once Dragon gave him the story. Alex rushed over there and called the station on the way back to the center.

All the time, she was wondering how quickly the authorities would trace this back to New Era. At first she thought it would happen immediately. But now she's wondering if the Wallaces even told anyone about the work they'd been doing. They were getting containers of food from the center, but those were carefully left unlabeled. The police already knew about the food program though. Something like that was bound to pick up some attention. But the Wallaces didn't need the food—only kept it in the apartment for the guests they were housing.

Alex knew of only two couch surfers who slept at the Wallaces', Dragon being one of them. They had just started supporting New Era in that way, though they'd been giving money for over a year. That's all she knows. She will have to talk to Tez once things settle down, to see if there is any cleanup to be done at the Wallaces' once the police leave the scene.

Alex puts a hand on Dragon's shoulder. He jumps at first but then sees who it is and calms.

"You okay?" Alex asks.

"I'm okay."

The way he says this breaks Alex's heart. This child, this adolescent, has seen a lot of death in his life already. This is deeper than shock, though that's there too; this is heartbreak and the sort of numbness that comes from someone used to tragedy.

"I'm sorry this happened," Alex says.

"Me too," Dragon says. "What happens when Tez finds out who did this?"

Alex shakes her head. And it is true—she really doesn't know—but she is worried about what Tez will do. He doesn't seem particularly violent. But she knows he is a monster, has known from the very beginning. This killing is more than a little thing for him, for what it represents.

"Dragon," Tez says, "Kwame here is going to set you up with a new place in your rotation. You'll spend the night there." He adds, "Don't tell anyone about what has happened. We need to keep this quiet for now."

"I won't tell anyone," Dragon says.

It is clear that he has no one to tell, which breaks Alex's heart again.

"And, Kwame," Tez says, "when you're done, call up the fund and ask them for a burial loan."

"On it," Kwame says. He retrieves the boy, and they leave the conference room. Alex likes the way Kwame is talking to

Dragon as they go, calm and gentle without playing up (or playing down) what has happened. Steady—something Dragon needs right now.

Tez and Alex remain.

"You think we'll get out of this without suspicion?" Tez asks.

"No, not forever. But that's only if the police decide to cover the case. I took a quick look at the apartment," Alex says cautiously, "and the words *monster lovers* were written on the walls."

She's glad Tez doesn't follow up by asking what the words were written with. Instead, he says, "They might drag their feet on this one. Let's hope they do."

17

A memory: Alex's mother coming down from her bedroom for dinner. The first time in months, her skin glowing. Alex was surprised by this, by the smile plastered to her mother's face—inexhaustible and enough for everyone. Her mother telling stories about when she was young, and Alex's amazed laughs. Her mother superimposed, each stratum of her overlying the last like translucent skin, so Alex can see the woman she was and the girl she was before adulthood and sickness took her away. Her mother came down for dinner every night after that. She didn't come out for breakfast.

But Alex slowly grew fond of dinners with this very different woman. Her skin so bright. Her eyes so present. Her father seemed to like this different woman too, and Alex could tell that he knew parts of her before, sometime in the past when Alex wasn't even a desire for either of them. Her father laughing and her laughing, and her mother with those arms—spindly before, now rippling with lean muscle—telling them a story about the summer she spent on boats sailing through the Caribbean.

One afternoon, her father texted that he'd be home late. The housekeeper came over at her usual time to see about the house. While she was there, Alex's mother called her upstairs. The housekeeper went up the stairs, and Alex spent the next half hour on the couch, trying to listen to what was happening. But eventually, she fell asleep. She woke to a dark living room. The housekeeper must have left already, because the lights were off, the house silent.

When Alex's father came home, he exchanged a few words with Alex. She saw the worry on his face before he rushed upstairs. He came back down moments later, his expression hard. He went out on the porch to have a hushed conversation over the phone. Alex couldn't hear, but she recognized the frantic tone of her father's voice. All through this, her mother did not come down the stairs.

A memory: Alex as a teenager. Her father away on a business trip. People came in and out of the house to visit her mother, who Alex hadn't seen in several months now. They went to the basement door, punched the code that now kept her mother below. They opened the door and descended the stairs. Alex sometimes watched them do it. She sometimes replied pleasantly when they attempted small talk. But then they would go down into the basement. The door would lock. And no matter how hard Alex listened, there was no sound from down there.

One day, Alex didn't see one of the people leave. She didn't always hear them go, but she was almost positive the door had not opened again since the woman went down. Alex waited until late in the night. She descended the stairs from her room and approached the basement door. "Mother," she called out. But her mother didn't answer. She never answered.

Another person came by the next day. He seemed anxious when he entered the house and didn't make small talk. He punched the code. He walked down the stairs. She heard his steps disappear into the silence below. He came back up shortly after but didn't say anything to Alex. He just left the house. His face was carefully neutral, but Alex could see that he was sweating. He didn't return.

No one came the next day.

Alex woke late that night and went downstairs. She pressed her ear up against the door. She didn't know why she was doing this. But then she could hear something. Finally, there was sound. It was her mother calling her name, begging her to come down. Alex knew the code. Some of the people who visited weren't careful. But another sense took over—one she didn't even know she had—and she resisted her mother's plea. She wondered again what her mother looked like, down there in the dark.

That next night, she woke up to an empty house. Quiet, but it was always like this when her father wasn't home. Either her mother didn't make any noise, or the basement door muted it. She got up, pressed her hands to her stomach to stop the ache. It didn't help. She did a mental inventory of what was in the fridge: tuna salad from a couple of days ago, steeped in globs of mayo, the way she liked it. She would have gone straight to the kitchen, but something told her to check on her mother again.

It was a habit. Alex wasn't really checking on her. She never went downstairs, even though she knew the code to the door.

WE ARE THE CRISIS   153

She pressed her ear against the wood. Again she heard something scraping deep inside the basement, and her mother's voice calling out to her by name.

"Come down," she said. "Come down, my little Amie."

Only her mother called her Amie. She hadn't heard the nickname in months, since the last time her father allowed her mother upstairs. Then, her mother had worn a look on her face that Alex didn't recognize. Her dad had seen it, too, and had kept her in the basement, saying for months that her mother was too unwell to come up.

But here Alex was, listening to her mother calling her name again, and she was surprised at how much she wanted her mother to be with her, not trapped behind a door in some basement. She remembered that feeling because it was the last time she felt that this was her mother and that there was some version of reality in which Alex could be her daughter, loved and cared for, doing the sorts of things other daughters and mothers did together. Alex hoped she would go down there and see the mother she wanted. She hadn't forgotten that look her mother had given her right before she was taken downstairs. Alex had put it away, like all the other unwelcome realities that lived inside her and around her all those years. She had grown up too fast and suddenly was aware of all the things she had missed out on, the quiet needs she had buried deep down in the most recondite corner of her heart, like a tiny luminant pearl.

Somewhere in her mind, Alex must have known there was danger, because she didn't punch in the code right away. She hesitated at the keypad, her hand hovering very close to the keys. Her fingertips buzzed with anticipation. She swore she could feel the pull of it, like gravity or magnetism.

It was luck or something like it that brought her dad home. He flicked on the light, the front door still open. He had a thin sheen of sweat on his face. In that moment, Alex knew what her father already knew: that the door was for keeping in just as much as for keeping out.

"Where's the attendant?" he asked.

Alex shook her head and said she didn't know. There had been no attendants for days.

"Did you see the last one leave?"

"Yes. But I didn't see the other one leave."

Now her father was burying some emotion. He was good at this, but Alex knew her father, knew when he was hiding, because she knew when he was not.

He said, "Go upstairs and get to bed."

Alex considered arguing, but the tone of his voice stifled any response. He wasn't loud; the threat was in the low pitch, the forced calm. She turned and climbed the stairs.

She took a shower first, locking the door so he would be forced to use the bathroom downstairs—a little rebellion. But she didn't want to see him or hear him once she shut the door. Her anger pushed all the subconscious fear out of her. She wanted different people to love. She imagined herself in a different house, with parents who invited friends over—not neighbors or coworkers, but real friends. A family who went on trips together and took her with them. She wanted and she wanted. A well was opening inside her, pouring out all the want. Alex stayed in the shower, let the water wash over her for she didn't know how long. She considered putting on her pajamas and stomping right back downstairs. But even in her rage, she lost her nerve. She decided to wait until he was asleep. He didn't know she had the code. She could go down and visit her mother without his ever knowing. It could be their little secret. She had built the whole conspiracy up in her head: how she and her mother would keep the secret all the way until she left for college; the night it would all come out, when she came home for Thanksgiving (or Christmas—she couldn't decide which she liked better), and she'd be drunk and just let it slip; and Dad, angry at first but seeing no harm in it, especially after all this time, would laugh quietly to himself. (She didn't know how she got this image. Dad never laughed. Not anymore.)

But when she came out of the bathroom, the house was quiet again. She crept back downstairs, being as quiet as she could. The light was on, but Dad wasn't there.

"Dad," she said softly, and then louder so that her voice carried through the house.

Again she felt the chill, the half-buried fear of something she couldn't name yet. She went to the door, listened again.

"Mom? Dad?"

"Amethyst," came the voice from deep inside the basement. Her mom, but with something else behind it. As if she were being puppeted.

She didn't think any of this back then. She didn't have the words for it, and for a long time after, she wouldn't remember that night.

When Alex did remember, it was crystal clear, as if it had happened only the night before (some side effect, Aura said, of memories stolen and returned). What she had felt when hearing her mother was a desperate urge to see her father. She punched in the code and ran down the stairs. It was all very fast, not like in the scary movies. She was too worried to inch her way cautiously down into the room.

The scent hit her nose first—coppery and damp, overlayed with decay. Like a dead rat in the walls. She slipped forward on something wet and tumbled to the floor. Her hands landed in something dark and slid. The whole front of her shirt was now wet and sticky. Alex looked up, taking everything in: her mother standing against the wall, the stone behind her cracked, the metal bracelets around her wrists, attached to a chain. Her mother was swaying in place, head pointed up to the ceiling. Alex's father was also there, lying on the floor, a pool of something dark beneath him. Alex understood immediately, and she knew what she had fallen into. She tried to get up and slid again. That's when she saw the attendant. Crumpled against the far wall, half covered in shadow, one eye open that had turned gray, misted over with death, and a mouth open and contorted, like a Halloween mask ready to be worn by something living. But there was no life beneath; the oppressive scent of death pulsed off her.

Alex didn't scream. She was in shock, she thought. And she didn't try to get up again.

Her mother looked down at her. She stepped forward, and then Alex saw the chain dragging on the floor. She saw the two holes in the wall where her mother had pulled them free. Now she could get a better look at the crack in the foundation. Her mother had done that. But how? She considered all this in stunned silence.

Her mother was slowly coming toward her. Alex wanted to call out to her mother. She wanted to use her sweetest voice and call her mother back to her body. Because the thing that was coming toward Alex was certainly not the mother she knew.

"Amethyst." She was smiling. The smile should have been friendly, open, even kind. But something about it was all wrong. Tears fell down Alex's cheeks. She was shaking.

"My little girl," she said. "You keep getting so big!"

Alex finally managed to push herself up off the floor but immediately fell back onto her butt. Most of her clothes were now black and sticky with blood.

"Your father had an accident, but it's okay," her mother said. "When we go upstairs, I'll call for help. But we can't be here when the ambulance comes. Do you understand?"

Alex shook her head.

"Harriet over there had an accident. I've been down here with her for too long. They won't understand. We have to run, sweetheart. Will you come with me?"

Had she *ever* called Alex sweetheart? Alex tried but couldn't remember, couldn't recall a single thing. All memories of her mother had been swallowed up by the thing in front of Alex, wearing her mother's face.

"What happened to you?" Alex asked.

Her mother frowned at this, in almost real sadness. "I am your mother, of course. Quickly, Amie, you must decide."

Alex would eventually come to know that vampires weren't soulless and that she had to unlearn a lot of other nonsense she had picked up from watching films and reading books. It was their priority that had changed. The blood supersedes everything. Other instincts—other emotions, like love—come second. She really was her mother, really did love her. But other priorities were competing for limited space at the moment. How long did her mother wrestle before killing her father? How long did it take for the hunger to win out? Was she still hungry when

Alex came stumbling down the stairs? And how long would it take with Alex before the hunger won out again?

"Decide."

Alex couldn't. Tears blurred her vision.

Alex's mother grew impatient. "You're wasting time," she said. And then it happened so quickly, her mother leaping over her as she lay crouched on the floor, as if Alex didn't matter at all. By the time she craned her neck to see where her mother had landed, she was gone.

She didn't know how long she sat there in the basement with all that death around her. When Mister came, he descended the stairs and scooped her up without a word. Another man was there waiting, and after a nod from Mister, he went down the stairs. He never came back up again. Later she would know why: He had walked down the stairs only for her benefit. This man could turn to smoke.

A woman was sitting at the kitchen table, and Mister took Alex to her. He set her down in a chair. The woman was impossibly frail. Skinny limbs, a sunken face: the Bone Witch. She had an old book open in front of her. She whispered to herself, not even looking up at Alex. She would have been frightened if Mister weren't there, his hand on Alex's shoulder, talking to her. He had given her another puzzle to solve and was talking her through the logic of it. He said nothing about her father, nor asked her where her mother had gone. He seemed completely uninterested in what had occurred in the house. Alex looked to him for how she should respond to all that had happened. She looked to him to see if she should cry. She wouldn't cry for a long time after. She didn't notice when the witch took the memory from her. One second, Alex was at the table, and the next, she was lying in bed feeling dizzy and unable to sleep, not knowing what had happened or how she got there.

When Alex called out for her father, Mister appeared in the doorway. He told her what had happened. There was an accident at work. Her dad was in the hospital.

"I want to go see him," Alex said.

Mister shook his head. "In the morning."

It didn't make sense, but somehow she understood that they couldn't go to the hospital.

"Get some sleep," he said.

Before, Alex couldn't sleep, and then she could, slipping right into dreams. She didn't wake up until the next morning.

But by morning, the story had changed. Her father had died during the night. No, they wouldn't go to see him. No, Alex couldn't stay with her mother; she was unwell. Mister would have some people take care of her if she was found. This didn't make sense either, but Alex couldn't think why.

Later she would replay that night in her mind, looking for inconsistencies. But her mind would bend around that night, tie itself in a knot. Frustrated, she would have to wriggle free each time. The effort exhausted her and gave her headaches. Eventually, she stopped punishing herself with her suspicion, and the headaches stopped.

The meeting for the Federation of Greater Boston Cooperatives is being held at Renegades, a local cooperative brewery and pub. It's a big place, located in the heart of downtown Boston, a few minutes from Park Street and the Boston Common, making it the perfect centralized location for the Federation's meetings.

Renegades can afford such a coveted location and square footage by being publicly funded. Investor-members number in the thousands, with some of them putting in tens of thousands of dollars. It is what insiders would call a multistakeholder cooperative since the membership includes workers, consumers, and a significant investor class. A place like this might not have been possible only a decade ago, but the cooperative movement in the city has been growing. Many of the investors in this pub are worker-owners themselves or members of consumer or producer cooperatives.

On the first Tuesday of every month, the Federation meets

to discuss matters of business affecting local cooperatives, but most of the time is occupied by small-group socializing.

Because this meeting is happening so soon after the murder of the Wallaces—now known to everyone in or out of the movement—much of the preliminary conversation consists of speculation about what happened.

Dragon has found a corner to disappear into. The back room of Renegades, full and pulsing with people, appears as if everyone is engaged in some arcane dance. People float purposefully from one group to another, and once again Dragon feels outside the flow of things, with no internal sense of how to join the stream. Although voices are hushed, it is clear what everyone is talking about.

Tonight's meeting has pizzas for the attendees. They are on serving trays on one long table opposite where Dragon is sitting. Some people are still eating, but most have shifted to drinking what Dragon knows to be beer. They are holding their pint glasses in their hands, taking small absent sips. Dragon has no interest in beer. He has already eaten two slices of pizza and considers getting up to grab one more. He isn't hungry, but his stomach feels lonely.

"Are you okay?" someone asks him, and he turns to see Alex standing there. She is looking down at him, her expression unreadable, though she is clearly picking up something from his face.

Does he want to tell her that he thinks it's his fault? Someone must have followed him home, knowing what he is. How would they have known? He has tried to answer that question again and again. Dragon doesn't feel as though he belongs to this surface world, and he doesn't imagine that he is hiding it very well. His best guess: They must have known because it is obvious. The Wallaces risked their lives to provide him a place to stay a few nights every week. And what is their reward? To be punished in his place.

Dragon shakes his head. "I'm okay."

"These things must be boring for you, huh?" Alex says.

"No," Dragon says. "I don't really know what they are."

"So, confusing, then."

Dragon nods.

"Trust me. It is simpler than it seems. All the time, the same human dynamics are playing out. Power struggle is everywhere, even here." She looks at Dragon, decides something, shakes her head. "Never mind. I'm thinking out loud."

Dragon says, "I think I understand." Then he says, "I'm not good in social situations, so the, uh, dynamics all seem strange to me."

Her attention is now completely on him. "You *are* something, aren't you?"

Someone is calling the room to attention, and cluster by cluster, the conversation dies down. To Dragon, it is like watching a complex piece of music fade out, strand by strand.

"Calling our meeting to order," says the youngish brown-skinned woman at the front of the room. She is of a complexion unlike Dragon's and has a quality to her voice that marks her as coming from somewhere else, though Dragon couldn't say how far away.

"First, an update on the cooperative stimulus legislation," she says. "Five million more dollars to invest in cooperatives across Massachusetts."

Applause, and a wave of chatter moves through the various

groups. Again, Dragon marvels at the dance of it, this swelling up of human passions. Just as quickly, it ebbs away as the woman continues.

"We have Debra and Jaden to thank for working with Congresswoman Hilford to fine-tune the proposal, and particularly for incentivizing cooperative conversions for business owners nearing retirement in Greater Boston. A win for many workers—or should I say, future worker-owners."

More applause, and a few cheers and whistles. Dragon is unmoved by their enthusiasm, mostly because he doesn't understand what makes the proposal so important. He looks to Alex for confirmation. She is smiling, but it doesn't look real to Dragon. Watching her, he feels an itch in the back of his mind that he can't reach.

The woman makes more announcements and then passes the microphone to someone else. This older woman's skin and features are more like Dragon's, and she has a trembling voice that somehow pulls everyone in.

She says, "We all know what happened a few nights back. I will spare everyone a rehashing of the gruesome details. The Wallaces were good people and deserve to be remembered well."

Dragon looks down at his hands.

"This city is becoming a terrifying place to live. Hysteria about monsters has been driving people to do unspeakable things. As far as I know, the Wallaces weren't monsters, weren't a threat to anyone. Their activism with New Era had nothing to do with monsters either. So why this senseless violence?"

Dragon feels the pinch of guilt he has trouble unraveling from himself. He is also suddenly afraid. This woman, these people in this room—what would they do if they knew what he is?

He spots Tez in the crowd, sipping from a large beer mug, eyes keenly focused on the speech up front.

"We need to watch out for each other, protect each other from these sorts of attacks."

Someone interrupts, and it isn't Tez, as Dragon expected. Heads turn to the back wall.

"Ridley, for those who don't know me. I co-own the bookstore in Union Square, in Somerville. I don't mean to speak out of turn, but when we say 'protect each other,' how far are we willing to go?"

People look uneasy at the question, but no one asks for clarification. Dragon has attended a couple of these, but he doesn't recognize this person.

Ridley doesn't speak again, only gestures to the person beside him.

Someone else steps forward and starts taking off her clothes. By her expression, it would seem that she isn't doing anything strange at all. The rest of the room shuffles, uncomfortable, but still no one says anything. People stare dumbly at each other or down at the floor.

"My name is Rebecca," the woman says, "and I am a monster."

The audible response from the group distracts Dragon as the woman takes off the final item of clothing.

There is no more preamble after that; they all watch her shift. It happens quickly, and even for Dragon there's a moment when reality seems to skip forward—some fraction of time lost. A wave of dizziness washes over him and away.

The wolf now in the woman's place is beautiful. There is no other word for what Dragon is seeing. She sits next to Ridley and quietly turns her head from right to left, taking in the crowd. The space around Ridley and the wolf has expanded—an involuntary pressing-back, away from the source of the new strangeness. Dragon is looking everywhere, and eventually his gaze rests on Alex. She is standing in the same place as before, but with her head lowered. And her expression is what, exactly? Something complicated, and again Dragon feels the certainty of how little he knows about human beings.

"You can look at her," Ridley is saying. "That's the whole point. See that she's not dangerous."

The room is silent, noise from outside seeping in to take up the void of sound.

"I'm a monster too. I know at least a dozen personally, but we're all isolated. It has been difficult hiding this from a movement I love."

Ridley smiles, and the action seems private somehow, directed inward, at himself. Dragon can't say how he knows this.

"A monster I know very well made a similar confession to me a few years ago, when I didn't know better. I'm not proud of my reaction. I hope you will have a different one."

Someone opens the door and escapes into the pub outside the back room, her footsteps disappearing into a wall of sound as the door closes behind her.

The quiet that follows is tense, the discomfort a palpable aura over the whole room.

"I know that what happened to the Wallaces was terrible. I knew them well, as some of you know me. They understood what New Era is, and they weren't shy about being pro-monster. I am asking the Federation to take a similar stance."

"This isn't the way to ask us." It's the young woman who spoke before. "Surprising us with this display."

The wolf stands, and a collective flinch passes through much of the crowd. She steps out into the center of the room and lies down, resting her head on her paws.

"You think you're the vulnerable ones here," Ridley says. "But you're not. *She* is. Rebecca has revealed herself to a room full of people here without knowing what is in any of your hearts. I know this isn't the appropriate way to do things. But we're desperate. We've been trying to understand what's happening around us, but we need help. The known world is terrifying, but there are rumblings coming from places we don't know. We need support. And visibility. I'm sorry."

The apology takes the breath out of Ridley, and he is staring around the room with an expression that is almost pleading. Dragon realizes that he likes Ridley's face and the red paleness of his lips. Dragon is shocked at the feeling he gets next, so different from his normal feelings toward other people. He looks away from Ridley to catch hold of himself.

"I'll support you," says a familiar voice. Dragon looks and sees Tez stepping forward. He walks over to where the wolf is, kneels down in front of her. "Can I touch your head?" he asks. He extends a hand but waits. The wolf lifts her eyes, and then her head to meet his hand. "I won't insult you by petting you," Tez says. "Just saying hello."

"Anyone else?" Ridley asks.

There's a moment's pause before another hand goes up, and then another, and then many more. A few stragglers reluctantly raise their hands.

"I have family," someone says, apologetic. "This is dangerous."

Ridley nods, and the expression on his face is true sympathy. "I won't speak a word about who gave their support here.

I hope that this extends to all of us. Rebecca and I share in the risk. You can change back now, Becca."

The wolf stands, and reality skips again—the naked woman reaching for her clothes. She dresses quickly but doesn't appear nervous. Dragon feels himself wanting to watch her get dressed, just for how unusual the moment is, but he thinks it kinder, more respectful, to look away, so he does.

"We'll get going," Ridley says once Rebecca is dressed. "I hope the rest of the meeting goes well."

Silence follows them out.

19

A week after her father died, Alex moved in with Mister in a large house in Watertown. It was barely furnished when she arrived. He'd gotten a whole new place to put her. Or at least, that's what Alex thought back then. She had a retinue of house staff to look after her. Tutors in every subject. Dozens of them. Her whole day, weekday or weekend, was scheduled for her. Piano, then English, then math, then art, then tennis on a newly made court out back. Lunch, then physics, then history and sociology, then fucking archery. On Tuesday and Thursday nights, she had strategy.

With the house and the schooling and the new life came a new name: Alexandra.

Yes, it all seemed strange. But Alex had never spent time with someone as rich as Mister. She just thought this was how rich people parented children. Alex made up a story she liked. She still can't tell if it was magic or spun up out of convenience.

Alex had come to learn that Mister belonged to an organization that did this all the time—paid attention to schools all over the country, tried to pick out who had the right combination of family connection and innate brilliance to become someone formidable in their various spheres of endeavor. Extra attention was placed on politics, but intelligence dynasties also got their due. The sort of people who could slip into different shadows and do the sort of covert work the organization needed done. Alex's father was intelligence, and—she hadn't known this when her father was alive—so was his father before him. Alex was her father's only child, and she was already showing the sort of sharpness needed for that kind of work. It didn't matter that her father was dead, and her grandfather long dead, before she was born. Mister knew all the same people her father had known and could grease the wheels of power for her.

So no, she didn't know she was being groomed until much later. Most of that she pieced together herself. And then she pieced together memories from her childhood to figure out the rest. Those parties he held where he would cart Alex around from group to group. The other children there, forming their own strange networks of wealth, power, and privilege. The other children, who had never glimpsed this world before, sitting in their corners, trying to take it all in before some old man—shit, when isn't it an old man?—came over to chat them up.

As a teenager, Alex thought it was some creepy sex thing, and then she tried to avoid the parties if she could. Sometimes people looked at her as though she was something they could use, and she didn't like how that made her feel. Worse than that, she didn't like that she didn't know how they planned to use her.

During that time, Alex met a girl who would become her

only friend her age until she went to college. She met Shaya at one of those parties, of course, and then Mister would arrange these weekend getaways to the mountains. Different one each time. The man had a cabin on every mountainside, and where he didn't have a cabin, he had a resort that knew him by name. Those trips were always wonderful, mostly because he let Alex and Shaya do whatever they wanted. They ordered the weirdest thing on the menu and almost burned down two of his cabins. Shaya had parents. Living ones who loved her in their own way. They were both politicians. Her mother was a senator, her father an ambassador to somewhere, so they were always traveling. And now, because Shaya had had a huge fight with them about it, she was staying in the Boston area with her father's sister, who Shaya always referred to by name or as "father's sister" and never her aunt. They didn't get along.

Alex and Shaya spent a lot of weekends together, and then, once Alex got Mister to let her go out after homeschooling sessions—always with some brooding escort standing around—Shaya and Alex would go to movies or little dinky restaurants, or to the mall to look at boys—and sometimes, for Alex, to quietly look at girls. They got close, and for a while she had a crush on Shaya that she convinced herself wasn't a problem. And mostly it wasn't.

They fell out for the reasons that people fall out who come from different worlds and want different things—and, Alex would come to learn, were fated for different lives. Alex was who she was, and Shaya was who she was. Shaya was a serious person, and Alex wasn't, not then. Shaya had big goals; she could never figure out where she started and her parents ended.

Alex supposed she was like this too. She watched spy movies, imagining herself in faraway places, neutralizing strangers who were trying to kill her. A lover in every city in every country. A bag of money stashed under the floorboards, secret compartments, safes in banks where men with gelled-back hair stood aside while she viewed the possessions of her various selves.

Childhood is a lot of playacting for the person you're going to be. And if you're lucky, you get to play that person in real life. And if you're *really* lucky, you actually like that person you imagined yourself to be, the person you become. If you're lucky, the life you made up is actually one worth living.

Shaya ended up doing well for herself. A prominent congresswoman, one of those people with a finger on the pulse of the young people and who was charismatic enough and passionate enough that people overlooked that she didn't come from a hard life, or a difficult childhood where food wasn't always on the table. It helped that she was not white; it undercut some of that privilege.

But Shaya, too, had been groomed. They met at one of those parties, and they both went on to be what they had been groomed to be. Shaya went to an Ivy League school. Alex went to a school with a good criminology program. Mister didn't advise her on anything, but by then he didn't need to. Set a person well on their path, and they'll follow through on sheer inertia.

He did offer to talk to people at her top-choice schools, and whether he did, she never found out. She told him not to, at the very least. She still got into every school she applied to, which always made her a little suspicious. She told herself it was about her scores, her essay. But she knew enough now to know that she didn't have enough extracurriculars to give her the edge over other high-achieving applicants. No way to know for sure, but her suspicions lingered.

Sure, Alex and Shaya talked about going to the same school. But Alex wasn't interested in Brown or Harvard or Cornell. She wanted something less attention-grabby. Shaya wanted the biggest institutions in the land. Alex applied to the top choice on Shaya's list, got in, almost went, but she took a walk one day, and by the end of that walk, Alex knew they were headed to different places. She didn't want Shaya to carry her through life as her shadow friend, her girlfriend no one understood. "Why do you even still hang out with her?" And later, when they were older: "She seems nice, but she's not like you, not like us."

Yes, it was a defense mechanism. Everyone else had left Alex. She loved Shaya and didn't want to lose her. So Alex got herself lost instead.

And then, junior year, the two suits outside Alex's classroom.

It was a paper Alex wrote that got their attention. Or so the story was at the time. It was about terrorist organizations and their similarity to other clandestine groups. Terrorist groups and organized crime, Alex wrote, need to have secrets, even from people within the organization. In this, they mirror other secret organizations of the more benign variety. Alex referenced secret societies and made comparisons to the mob, explored the rituals that both used to inspire loyalty. She wrote a whole section about spiritual cults. Her professor, who she later learned was sometimes contacted by intelligence agencies for psychological profiles, took an interest.

Alex's major was in conflict and terrorism, but she took several classes in criminology and a few in social organization under an eccentric professor who later infamously disappeared. Professor Flood got Alex interested in secret groups, but she found that her interest gravitated toward the more dangerous end of the spectrum. The garden-variety secret societies didn't hold her attention. Their actual impact on society seemed too nebulous and opaque, which she read at the time as being a lack of impact. (Now she knew how wrong that line of thinking could be.)

Alex spent most of the paper trying to use social organization theory as a lens to study extremism, how one might read the less transparent aspects of recruitment and indoctrination.

Professor Carter wasn't particularly interested in or impressed with the social organization stuff. But he was interested in Alex's passion, the way she argued her points—particularly the way she incorporated real data to create an algorithm to judge whether a political society might turn toward real violence.

He kept her after class one day and offered a few more thoughts on the paper. A week later Alex found two people standing outside the classroom—a man and a woman.

"Want to grab a drink?" the woman asked. It was 6:00 p.m., so not an altogether unusual offer—if she knew who the hell these people were.

"You can pick the place," the man said. He had a thick mustache and no beard.

Alex usually disliked the look, but it worked relatively well on the guy. He had on sunglasses, which he took off—brown eyes. The sunglasses were a red flag—it was too late in the day to be wearing them for any reason except to conceal one's features—but his eyes were kind.

When Alex continued to hesitate, the woman finally introduced herself.

"Sorry, I thought you were expecting us," she said. "I'm Rosie. And my colleague here is Thurmond."

What a name, Alex thought. She also got stuck on the word "colleague."

"Okay," Alex said, finally, and led them to a favorite spot across the street.

In the low light, they ordered drinks. Alex considered ordering her usual Ace cider, but she decided to pick an expensive beer from the menu. The woman ordered an Allagash White, whereupon the man went through the whole menu, back to front, during which Alex watched the waiter's expression move through all five stages of grief. He finally ordered a Negroni, which wasn't on the menu, but the waiter grudgingly brought one anyway.

As all this was happening, neither stranger broached the reason why they had asked to talk with her.

Rosie—and Alex was certain that couldn't be her name—asked a few casual questions about her study. Alex answered the woman but didn't linger or elaborate, letting the conversation slip back into silence. Alex didn't squirm; she watched them both with unselfconscious interest. Thurmond was amused. Rosie tried again and again to move the conversation into polite generic territory.

"Let's have it," Alex said, finally too annoyed to keep the ruse going any longer.

Thurmond laughed, sipped his drink, and made a face of dislike. He put the glass back down on its coaster. "Well, you're everything we hoped for," he said.

Rosie leaned back in her chair. Alex saw the moment when the shroud slipped away and the real woman revealed herself. She didn't smile or laugh—just raised her eyebrows to Alex as if to say, *Now we're really seeing each other.* "We want to offer you a job after school."

"What kind of job? Obviously not a typical one."

Thurmond tried his drink again, groaned but didn't quit. His eyes went to Rosie. So she was the boss here.

"You're right," said Rosie. "It is the sort of job we can't explain straightaway."

"Actually," Thurmond added, "it's the sort of job you don't explain at all. Until you've passed the necessary tests and checks, you won't even get the chance to figure it out on your own."

This stopped Alex from asking which federal government initialism she would be working for. She was hoping CIA. Then she felt silly for that hope and pushed it out of her mind. She was grateful she denied herself the possibility of asking, because it felt too much like what someone in a spy novel would ask. She didn't want to seem like the sort of person who read spy novels. She wondered if real spies worried about things like that, constantly comparing themselves to their fictional counterparts. She knew too many spy books and movies, had filled her head with the stuff.

"For the government?" Alex asked instead. Only a little better than her instinctive question, but there were only so many ways this could go.

"Yes," not-Rosie said. "You'd have to come in for us to lay it all out. But it is a solid offer. Good benefits."

"But I'd never be able to talk about it."

Thurmond was finished with his drink and was frowning with disappointment. "You can talk about it, sure. Just not with your family and friends. Colleagues with the proper clearances. But you don't really have close family, right?"

Alex shrugged. She was done with her beer but reached to pick it up anyway. She stopped and tried to hide her slight embarrassment.

For the first time, Rosie smirked, watching her.

Thurmond continued. "You'd be able to talk to your superiors, people on the same assignment as you. That's it. From now until the end of your life."

Rosie said the next line in their recruitment pitch: "So, what do you think? We don't need you to answer right away, but we're here to answer any questions you might have."

"If you *can* answer," Alex added.

Rosie let her gaze linger before saying, "You have a reasonable poker face. Too many tells, but we can work on that."

Now this sounded too much like a spy novel, and it gave Alex the nagging suspicion that Rosie/not-Rosie was playing up the fantasy as bait. The stubborn part of Alex flared: "Is that all you wanted to talk to me about?"

"Pretty much," Rosie said. "Unless you're willing to say you're interested. Then we can proceed to the next part."

A bunch of fraternity bros (Alex wasn't certain, but they had the look and the vibe) were sitting at the table opposite theirs. They were laughing loudly, one banging his hand on the table in the midst of a story. That was what finally broke the whole illusion, this cloak-and-dagger game they were playing. Suddenly, Alex felt like just another young girl wanting to feel important and thinking this was the kind of thing that made a person important. A dangerous job with access to secrets. But the likelier truth was that she would be another cog in a bigger wheel. Valuable maybe, if she performed well enough, did a convincing enough dance for whoever was on the other end to judge her worth. It made Alex angry, this projection of herself, at once greater and lesser, and then made her angrier for being angry, for engaging in this elaborate fantasy without even knowing why she was here or who she was talking to. And then frustrated. Any answer she gave now would feel like a child's response. They had more power than she, no matter what she did. Leave or stay, Alex was on the losing end.

"You got my drink?" Alex asked.

Rosie nodded, and her smile was the final dagger.

"Goodbye, then." She started to walk out.

"I knew your father," Rosie said.

Alex stopped and turned back.

Rosie smiled again, meeting Alex's eyes, and it was the closest thing to something real that Alex had seen from the woman so far. "Can we start over?"

A year later, Alex arrived at a hotel outside Arlington, Virginia— the sort of nondescript place where people host conferences in fields that no one but the people working in them understand. While Alex was there, she passed people in the halls sporting badges bearing their names and the words *LLA Eastern Conference* and a line drawing of a bird soaring over a mountain. She had no idea what the initialism meant and couldn't glean anything more from the attendees. Their conversations floated well above her head as she listened in breakfast lines or elevators. She detected their awareness of her, the way their eyes would glance over in her direction. Whatever they were, whatever they were doing, it must be a cover for something else.

Alex was there for her own secret reasons. In conference rooms and hotel rooms dressed up as conference rooms, she underwent interviews. The questions these suited men and women asked her were hard to decipher. Had she ever worked with terrorists? No, she answered. She hadn't. When she was a child, did she play an instrument? That question she answered quickly: yes, a clarinet. And then she spent the rest of the day wondering why they'd asked.

She took polygraph tests. They had her speak to a psychologist about her childhood. Alex's mind slid over the questions about her mother. For the life of her, she could not remember how she had answered those once she left the woman's—Alex assumed it was hers—hotel room. In the hall, she felt dizzy, her head throbbing. She left the hotel just as the LLA Conference people were leaving. At the airport, she saw several of them ahead of her in line at the kiosk, and then a couple at her gate waiting for the plane to arrive.

A woman with dark brown hair and full lips sat next to her. Alex recognized her from the breakfast line, the way she heaped mushy eggs onto her paper plate.

"What were you doing there?" she asked.

Alex looked up from the fantasy novel she was pretending to read. "Sorry?"

"I saw you at the conference," she said. "But you're not one of us."

She said "one of us" in the way Alex imagined a cult member might. But her smile was completely innocent, mundane. She waited for Alex to answer the first question, even though she hadn't repeated it.

Alex considered the story she'd rehearsed. "You know, sometimes I just get this feeling. Like I need to go somewhere? But I don't know where I want to go. So, I pick somewhere out of the way, book a hotel for a few nights, rent a car, and go driving in the area, stopping anywhere my gut tells me I should stop."

"Sounds lovely," she said. "Almost like something you just made up."

Alex stared into the woman's eyes. She had the same innocent expression as before. Her eyes were dark brown, and usually Alex would decide on that alone that they were unremarkable. But they had this sharpness. And her eyes were sort of big, actually, like a doll's, but she wasn't doll-like in the typical sense. Where a doll might appear oblivious or ditzy or inanimate, the woman possessed the opposite of all those qualities, and that fact was present in her eyes.

"I'm Georgie," she said.

"Amethyst."

"A lovely name."

"How about you?" Alex asked. "What were you doing there?" A ticket agent said something over the intercom, but she was positive it had nothing to do with her, so she ignored it.

Georgie didn't stop smiling, but her eyes narrowed. The effect made them look more average and at the same time less natural on her face.

"The LLA Eastern Conference," Georgie said.

"I never could figure out what it was a conference *for*."

"Well, I got one of those conference schedule things in my bag somewhere." She ruffled through her purse for a while. Alex watched her at first, then thought she was being impolite. She returned to her book.

"Ah, can't find it," she said finally. "Must've thrown it away."

"I never hold on to those things myself."

"Oh yeah. What do you do?"

"I'm a student. Final semester."

"What major?"

"Criminology."

"Sounds lovely."

Alex raised her eyebrow, puzzled. "You're the first person who's ever said that to me."

She laughed. "Well, it's something I say. When I'm nervous. Like a personal tick. You know, like how Owen Wilson says 'wow' all the time?"

Alex would have asked why she was nervous, but then she noticed the woman was staring at her lips. It might have been bad timing, but it made the rest of the impromptu interaction make more sense. Other people managed it all the time, but other people hardly ever engaged Alex in spontaneous small talk.

"You never answered me," Alex said, seizing a bit of the power she now thought she had. "What do the people at the conference do for a living?"

"Oh, right. All sorts of things. We're a conference on cooperatives."

Alex nodded. "You mean, like grocery stores?"

"No, not just that. Purchasing co-ops and housing co-ops and worker-owned co-ops of all kinds. Bakeries and bike-repair shops and tech co-ops, and quite a few credit unions, and, yeah, some co-op grocery stores."

Alex remembered an article Dr. Flood had assigned that she never finished reading in its entirety, mostly because it sounded like nonsense. Something about a solidarity commonwealth. But Alex had seen cooperatives pop up a few times in the article. "Sounds lovely," Alex said, maintaining eye contact. "And what do you do?"

Georgie laughed. "I own a bakery with four other women. Out in San Francisco. Yeah, I know. Far from home."

"How did you all manage that?"

"We sort of found each other. We were all into baking, attended a couple of common meetups in the area. And, well, one of us—I don't remember which—brought up the idea of renting a space and starting a bakery together. And so we did."

Alex looked at her for a long time, trying to fathom what it must be like to have that level of trust in other people—in virtual strangers, by the sound of it.

"You're looking at me like I'm crazy," she said. "We've been in business now for seven years. I've never been happier."

That only made Alex more suspicious. It sounded to her as if the woman was evangelizing. "But you all must have conflicts."

The woman looked down at Alex's lips again. "If I had a dollar for every time someone not in the movement has asked me that question . . ."

"The movement?" Alex repeated before she could stop herself.

The woman shook her head. "Yes, we have conflicts. We just work them out. Like adults."

A thought occurred to Alex. "Aren't you heading back home?"

"No, I got some family in Boston I'm visiting. My aunt . . ." She paused, looking Alex in the eyes. "She's *touched*."

Alex blinked at her.

She caught the change in Alex's expression. Her eyes widened. "Sorry, I thought . . . well, never mind."

"What is it?"

She did something strange then. She touched Alex on the hand. Alex startled.

"Sorry," she said. "Uh, well, this is embarrassing. Please forget I did that."

"Why did you? Why did you do that?"

Georgie was blushing, her cheeks very red. "I don't. I just, ummm . . . It was nice talking to you." She stood up and went to the restrooms, and Alex didn't see her again until Alex was putting her carry-on in the luggage compartment above her seat. There she was, a few seats back, trying and failing to seem as if she weren't looking at Alex. The entire flight, Alex could feel the woman's eyes burning into the back of her head. Alex usually would have tried to sleep, but she kept going over what the woman had said and the feel of her touch, the quick surge of heat that went through her.

When the plane landed, Alex rushed out, trying to get her luggage off the carousel quickly and avoid a further encounter. But there the woman was again.

"I want to apologize," she said. "That must've been strange."

Alex glanced at her but kept watching for her bag. "It's fine. Don't worry."

"It's just," she said, "I don't know if you know, but . . ." She trailed off, as if unsure what to say next.

The whole thing was terribly uncomfortable. "Look, I don't know what this is about—"

"You have a hex on you," she said. "I thought it was the gift at first, but it's not. I'm not good at this. I'm learning from my aunt." She was talking fast now, hardly sparing the time to breathe.

"I don't know what you're talking about. Please leave me alone." Alex raised her voice at the end of the last part, and Georgie stepped back in surprise.

"Sorry," she said. "But please."

Alex was scared of something, and she could feel the little

hairs on her neck rising—some danger from beyond her senses closing in on her.

"Okay," Alex said. "I'm sorry too." She walked to the other side of baggage claim.

Alex thought it was over, but the strange woman caught her again on her way out the terminal doors. "My aunt's name is Aura Lane. I know. Not subtle. She lives in Jamaica Plain. Clarence Road. Apartment three-A. She can help with whatever's hanging off you."

Alex rushed past her and boarded the Silver Line.

She wouldn't call Aura Lane until many years later, assuming that Georgie was crazy. That changed when Alex joined the Order and met the Bone Witch—the frail body, long, bony hands always clasped around her hex book—and recognized something there that made her feel as if she had been violated in some unnameable way. And she would find out why once that rogue witch lifted the hex, but she would never let on to Mister or anyone.

She kept the secret and savored it because it was something that truly belonged to her. Only hers. And one day she would know exactly how to use it.

She had no one in her life she minded losing. No one who would miss her when she was gone.

Alex believed that trauma imprints on the soul. The story of how her parents died was painful enough, devastating enough to make most kids grow into fucked-up adults. But somewhere deep and dark, beyond her mind, in the cells of her, Alex knew what had happened to them. And she didn't want to trust anything the world gave her, because she knew what stirred beneath all of it. Ruin. Oblivion. Alex knew her entire life had been a lie, where she knew nothing worth knowing about the people she loved, who were meant to love her. Mister was the final straw. Alex had looked up to him. And he was right in the middle of that gaping hole in her memory. He had done it and stood there and told Alex the story afterward. And because the spell had required it, she accepted it. But her essence had not. Who she was beyond the machinery did not.

Why didn't she leave then, knowing that she'd been pried open, her most formative experiences torn from her mind? Why didn't she leave as soon as she realized that Mister had been grooming her all this time? Why did she keep walking down that road?

Because, Alex knew, there was no escape but true escape. She was exactly who Mister thought she was. She wanted to know the real face of the world.

The night it happens, Alex is outside, parked in her usual place outside the community center, a cigarette dangling from one hand.

Tez comes down from the community center and crosses the street at a leisurely jog. Alex's window is down, and so he stoops to talk, looking out at her from under furrowed brows. "You think you could take me out of the city?"

Alex nods, says of course. "What's it about?" she dares to ask.

"I'll tell you on the way." He runs around the car and drops into the passenger seat, shutting the door.

"So now, then. Okay."

He actually doesn't tell Alex on the way, other than that he is meeting someone.

When they arrive at the apartment building, she asks, "You need me to come up?"

He nods gratefully. "Thanks. It'll be quick."

Tez's expression when he knocks on the door confirms everything for Alex. He places his head close to the door as if listening for movement on the inside. And his body is wound up to kick down the door. Alex thinks quietly to herself that there is no other world she belongs in than this one, where violence is always a moment away. She readies herself as well, and when Tez kicks the door down, she follows him in without a word.

The man is still stumbling back until the side of his body finds the couch, and he slides ungracefully down the side of it to the carpet. He pulls himself up again and tries to put his hand to his face, but Tez forces it away and catches him by the neck. Alex feels it in her own body when he slams the man against the wall, and she isn't surprised when his eyes roll back for a moment in pain. It vaguely occurs to her that he might have a concussion. He'll need to go to the hospital.

"I don't need to ask, because I can smell it on you," Tez says. "But nod if you know why I'm here."

To the man's credit, he doesn't pretend ignorance. Hard to do with a hand to his throat. Another thing they get wrong in the stories. It's a toss-up whether a person will lie or tell the truth in a moment like this. Often defense mechanisms take over unless you train against them. This man had chosen compliance and acceptance of his situation, which is smart. A lie might have ended with him dead on the floor.

"You will turn yourself in?" Tez says and releases him.

He chokes for a moment and nods, his face sweaty.

Alex stands back, still saying nothing, but she takes a glance out into the hallway and then tries her best to close the door. When she can't, she leans against it.

The man says, "It wasn't just me."

Tez leans in again. "We'll find the other ones, don't you worry."

Alex feels a twinness: Herself standing there waiting, but also the feeling that she might not be here at all—a floating camera, a hovering ghost. A witness peeking through from a rent in the fabric of space-time.

Tez steps back. "Go today," he says. "Once we leave."

Alex takes a breath, lets in some relief. This will be the end of it.

But then the man allows his true emotions to show in his face—the humiliation of having a monster, this thing he hates, come into his home and violate him. He doesn't speak, but it is obvious that he will not let this go, will not turn himself in once they leave.

Tez looks back at Alex, and his expression is almost apologetic. The rest of what he is saying with his eyes surprises her, and she understands that she is completely out of her depth here, perhaps always has been. The things she doesn't know can swallow her whole.

Tez shifts in his clothes, and the creature that spins into reality turns the cloth covering its body to tatters. He leaps at once, the change completing itself as the massive black cat makes contact. The man puts his hand up again to cover his face, but it does less than nothing. The cat tears through the hand, catching it and separating it from the man in a movement so quick, Alex doesn't register what has happened until the hand arcs through the air past her. She doesn't see when Tez bites down on the man, but she sees the head in Tez's mouth. He twists it off as he holds the man's body steady against the wall with his front paws. No time for anything but a yelp from the man, and it is unclear which part of the attack has caused it. Wet tearing sounds fill the room, bouncing off walls. It takes . . . *seconds*—not even a half minute. Alex is somehow still upright, but her legs are shaking. Tez releases the man's body, drops to all fours with the head still in his mouth. The body slides down the wall, blood flowing down from where the parts are missing.

Tez spits the head out, and Alex has to look away as it rolls into the dining area of the small apartment, fetching up against one of the chairs. Nothing of the scene looks the way it should. Bodies don't fall apart this way. But Alex now knows that sometimes bodies *do* fall apart, that this man's body has done so. She tries to shake the wrongness of how it happened, but can't. The whole scene feels like a lie; she keeps looking, hoping for the curtain to fall.

Tez shifts back into human form as quickly as he changed out. Alex distantly registers that she didn't get a good look. She can remember the color and size of the cat—black as India ink and bigger than just about anything alive she's seen—but her mind went spotty as soon as he made the change and is only now coming back to itself. In human form, Tez looks at her. His shirt is hanging off him, his pants torn and resting on the floor in a puddle of the man's blood.

He is saying something, but despite herself she's fixated on his nakedness.

He repeats, "You there?"

Alex opens her mouth to answer, but a voice not her own fills the room.

"You've made a mess for all of us," it says.

"And that's why you're here to clean it up," Tez answers.

"What?" Alex says, the question coming out as a whisper. She looks around for the source of the voice.

"This might be bigger than I can manage."

"Please. You've managed much bigger things."

The voice is coming from . . . the kitchen counter? A spider is there, watching her. Willful disbelief makes her almost look away, but then—

"You both should go," the spider says.

"Give me a second," Tez replies. "I'm going to find some clothes." He looks at Alex. "You going to be all right for a moment?"

Alex nods distantly. She is in shock, she observes. It feels like someone else observing it and slipping the thought into her brain from outside.

Tez disappears down the hallway and opens a room at the end.

Alex is alone with the spider. Seconds pass, the glowing, multifaceted red eyes observing her. The spider, about the size of a tarantula but nothing like one in appearance, has wiry hair covering its body. But the hair is wrong. It looks . . . oddly metallic.

"Who are you?"

The spider voice comes out tinny but clear, with a slight accent she has heard before: "Try to forget what you've seen here. It doesn't matter. *I* don't matter. It didn't happen."

She wants to say, *Don't tell me what to do,* but it sounds childish. And Alex will not give more of an upper hand to this thing she doesn't understand. She adjusts her body to stand straighter, try to take control, try to understand. Consciously she steps away from her own fear. Later it will be there waiting for her.

Tez comes out in a shirt and pants too big for him. He touches her shoulder, and she flinches slightly.

If he noticed, he doesn't acknowledge it. "Let's go."

Alex follows him out. As they leave, the door starts to close behind them, but Alex spares a moment to look back, sees that the apartment is suddenly, inexplicably infested with ants—on every surface, a great mass converging on the man's remains. Their abdomens are glowing like the spider's eyes, bathing the apartment in sharp red light. The brightness blinks out as soon as the door closes shut (somehow, though it couldn't close before), and Alex has another feeling of vertigo, as if someone has turned the jar she's in sideways.

They descend the stairs.

THE COMING STORM

MATTHEW REED AND SONDRA PAIGE
SAINT THOMAS, USVI
EARTH 0539

NOVEMBER 5, 2026

The dream again.

Matthew shudders awake. Sondra is still resting beside him, and so he breathes a sigh of relief. All this time, and still it reemerges, a breaching whale from his subconscious—this memory disguised as a dream. Or something his mind has made up to fill in the gaps of who he is. He'll never know for sure.

He's careful when he leaves the bed, spares a moment to watch Sondra's sleeping face, softly illuminated in the predawn gray. He wishes he could touch her head and somehow read what is happening behind that face. He knows she has her own troubles, but more often than not she keeps them to herself. They love each other, of course, but there is still so much distance, so many secrets, knowable and unknowable depths to be plumbed.

On soft feet, he leaves the bedroom and goes to the kitchen to start a pot of morning tea. He puts the loose leaves in the water as it boils, turns the stove down low. Matthew doesn't like coffee, though Sondra enjoys it some days. He does like his tea strong and dark, with a mix of oat milk and lactose-free milk so he doesn't upset his delicate intolerance. He makes them each a cup and starts drinking his while passing the time flipping through reels on Instagram. He shouldn't start the day this way, but he doesn't want to be alone in his own mind, trapped with those old mysteries.

He lingers on one reel. The caption on it reads, *When your wife is a vampire.* In the short video, the husband turns off the bedroom light and yells out in pain. He flicks it back on, rubbing his neck. His wife is asleep. He looks around, confused, turns off the light again. The series of events repeats two more times—the yelling out in pain, the light turning on, his wife convincingly feigning sleep—before the husband turns on the light and finally lunges at his wife, pretending to bite back. She leaps from the bed, laughing. The video has one million views.

Matthew considers saving the video by sending it to Sondra, but he doesn't think she'll find it funny or interesting. For Matthew, it is a sign of times changing. He glances at the comments. Divided, as always, so maybe the times aren't changing as much as he'd hoped. But for this to get so many views, for the channel to have so many subscribers . . . He's seen other videos featuring these same two people before, but this is the first one that is explicitly "monster-positive." Could it be called that? Monster-friendly, at least.

He closes Instagram, puts his phone away. He's wasted too much time thinking about it.

The bed creaks, and moments later he can hear Sondra walking out of the bedroom and down the hall. His first vision of her: yawning, hands outstretched, beautiful.

"Good morning," she says through her yawning and stretching. Her hands fall to her sides with a soft slap. "What's for breakfast?"

Matthew shakes his head.

She frowns. "You mean you didn't even fry an egg?"

"I wasn't hungry. I made tea."

Still frowning, but when she reaches out to him, she touches his hand. "Thank you." She goes straight to the fridge and rummages about. "You having trouble sleeping again?"

Matthew nods. "The dream came back."

"Really? It's been months." Sondra places the carton of eggs on the kitchen island, in front of Matthew. She pulls her favorite cast-iron skillet from the drawer below the oven—a smaller one, with room enough to fry two eggs. "Want one?"

"Sure."

"We still have a little of that butter bread, if that's fine."

"More than fine."

Sondra oils the pan, turns on the burner. "You think it has to do with the monster vote?"

"Probably," Matthew says. "Would be nice to have a friendly face in the chamber."

Sondra is quiet. She cracks two eggs. The sizzle is like music.

"I'm not saying you have to sit in or anything. I know that makes you uncomfortable. I just wish—"

"I know what you wish. But it's better that I'm not there in any capacity."

Matthew wants to ask questions, but he knows not to. She won't answer him anyway. He sighs instead. "Smells good."

"It's just eggs."

"Sure, but yours always come out better than mine."

"You want bacon, don't you?"

Matthew smiles to Sondra's back, but her head is nodding. He has no idea how she can tell what he's thinking even when she's not looking at him.

"It'll be okay," Sondra says. "You'll do fine. Even if it fails this time, there'll be other opportunities. Progress is a long road."

Matthew admires her pragmatism, her ability to see change through a long lens. He is too impatient for that. He doesn't feel it in his bones. He understands urgency, understands that human beings have so little time to accomplish their many goals. Maybe that is where the difference comes from. Sondra is human, and something more.

"Plans for the day?" Matthew asks.

"Some work with Solidarity Commonwealth VI. Then I'll probably go see Mom."

"How long do you think you'll wait before you bring your uncle to see her?"

"Whenever she insists. Whenever he gets up the courage to ask me about her."

"I know you think he knows already—"

"He does."

"Right."

"I don't know what it is—fear or pride or whatever. But every time I go see him, I can see the question right there, begging to come out. He holds it in every time. I'm not going to push."

"Seems like the mature option." Even as he says it, he knows he is just performing the right words to say to her in the moment, the words she needs. Fear and pride aren't only in her uncle; Sondra has more than her share. But he won't push either. He has worked hard for the trust he's gained with her. So many secrets, but every day a little less distance between them.

Sondra puts some bacon on his plate with his fried egg and butter bread. She takes the chair next to him—more a barstool than a real chair. It bothers Matthew's back, and he's thought about replacing them, but Sondra likes them, and she doesn't seem to get lower-back pain. The perks of being a woo-woo.

"I'll be off," Matthew says after shoveling down his breakfast. "Heading to the office."

"Have a good day," Sondra says.

Matthew takes a speed shower and is dressed in fifteen minutes. Starched shirt and pants from the dry cleaners, which will soon be a worker cooperative if Sondra and Solidarity Commonwealth VI get their way.

He passes her on the way out, sitting on the couch. She smiles up at him and gives him a kiss.

When he's gone, Sondra sits in the living room, listening for a moment to the empty house. She can't help but smile a little. These are scary times, but she's managed to carve out a small corner of sanity within them.

Matthew and Sondra had spent most of their early dates debating. Matthew would come over to her place and cook because it was less stressful than going out and perhaps being spotted by nosy people who would then be up in their business. It would get back to colleagues in the legislature in no time. But the added benefit was that they could debate openly without drawing attention from anyone.

"I think statehood is loud power."

Matthew put down his fork. "Say more."

"Grabbing at that only hardens the resistance against what we can do in the here and now. It looks good on paper. Statehood might allow us to vote for president, have voting representation in the Senate and the House. But no move comes without drawbacks. We can see that states have their own struggles. Being a territory gives us a certain degree of autonomy. If we use it wisely, quietly, we can build power that would make a move to statehood advantageous in the long term if we decided to make that choice. If we're strong, our choices would be ours to make. I wish you could see that statehood isn't the same as cultural power. Cultural power can't be bought with gestures. It has to be bought with effort, solidarity, consensus."

She paused to eat some of the fettuccine in white sauce. This was their fourth date. Matthew had cooked chicken alfredo, the chicken blackened with jerk spices and scotch bonnets for a bit more of a kick. He had a few signature dishes during those early dates, and later he'd try new ones he made to extend his repertoire. He was really trying to make a good impression. And he did. But Sondra thought he was a good cook when he made new meals, and a great cook when he relied on his staples and his gut. The chicken alfredo was one of his mainstays—something he could make without thinking, and it would taste like heaven every time. Even though they were at her place, he was all dressed up—in shirt and tie, even—clearly trying to maintain a good impression. Sondra had deliberately chosen a T-shirt and jeans.

She took a bite of food before Matthew spoke. He was smiling, looking at her.

He said, "It is terribly condescending to say that we don't have the power to come to the table and demand statehood.

And it is terrible to ask that we continue to exist without the power to choose our overlords."

"But you hear that, right? Why *have* overlords?"

"We will have them regardless."

"That's where we disagree," she said. "All power is topography. All power tells you how to circumvent it if you study it long enough. Real power isn't in the landscape. It is in the body and in the mind that understands the landscape. We're not beneath it. It is beneath us."

"So, independence, then?"

Sondra smiled. This was her secret hope (someday), but she didn't dare say it out loud. Not yet. "I want us to be strong no matter what title we have, independent of title. So that when we choose, as a people, eyes wide open, our choices will be ours, made through full knowledge, true knowing. You can't get there by spending yourself on gestures. The work is harder, longer. No shortcuts."

"I don't understand this 'gesture' stuff. What do you even mean by that? It isn't a *gesture* to be equal under the law."

"What is the law? Did you write the American laws that you want so desperately to be a part of? And what's the point of fighting for statehood if you can't get there. Do the work to make sure you can get there, and then consider if *there* is even where you want to get."

"Your way takes too long."

"My way gets us there."

"You're being moderate."

"You know I'm not a moderate. You're frustrated or you wouldn't be saying that."

"What are you, then?"

"I don't let my idealism convince me that a mountain is just a hill. Reality doesn't change because you're hopeful."

"And you know what reality is?"

Sondra frowned. She could feel the conversation edging toward hostility. She looked at him. He had stuffed some fettuccine into his mouth and was chewing vigorously. She held the silence, and he held her gaze. He was patient at least. Maybe she had been underestimating him.

She said, "I know I don't know the reality. But what I can see of it is jagged glass. I'm not running out there barefoot. If you go out there now, you won't get what you want. You don't know what will come up to meet you. You have to be prepared."

He continued his silence, drinking some of the red wine he'd bought for the occasion. He looked down for a moment, going into himself. When he looked at her again, his eyes were kind. "I was wrong to call you moderate. Just then you sounded like a revolutionary."

Sondra laughed to conceal her embarrassment, but he held her eyes again, not blinking or looking away. She let the axe fall. "If that's what you want to call it."

"You are," he said. And then later, in bed: "I know you believe in having a plan for everything. But you must agree that with some things, the only way you can learn is through doing."

They were naked, curled up under the sheets together. She was sweating, the heat from sex still radiating off her skin. He felt warm to the touch, his chest hair slick from the exertion. She liked it.

She said, "I used to think that way too. Do to learn. But sometimes thinking is learning, knowing when not to waste what you do."

"Say more."

How open he was! Sondra asked herself if she could consider him more than an adversary she was trying out a flirtation with. Yes, they'd had sex, but she wasn't about to make it anything more than that. Or so she tried to convince herself. When she talked, he listened. He was more of an idealist than she was, but he knew how to set that aside, consider another view of the world.

"Power," Sondra said, "is almost always negotiated unless your life is on the line. The powers that be, the ones that run the country we consider our owner, the laws that hold the whole sprawling mess together, form a landscape if you can see it. An obstacle is a hill, a log, a flowing stream. An impasse is a mountain, an ocean. All these intersecting systems are the topography of the intangible contract that binds the world. Pretending a mountain is a river you can swim across will only give you a concussion. It isn't about who has power over you. It's about how you navigate the landscape of power. That simple reconceptualization has saved me a lot of headaches. Building the means of moving along a landscape, learning how the wind turns or when a storm is coming—all those individual actions develop a keenness, a sense of who you are. What's you, and what's geography. It expunges one's shame over not leveling a mountain that need only be climbed."

"The landscape metaphor again." He was silent for a moment. "Nothing can be that simple."

"Never. What I'm describing isn't at all simple. But you don't beat yourself up just because things are complicated. Complexity has nothing to do with you. It just . . . *is*."

He was quiet again. It was the strangest sort of bedroom

talk. Most other senators couldn't get into the weeds like this with her, and so she knew they weren't worth her time. Sondra could feel herself shifting with Matthew, opening up.

"You awake?" she said, testing.

"I'm taking it in. There's more, no? I want to hear it."

Sondra explained that once you considered the world this way, saw this realm of intangibles as something to climb, to cross, to build boats and bridges and vehicles to traverse, it became less about pragmatism versus radicalism. All things were a matter of physics. The problem was that this landscape wasn't easy to see. There were gaps everywhere, unknowns, uncharted territory. Those parts you had to feel your way through with your hands or find a flashlight, or, better yet, wait a bit until daybreak. By the time she was done, they were swimming in so many metaphors that she could feel herself losing her grip on it. She had never explained it so deeply before. No one had let her get this far outside her own head.

Sondra was getting cold, so she pressed herself closer to Matthew to steal a little more of his warmth. She felt his body respond to hers, felt her own body respond to his. He turned to her in the dark, pressed his lips to hers. She expected him to go further.

Instead, he said, "So you're saying statehood is a mountain, and we need climbing gear, a plan to get up the mountain, food for the trip?"

What a strange mix of emotions: intellectual excitement and sexual frustration at the same time. She thought on his words before speaking. "Or we need to know if it's even worth climbing. I know this is going to sound terrible, but we're on fertile ground here—a place where, if we found the will, we could become a people strong enough to leave this metaphorical Earth if we want. But I don't think we know what we want. Not as a collective. I want us to find that out. But first we have to heal each other so we can listen to each other."

"It doesn't sound terrible," he said. "I still think you're underestimating the importance of agency, even symbolic agency. I think you might be missing how a win like that could open up the opportunity toward healing. But I don't disagree with you either. I'm torn, unsure, in a way that is always a good thing— it means there's something still to figure out."

Sondra smiled to herself. The truth was, he had somehow made her unsure as well. Was she right? Or was he? Were they both? She didn't reciprocate his generosity in the moment. But she thought, this was a person she might be able to build a life with. Here was someone she could share her dream with. Someday. The thought, even as she had it, terrified her. She wanted to get up out of the bed and put her clothes on.

In the dark, she could feel his entire body, even though only their arms touched. His outline was as vivid to her as her own, and it felt more as if she were swelling and shrinking in response, her limits a blur or the lapping of weak waves in and out against a shore. His shore? She was drunk with something, that was for sure. She felt closer to the world of atoms and magnetism and exchange of energy. She was more than she was, and aware of her smallness—insubstantial and infinite.

"You've gone quiet," he said, testing her now.

"I'm thinking."

"Thinking about what?"

"You want to spend the night? If you have to go, that's fine too." What was this? Butterflies? Sondra wanted to jump out of her own skin.

Matthew didn't let too many seconds pass. "Yes. I can stay," he said.

Finally, to Sondra's relief, they had sex again.

After he proposed, Sondra sat Matthew down and told him over dinner—at his dining table this time—about her parents' disappearance. She omitted so many things. She didn't talk about Sonya or the Order of Asha. She didn't say she'd found her mother in some strange apartment thousands of miles from home, with the stink of foul magic on her and a fraying mind. It would be a while longer before Sondra told him that part. Secrets on top of secrets she kept for herself. But she did tell him her tenderest secret then: that she had lost her family and it had left her with a gaping wound at her center. She had run from every intimacy throughout her adolescence and her twenties. She had planned to run all the way until age took her. But she had found him, and she wanted to share some of herself, and she was afraid of that feeling.

His response made Sondra know she would marry him.

"My mother left me when I was a baby. I have memories of her face. It should be impossible, but it is frozen in my mind. I have a memory, before she walked out on me and my father, of her telling me that knowledge is pain. I spent almost a decade trying to find her. It was like she stepped off the edge of the earth.

"I don't know what it's like to lose two parents. But I know a bit about having a hole nothing can fill."

Sondra didn't believe in soulmates or any of that bullshit.

But she did believe in being with another person who could understand the harder things to understand. She just didn't know she believed it until that moment.

"You keep surprising me," she said.

"In a bad way?"

"No. In the best way."

Sondra's day, once Matthew has gone to work:

10:00 a.m. Stop by Joseph Dry Cleaning and try to convince the elderly owners to convert their business into a co-op.

When she enters, Dana is up front, staring at the phone in her hands.

"Afternoon, Dana," Sondra says.

Not looking up from her phone: "Afternoon."

Sondra waits.

When Dana finally glances up, her demeanor changes. "Senator."

"Former," she corrects. "Ms. Joseph in?"

"In the back."

Sondra continues to stare. She says, "Could you get her for me?"

Dana blinks. "Oh yeah. Ms. Joseph! Senator Paige here to see you."

Sondra smiles. "That works too."

Ms. Joseph appears from the back in seconds. "Why you yelling down the place?"

"Sorry," Dana says. "Senator—"

"I heard. You here to try to convince me to sell to my employees again?"

Sondra straightens. "Well, yes, in fact, I was. Did my colleague stop by to talk with you about the process?"

"She did. I'm not interested."

"Ms. Joseph—"

"I'm not selling to my employees. They good for nothing and will drive this place into the ground as sure as I breathe. Take this one." Dana startles when Ms. Joseph turns to her. "Bet she was on her phone when you came in, right or wrong?"

Dana doesn't say anything, slipping her phone into her back pocket.

Sondra isn't about to rat the young woman out. "Ms. Joseph, you're struggling to keep the lights on already, right?" Sondra doesn't need to wait for the answer. "That's why you're retiring. You're tired. Now, you can let someone swoop in here and buy you out—it won't be a lot of money—and then gut the business you've spent a lifetime building. Joseph Dry Cleaning has been in this spot since I was a little girl. Do you want to let that legacy die?"

Ms. Joseph looks around, uncertain. "Well, I don't see what else I can do."

"Solidarity Commonwealth VI has worked with the Virgin Islands Department of Labor to develop programs that could train your employees to run the business side of things. They already know the work."

Ms. Joseph laughs. "Sure they do."

"And our loan program can give your employees the starter funds to pay for the business at a competitive price. That's money that will go to you and Mr. Joseph. Money that could be put toward your retirement."

Ms. Joseph is quiet, hand to chin, considering.

Sondra rifles through her bag. "Here's my card. Just think about it and call us anytime."

Ms. Joseph takes the card, nods.

Sondra knows not to overplay her hand. "You have a good day, Ms. Joseph."

"Yes, all right."

"You too, Dana."

"Yes, Senator."

Sondra also knows better than to correct the young woman again. Leaning into her former position in this case can only work to her advantage.

In her car, she sends Jessica a text:

> I think we got them.

You sure?

> 75 percent?

Better than me. Ms. Joseph basically ran me outta there.

> She said she'll talk to Mr. Joseph.
> I know him. He's a practical man.
> He could get her over the line.

Sondra adds, *I think.*

> Well, that's why you make the
> big bucks.

It's their in-joke. Neither of them is making the big bucks running this nonprofit. In the beginning, Solidarity Commonwealth VI's main objective was to help people procure the funds to start co-ops. Part community fund, part policy advocate, the nonprofit had quickly found it easier to encourage businesses on the verge of collapse, or whose owners were at retirement age, to convert to cooperatives by selling to their employees. It was easier to get government funding and community buy-in for businesses that were already a part of the community.

Not that it made their job easy. It was still difficult to convince traditional small businesses that a worker-owner model could be stable.

Jessica sends another text:

> Inbox getting full. I gon spend some
> time in the trenches, but Andre need
> picking up from school at 2:30.

> Okay, I could drop in later
> this afternoon.

But a couple of other things first:
12:00 p.m. Stop by Forbes Bakery Cooperative and get a beef pate. No, get two of the pastries.
12:30 p.m. Visit Mom at the Bordeaux Compound.

Sondra knocks before entering her mother's room. Her mother doesn't look away from the window—so used to this routine that it isn't worth the effort.

What she says is new. "I'm ready to see him."

Sondra places the paper bag, already greasy from the pate inside, on the dresser by her mother's bed. She's already eaten hers, the spiciness of minced meat and the buttery taste of the fried dough still lingering on her taste buds.

"Who do you want to see?" Sondra asks.

Her mother turns away from the window, her expression sharp as shattered glass. "How is he?"

No use pretending. "He's fine. Or was the last time I saw him."

"His leg."

Sondra is constantly reminding herself that she must be delicate with her mother. She chooses her next words carefully. "A little worse than before."

"A *lot* worse. He's been hiding the damage from you."

No, even her uncle's pride cannot hide the damage from her. They are all inheritors of the ability to smell magic, both the good kind—healthy and vibrant—and the bad kind that turns in on itself or eats the host. The curse on her uncle's leg is the latter.

Sondra sits on the bed. "He ever tell you how he got it?"

"Your uncle is a private man," she says. "He said it was an obeah woman. But he spent some time on the mainland looking for our brother. Went, and came back with a slight limp. I didn't before, but I recognize the work now."

The Bone Witch from the Order of the Zsouvox? Sondra chooses to leave the question unasked. She can feel that madness crawling up her back, and she wants nothing to do with it. She wants to ask if this was the beginning of what would become the abduction—her uncle going to the mainland and unwittingly bringing back a passenger with him. Is that how they found her mom and dad? Is that part of her uncle's secret shame? She wants to ask all this but doesn't. Her mother is delicate. Her mother likely doesn't know.

"I want to see him."

Sondra blinks. "To ask him about his leg?"

"No. I want to see my brother."

"I don't know if that's a good idea."

"We've been apart for a long time. And some days I don't know where my mind is." A sudden hardness to her face. "But I'm still your mother. And I want to see my brother."

Sondra knows there is no use, but she wasn't prepared for the sadness she feels. Why would she feel that emotion? But instantly she realizes she has gotten used to her mother being hers and only hers. And that thought leads to another—of her sister, who has not visited their mother since she arrived at the compound. Sondra has no idea why.

"I'll need time to prepare," Sondra says. "Give me a couple of days."

She can see that her mother wants to ask, *What for?* But she doesn't. She lets Sondra have this, and Sondra is grateful. "How are you doing today?" Sondra asks. The customary question, the one thing she asks every time she comes here.

Her mother is suddenly avoiding direct eye contact, so Sondra knows her answer won't be altogether truthful. "It's a good day."

On the walls are small paintings on stock paper. Watercolors. Sondra's mother used to paint when Sondra was a child, but her mother was always too busy to keep up the habit for long. Now, here, where there's nothing else to do, she can cover the walls with her work.

"Okay," Sondra says. "I'll be back soon."

"With my brother."

"Yes."

"And your father?"

Sondra stiffens at the question. Her mother hasn't asked about Sondra's father in months.

There is no good news and nothing Sondra can do to soften the blow. "He is still lost, Mom."

"Not lost," her mother says. "Locked away."

Sondra watches her mother. She's never said this before either. Today is full of surprises. "Mom."

"Don't tell me I don't know what I'm talking about. I remember more every day. Your father wouldn't let himself be used. And he wouldn't stop fighting them. So they had to muzzle him."

The way she says "muzzle" tells Sondra that what her mother is talking about is a particularly terrible form of magic.

"He's out there, and he's in pain," her mother says. "He's out there, and he's all alone."

What could Sondra say? She finds herself wanting to make all manner of promises. But this particular feat is beyond her powers. If only . . . She tries to put the thought out of her head. She'll never talk to Sonya again. Not if she can help it. But is she willing to hold this grudge forever, even if it means never seeing her father again? She can't find the answer in herself, so she steps away from the question so it can't hurt her.

"Let's deal with Uncle first. We'll figure out the rest."

Again, she can see that her mother has more to say, but she doesn't.

"Enjoy the pate," Sondra says, and leaves.

1:00 p.m. Drive home.

1:30 p.m. Spend the rest of your day answering damn emails.

This is most of her job for the nonprofit. Since it's just her and Jessica—and Reese, when he has the time—it means Sondra has to do most of the paperwork that needs to get in by deadline. She also must give most of the gentle nudges and do quite a bit of just answering sometimes good—and often stupid—questions about the legal parameters of co-op conversions. Occasionally, the nonprofit receives an email from someone looking into starting a co-op or converting their business. Forbes Bakery started from one such email. In those moments, she feels as though she is affecting the culture, changing people's minds about the benefits of solidarity economics. She's had her hand in creating ten co-ops so far. If she's lucky, Joseph Dry Cleaning will be their eleventh. A drop in the bucket, but with every conversion or new co-op business, word of mouth spreads. She is waiting for the shift change, when all these separate stories coalesce into a genuine movement. Every time she opens the nonprofit's inbox, a part of her is hoping for a flood of enthusiastic emails on the other end, community members interested in helping fund or start co-ops. It would be a terror to answer them all, but finally the good kind after so much of the not-so-good.

She opens the inbox with this hope in the pit of her stomach. There are twelve emails to answer—all busywork.

She huffs and gets started.

After she's gone through eight of them, she checks the time. She could call it a day, get dinner started. Her days are like this now, setting her own agenda. A benefit of running a nonprofit that includes only yourself. A benefit and a curse.

5:30 p.m. Make dinner.

She decides to make spaghetti and meat sauce because it's easy.

Matthew is home by seven. Over dinner they talk about their day.

"I saw Bishop in the hall today," Matthew says.

"Oh?"

"She didn't reply when I told her good afternoon. I think she's going to oppose the bill."

"But you knew she would."

"I knew she *might* oppose it. But I think we're in for one of her speeches."

"Well, you know Bishop."

"But to openly ignore me? What if she's plotting something?"

A thought crosses Sondra's mind that she shakes away. "I'm sure she has some plan in that big, empty head of hers. But you're smarter than she is. You can handle whatever she decides to throw at you."

"Maybe," Matthew says. "Or maybe she has backing from some of the other senators, and I'm walking into an ambush."

"Keep a cool head," Sondra says. "You do what you can and leave the rest for future battles."

Sondra notices his stifled rebuttal. "Okay," he says, and with it comes a sigh. "Really miss the days when you were there to keep everyone in order."

"Your job now."

"Well, I'm terrible at it."

Sondra touches him on the cheek and gives him a smile.

"You have that hopeful idealism on your side. The people love you more than they ever loved me."

"That's because they don't know what's good for them."

She recognizes when he is sucking up to her. There is no way Matthew would ever doubt the wisdom of "the people."

"How did it go with your mom?" he asks.

"She's ready to see her brother."

"And you'll let her?"

Sondra nods. Her stomach wobbles as she confirms that yes, she will actually let them see each other. And, worse, that it was never her right to stand in the way in the first place.

"I know you're worried about it," Matthew says, "but keep your head and leave future battles in the future."

Sondra laughs. "Shut up."

"Kiss me first."

She does.

The dream again. Matthew shudders awake, and this time when he looks at Sondra, her eyes are looking back at him in the dark.

"You were muttering to yourself." She adds, "And you kicked me."

"Sorry," he says. "What did I say?"

"Don't know. It wasn't really words. You were upset though."

"It was different this time."

Sondra breathes in. Then she sits up in bed, her back to the headboard. "Different how?"

"There was a creature outside. Gleaming eyes."

Sondra doesn't say anything, just waits.

He knows what the creature is, but he hesitates to say it. Sondra told him that she hasn't changed into a woo-woo since she was a teenager. Losing her parents killed that part of her. Matthew has never seen her in that form. In fact, for some time now, he has even forgotten that it is possible for her to change in that way. But he has imagined what it looks like, and he must admit that what appeared in his dream is how he thinks Sondra would look in that form. But what does it mean?

"Have you . . ." he starts, and moments pass before he has the courage to reattempt the question. "Have you thought about your other form since your mother has been back?"

Sondra seems surprised by the question. They don't really talk about this sort of stuff, not usually.

"I have," she says. "I decided to wait until my mother can do it again. I want to do it with her."

"Do you know when the last time was for her?"

"She won't talk about it."

Something in Sondra's tone tells Matthew to change the subject. He readjusts. "What does it look like?"

Sondra breathes in again, and the way her chest rises stirs Matthew. Not the best time to be having sexual fantasies.

Sondra says, "Well . . ." and then explains what her woo-woo form looks like: the pointed ears, sleek frame, spotted fur.

Not exactly what Matthew dreamed, but close enough to mean something.

"I think it was a woo-woo," Matthew says. "My version of one, anyway."

"You'd like to see it?" Her question has only a little apprehension to it.

"I would."

"My mom might be ready soon. Maybe by the time the storm comes. If it works out, I can show you."

A hurricane is on the path to make landfall, but he wasn't thinking about the storm and doesn't understand why Sondra would make that connection. "Your power is linked to storms?"

Sondra nods. "I didn't tell you that? I can change at any time, but it's easier during hurricane season, and much easier when there's a storm nearby."

"I see."

"So, my woo-woo is showing up in your bad dreams now? You know there's nothing to be afraid of, right?"

"It's not like that. I—"

"I know, I know. The subconscious likes to mix in our curiosity with our fears, our worries. It's what dreams do."

This sounds to Matthew like a deflection, a way to transmute the potential offense so that it doesn't harm either of them. He accepts the gesture with a nod.

"I would like to see you," he says. He almost says *it* but catches himself just in time, but could she have noticed the slightest hesitation in his words? In the dark, he can't tell.

Her next words: "It'll be okay. Everything. Don't worry."

Matthew's mind doesn't obey commands from himself. But with Sondra—her telling him not to worry—it works a touch more. He holds on to that small bit of reassurance.

They talk for several minutes more, and then Matthew can feel himself falling back to sleep. As his eyelids grow heavy, he thinks, *This woman*—how has she managed to make him feel so content, so quiet, in a life like his, in a time like this? She has saved him in more ways than she'll ever know.

"Thank you," he says. "I don't know where I'd be . . ."

"Without me," Sondra fills in. She knows he has fallen back to sleep, so she reciprocates quietly and to herself: *You came along when I needed you most.*

Sondra lies back down on her pillow, but her eyes stay open, anchored to a spot on the ceiling.

There's a lot to be grateful for, but she still has that sick feeling in the pit of her stomach. Ever since she was little and her parents vanished on her and Sonya, she's had this feeling that something terrible is right around the corner, always waiting. She would turn one bend and then another and the path would stretch out before her, but she always felt a future reckoning, her own body tethered to it by a string.

That afternoon in Boston, she thought it had come for her. But that wasn't it. Somewhere ahead, then.

Sondra shifts to her side to watch Matthew sleep, and as she does this, a familiar scent greets her nose. "Go away," she says to the darkness.

"What?" Matthew rasps, brought back to the threshold between sleep and the waking world.

"Nothing," Sondra says.

23

Sondra's uncle is on the porch when she arrives, sitting in the same spot he's always sitting in, drinking something from a large cup. No doubt, there's rum in it. She waves at him when he looks her way, likely catching her scent in the air.

"Hey, stranger," he says.

"Hey." As she steps onto the porch, she is thinking about all the different versions of herself throughout her lifetime that have done precisely the same thing, and in her mind all those selves are walking with her—her child self, with parents; her teenage self, parentless; and her now self, fatherless—superimposed. And her uncle too, every iteration of him, sitting in that same spot, drinking himself into oblivion on this hill. His life now, since he's retired, seems so small and ever shrinking. She feels a pull of sadness then. Eventually, like a candle burned down to its stub, there'll be nothing left.

"What's wrong?" He puts down his cup, watching her.

Sondra hates that he is so good at reading her face. "How's your leg?"

"You know. Worse every day."

Sondra is having a thought that is a fork in her own road. She has the power to open his world again, give back to him a little of what he has lost. If she can kill her pride. If Damsel would be willing and able to do it. Jesus, the thought of actually talking to Damsel . . .

"I need to tell you something," Sondra says, putting her distracting thoughts away for the moment. "You probably already know what it is."

Her uncle nods. When was the last time she tried to broach the subject? It had to be the weeks following the Boston Massacre, when all the dust had settled, and Sondra had time to talk to him. That conversation was all circles, both of them talking around the thing they actually wanted to say. She saw then that he didn't want to know, and she didn't want to tell him. She let it go that time, deciding she wouldn't bring them together until her mother was better. But later, when Sondra thought about the visit, the way he had avoided asking made her angry, and some part of her staying away and not sharing the truth was purely out of spite. A terrible, childish thing to do. She saw him a couple of times afterward, but with Matthew present. And they both let that be reason enough not to talk about the thing itself, no matter how badly they both wanted to.

Sondra takes a breath before saying, "She's in Bordeaux. Staying with friends who will keep her safe." That isn't exactly true—they aren't really her friends—but it isn't something she needs to get into with him.

Three years since she came home, and all this time he knew she was here and didn't ask for her once.

Sondra spent a lot of time wondering why he wouldn't, and two answers came to her: fear and shame. Sometimes these things can look like pride, but they aren't the same. She's wondering, Is it just her pride when it comes to forgiving Sonya? Or is there a bit of fear and shame mixed in as well—and shame at her own fear?

Her uncle still hasn't spoken. He sits there, looking down at the stained porch tiles, but really, he is looking into himself.

"I know someone there who can look at your leg," Sondra adds. "If you're up for that."

"I'll think about it."

"Which part?"

"All of it. I gon' call you tomorrow."

Sondra doesn't know what she expects. All this time, she is thinking only about what *she* would say, and how. She maybe expected a simple yes or no from him about seeing her mother, his sister, but this needing to think now seems just as likely a response from her uncle as a clear answer. Does it make her frustrated? Not quite, but she is feeling a little impatient and a lot disappointed. She wanted to see his face when he decided to see his sister—now she's certain that she never expected him to say no—but he hasn't given a single thing away.

"You had to know this was coming," Sondra says, trying to shatter the illusion they've been living in for three years, but more importantly, to force him into saying more than he's saying, stop him from hiding behind postponement.

"I don't know if I did. I assumed you couldn't get her back, or she was sick, or she was . . . dying."

Is he telling the truth? Sondra searches his face. "You couldn't've thought all that and not asked me about it. What was it, then? You were ashamed of giving up on her?"

"You a spiteful child."

"I'm not a child. And you never want to have difficult conversations."

"I was her older brother—"

"Are."

"—and I couldn't protect her. Couldn't even *find* her. We grew up together. I told our parents I'd take care of the family."

"Well, you tried. We all did. My dad did too. Sometimes you don't know what's going to happen. But you had a choice in whether you'd give up."

"Did you find him too?"

Sondra laughs, incredulous. "You mean to say, you were wondering that too and didn't open your mouth to ask?"

"Watch how you talk to me, girl."

"I will do no such thing. You left me alone with her to take care of. Coward."

This isn't going well. In every way, this conversation is a mirror of the one they had before, each of them digging their heels in on their own position, the gulf between their points of view unbridgeable. *Did* she want to understand him? *Did* she care what his reasons were?

"I'd like to see her," he says. "I'm sorry I've disappointed you. And *your mother*."

She looks at him, sees the genuine pain in the way his temple pulses above his clenched jaw. "She's not disappointed in you. She didn't want to see you either. Until she was well enough."

"Oh," he says. "Okay, then. When can I see her?"

"Soon. I'll talk to her again tomorrow. I'll let you know."
Sondra takes a pitying look at her uncle and turns to leave.

"We had a brother," he says, unprompted. "I had to kill him."
Sondra stops, turns back.

"He got himself caught up with an obeah practitioner, and things went bad. That kind of magic"—he shakes his head—"can mess you up in ways there is no coming back from. He went wild. And a storm was coming. Couldn't let him loose on an island of unsuspecting people."

Her uncle looks away to hide his face. "So I did my duty as I'd been told to do if it ever happened to any of us. A woo-woo gone mad is a dangerous thing. And then I found the practitioner and tried to take my vengeance. To my great shame, I couldn't."

Again, Sondra wonders, *Is this obeah woman and the Bone Witch really the same person?* But she doesn't press. She stays where she is, not saying a word.

"I hope you understand me a little more now. No excuse for how I been acting, but—"

"I understand," Sondra says.

"That's kind of you."

"She's healthy," Sondra adds. "Her woo-woo is quiet—been so since she came back, and through the last two storms."

"I'm glad to hear it."

"I'll be going. Let me know if you want my person to look at your leg."

Her uncle nods, but it is clear to Sondra that he wants to be alone. He is out of words. She is too.

Matthew is early to the Senate session. He takes his seat, watches the other early birds, but keeps his attention on his notes. People are talking, but their words travel to him as nothing more than murmurs.

This is it—the confrontation he's been waiting for. He has been talking about monster solidarity for a while, advocating for protections under Virgin Islands law. The public is divided, and so is the legislature. In the USVI, politicians are both callously distant and aggravatingly close. Chances are, he is related, at least distantly, to one of the other senators. The island is small, and so many of these politicians come from generations of prominence—well-known families with the sort of names that might help carry them over the line in an election.

It is a miracle Matthew got as far as he did, considering his humble background. His father moved here from Antigua a decade before Matthew was born. His mother was local, but she disappeared a long time ago, so he couldn't rely on any connection to her. His father didn't really know her background either, except that she was from a family with land in the countryside. She was excommunicated long ago, for reasons his father didn't know or pretended not to know. In either case, Matthew knew less.

Matthew is lucky to be here, and luckier still to have been able to maneuver his way into a second term and have allies within the legislature. But even among his friends, his support is divided, which means he is in for a hell of a fight.

The last senators file in at the top of the hour.

After all the preamble, Senator Francis is first to speak: "All I'm saying is, we need to know who these people are. It is no different from someone filling out their biographical information." He pulls out his ID from his wallet. "See, right here it says I'm a man, with brown eyes and black hair. My race is Black. It even has my height, though I'm hardly happy with that one."

Pockets of laughter erupt here and there throughout the chamber. Senator Francis is five seven—a couple of inches below the average. Hardly worth mentioning, except to use humor to undercut the dangerous implications of his argument. Hair color, even race, isn't as dangerous as having monsters reveal their backgrounds on their ID cards. Francis knows this; hence, the joke about his height and the ridiculous performance of pulling out his ID in the first place.

Matthew keeps his face blank as Francis continues. He knows Francis will not bring up the counterarguments to what he's suggesting. "Equal rights with equal visibility" has been the best argument Matthew has heard for his side. So far, espoused only by Senator Francis from Saint Thomas and Senator

Moses from Saint Croix. Everyone else is on the other side of the debate. No additional rights under the law. Don't even talk about it. Keep the monster side buried. Matthew has that in common with the opposition. He doesn't think monsters should be forced to come out openly. He does believe, however, that they should be able to receive protections with their identities kept hidden, which would be the most progressive argument in this circumstance. The bill his office has drafted asks for anonymity and protection, and harsh punishment for hate crimes against monsters, with the target's identity scrubbed from proceedings whether or not they have monster status.

The current split is the sum of all his fears, and a not-so-surprising undoing of all the work he's done behind the scenes with his colleagues. Francis was on Matthew's side until just a few days ago. Moses was completely on his side, as far as he knew, until this morning. Two other senators had switched seemingly overnight.

It isn't a complete surprise, because outside on the street are a few dozen anti-monster protesters—a small sampling of the greater number of constituents who do not want to see this bill come to pass.

Francis says, "I want our people to remain unharmed. This is a delicate dance here. If we have citizens who can cast spells on fellow citizens, I believe those vulnerable have the right to know who to avoid. If we have werewolves or whatnot among us, we should acknowledge the danger these individuals might bring to the innocent." He looks at Matthew and smiles sheepishly. "Not their fault, of course. But we know how unpredictable humans can be, the harm some of us have done within our communities. Monsters, well-intentioned or not, can't be treated as completely harmless." Senator Francis leans forward. "I yield the rest of my time to the bill's author."

Is this a kindness? No. His time is almost up anyway.

The chair says, "Senator Reed, the floor is yours."

Matthew stands, straightens his tie, clears his throat. "We have no evidence of anyone being harmed by a monster in the Virgin Islands. We have children's stories, but the law should not be based on superstition. We're grown-ups, and what we're facing is a grown-up problem. Leave the hysteria to the very young. We have a community to maintain here. Right now I can list several cases of harassment against citizens who were merely *suspected* of being monsters. Not proven, mind you. It is dangerous, irresponsible of us, to fuel further violence by not making a stand here. Many of us know well the cost of prejudice and subjugation. Our families are the descendants of slaves. Our whole history has been marred by the calamities of hate. We've lived in peace with our monster brethren from before we even knew they were there. I don't want us to become hateful, frightened people. I want us to be good to one another. Like it or not, the monsters in our community come from the same places we do, with the same histories. They are from the stories we carried over the sea with us. Now that we know they are real, we've had the good fortune of reuniting with a part of our heritage. We shouldn't treat our people the same way those stateside have been treating theirs. Love—that's who we are, and that's what we can give. We have the opportunity here to be the first community to pass pro-monster legislation. We'd be beating out even the most progressive nations in the world. That could be a legacy we can claim. The monsters aren't going away. They've existed in our families all this time, whether we acknowledged it or not. They're the ones most vulnerable in this transition. Let's do the right thing here, for the people we love.

"Let's show them we love them, the whole of who they are, and are willing to let them meet us on their own terms. We can handle it. I know we can. Thank you."

Matthew sits and registers the quiet that has taken over the room. It may not be enough, but he's gotten through, at least for the moment, to some people in the chamber. It likely won't turn the tide, but with luck, when he tries this again some of what he has said here will be remembered. He can hear Sondra's voice in his head telling him to be pragmatic. Everything can't be won all at once. Sometimes change needs to be gradual. Matthew takes in a deep breath. He has shown up, at least.

The chair gives the floor to Senator Bishop. It is true misfortune to be followed up by her.

Senator Bishop stands. "You all know the stories. A creature that can remove her skin and sucks blood. People who turn into savage dogs or wolves. Black magic practitioners, evil spirits. If even *some* of this is true of the monsters hiding in our midst, shouldn't we be prudent? How does it serve us to give these creatures the right to hurt human beings with impunity? We can't even ask them to reveal themselves? We must show our necks to prove what, exactly? That we love them no matter what evil they visit on us? If you all want to play the fool, leave me out of it. Me'n trying to get killed because you all want to treat monsters like cuddly kittens. We know better than to pet wild animals. And you want us to willingly lie down with creatures that are known to hunt human beings? What foolishness is this!"

Senator Bishop looks at Matthew, makes sure everyone can see her doing so. Again, he maintains a careful neutral expression. Inside he is reeling. Bishop often leans on her Saint Thomian English to emphasize her as a trueborn Virgin Islander for the people, but it's what she is saying that's so worrisome. All the points Matthew might make if he were on the other side. Appealing not only to her audience's worst fears but also (and especially) to their pride. No one wants to be a fool and risk themselves and their families because of it.

Bishop holds the silence for emphasis, her body relaxed as she searches the faces of the other senators. She lights on Matthew again. "Senator Reed has always had a gift for language. But it is pure hypocrisy for him to decry sane self-preservation as base superstition. And it is sheer folly to pretend that his idealism won't get us killed in the end. And, worse, he knows it. So does his wife, *former* senator Paige."

Matthew sits up in his chair. Where is she going with this?

"I always found it strange that Senator Paige stepped down the way she did. She was still very popular. She could have carried another election, I have no doubt. But she knew what we didn't. Senator Reed does too. It is the reason he is doing all this and assuring us of its virtue."

Senator Bishop turns her attention to the projector at the front of the chamber. No one has used it, but now Matthew's skin itches with anticipation, seconds before it turns on.

"You can play the video," Senator Bishop says.

Just then the black image on the projector blurs to life. On the lower right corner, he can see the date: November 5, 2023. There's a burst of sound from the speakers—screaming people and distant pops of gunfire—and on the screen people are running en masse through a park shaded with trees. The camera is shaky—likely someone's phone, but it's clear what is happening.

The surge of people slows to a few stragglers. People are on the ground barely moving, crushed by the stampede or hurt in worse ways. A woman pushes a body off herself and struggles to her feet. There's no need to pretend that this isn't who it clearly is. Sondra is distinctive, the profile of her face visible. Another woman is there, in a trench coat, one sleeve loose and flapping where her hand should be. Her other hand has a gun pointed at Sondra.

Suddenly, the woman with the gun is struggling with another assailant, this one invisible to the camera. The video ends with the invisible assailant breaking the shooter's neck.

Senator Bishop lets the murmurs in the chamber build without a word. She keeps her eyes on Matthew. "This the truth behind this bill. What was Senator Paige doing at a pro-monster rally on the mainland while acting as a sitting representative of the people of the Virgin Islands? And who is the creature that saved her life while so many died around her? I don't know the answers to these questions. But the VI people were kept in the dark so we couldn't ask no questions. We don't know enough about what is happening here to blindly sign this bill into law. And by the look on Senator Reed's face, neither does he."

25

"You should've told me."

He's circled back to this at least a half dozen times during their argument. Sondra is trying to be patient. "And if I had, you'd have the knowledge hanging over your head and be implicated right now. I was hoping your surprise would give you cover."

This isn't completely true. There is no way Sondra could have predicted that the news would come out this way, but she still kept the secret so she wouldn't have to lie when it all came out, which she knew it eventually would.

"They're not going to believe I didn't know, no matter how surprised I look. We're married. We share a bed. How would anyone believe you'd keep this from me? Even if you did."

Matthew glares at Sondra then, pausing from pacing around the apartment.

"Listen," she says, "at the time, I thought I was saving people. I had no idea I'd be in danger."

233 WE ARE THE CRISIS   233

"But you knew you'd be recorded."

"Once it happened, I thought I might be. It was a danger-ous situation that I wasn't prepared for. I stepped away from my work, a lifelong dream, because of this. So that everything I'm doing here isn't irrevocably damaged. An added side effect was shielding you. But this isn't all about you, and I won't apologize for making the best choice given the situation."

"The best choice would be to trust your husband."

"Your idealism clouds your judgment. In no reality would that have been the best choice. You'd ask more questions, and I wouldn't be able to answer all of them, and you wouldn't have been able to let it go."

"Don't play chess with me. I'm not a game piece you can move around because you think you know how I'll react."

His words pull Sondra back in time to the night after the protest and massacre. The expression in Sonya's eyes—that open hopelessness, wanting to say so much but knowing she couldn't. At the time, Sondra was so angry at being outside the inner circle and willingly put in danger, she couldn't take it all in. If the known world is topography to navigate, the metaphysical world must also be. She knew this already, but she didn't *know* it. She didn't feel it in her bones until right now.

She also remembers how much she hated all that self-justi-fication. People's lives were on the line, their futures. But isn't she playing that same game with her people? Isn't she playing that same game with Matthew now? But understanding Sonya doesn't make her right herself.

"I'm sorry," she says. "I promise I made the decision I thought was best. I can't pretend to know if it really was the best decision, but I didn't do it to hurt you."

"If this was just about this one thing, I wouldn't be upset. But you constantly make the decision to keep me at a distance. Since the beginning, I've had to figure out ways to get you to tell me things I should've known already."

"Known already," Sondra repeats. Should she be this angry about something so seemingly innocent? "What makes you think you're entitled to know these things about me? What we're talking about are life-and-death secrets. Since I was a child, I had to keep what I am from everyone. From friends. From boyfriends. From family who didn't have the gift. You have no idea the consequences of talking too much about what I am, how important it is to develop the practice of silence. How could you know?"

Matthew is looking at her, not speaking, and his expression tells her that she's stumbled onto the upper hand in the argument. She doesn't like how this makes her feel, as if she now has a weapon against him. So much of an argument is finding the right place to set your feet, with enough defenses that you can't be moved. But the cost is always there. Being right doesn't make you right.

"I don't think we'll resolve all of this tonight," Sondra says, exaggerating the tiredness she actually feels. "We should go to bed, work out what it all means in the morning."

Matthew maintains his silence.

"Are you okay with letting this rest for now?" Sondra says. "I really am sorry it all came out this way."

Matthew says, "Me too." He walks away, into the bathroom.

Sondra watches him go, but her mind is already worrying over something else. Not a lot of people know exactly where they live, but Saint Thomas is a small place. There will be blowback in public, but who might come knocking in private? Their security system will just have to do for the time being, give them the opportunity to feel out the best course of action once she knows how people will react.

She also anticipates other repercussions and has prepared herself. But she worries about Matthew. He isn't ready for this kind of fallout. Could she have prepared him better? So many questions.

Sondra hears the shower going and knows that he is going to need some space when he comes out. She decides to spend some time in the living room reading so he can go to bed first.

That's when she catches the scent of familiar magic. Oh God, not now.

Sondra goes to the door and steps out onto the porch. "You better be here about the video," she says.

Sonya says, "I *did* want to check in with you. Make sure you're okay."

"What for? You gon' make this go away?"

"I can't. Not this time."

"This the Order's doing?"

"The Order of Asha isn't involved here. This is the Cult. This legislation your husband is pushing don't sit right with their plans."

"Which are?"

"A monster-human war. At least in the meantime. While they work to make the Zsouvox whole."

"That's a lot you just said at once that makes absolutely no sense to me."

"It's as far as I can go."

"Sure, your contracts with the universe. Whatever that means. But that's not the whole reason you're here, right?"

"No."

"I don't want to hear it."

"You'll want to hear it."

Sondra glares into the spot her sister's voice is coming from. "Listen to me. I'm not going to let you manipulate me with information ever again. If you have something to say, I can't stop you. But I'm not playing any guessing games or waiting in suspense. You don't get anything from me anymore."

Another silence, this one shorter. "I think we found him."

God*damn* this woman. Sondra doesn't need to ask the question, but she asks anyway. Playing the game she doesn't want to play. "Found who?"

"You know who."

"Then why are you standing here telling me about it? Bring him home. There'll be no equivalent exchange. As I said, you get nothing from me. Bring him home to Mom so she can celebrate or grieve."

"It may not be a celebration. But it won't be grief."

"Jesus, can you say anything straight?"

"Is every exchange we ever have from now on going to be this hostile?"

"I don't know. Are you planning to tell me the truth about everything?" Sondra can hear the hypocrisy in her question, in her anger, but that knowledge is far away, drowned out in the other noise of the moment. She hasn't even fully processed the fact that her father is alive. How can she process it without considering what might be wrong with him, and the road he'll have to take, like her mother, back to wholeness? It is all too much. The anger is easier.

"Bring him home," Sondra says.

This silence is the shortest. "I will. I promise."

THE BLACK EGG:
PART TWO

26

When I come out of the shower, Gina is on the bedroom floor, pages spread out before her. I look back out into the hall, see no one, and enter the bedroom, closing the door gently behind me.

"What's this?" I ask. It's an inexact question (because I know what it is; I just don't know why Gina has spread out all my files on the floor).

Gina looks up, the ghost of puzzlement on her face. "So, I was reading stuff from the monsterverse again." That's how Gina describes the universe in which monsters are real—the monsterverse—and so it has become a special moniker for both of us. Not particularly imaginative, but a useful shorthand. "And I notice this passage. I reread it twice, not knowing why it was bugging me. Wait, let me finish. I didn't know why *before.* I just figured it out."

I'm listening to the house. I remember the sight of Mom standing in the dark hallway our first night here—the feeling

I got is still fresh in my mind, as if we'd been caught in the middle of committing a crime.

". . . only it's in her head. She doesn't say it."

"What?"

Gina sucks her teeth. "You not listening. Come here. Let me show you."

I lean down beside her. She points to two pages from two separate files. I follow her index finger from one page to the next, seeing the evidence for myself.

"You said you remember everything. How come you didn't remember this?"

I'm blinking at the pages. "I don't remember everything— just more than I remember when I'm awake."

"You'd think you'd remember the same words repeated almost verbatim in two different universes."

I shake my head. I don't have an answer for her.

"What do you think it means?" Gina asks.

"Nothing, probably," I say. A chill catches me, and what would have been a shrug turns to an involuntary spasm. "Things repeat themselves in other universes all the time."

"Sure, but not something like this. It's too . . . odd."

"It isn't really that strange."

"You lying," Gina says. "To me or yourself. Which is it?"

I shake my head again.

There is a knock at the door.

I look to Gina, put my finger to my lips. It comes again before I reach the door. I'm still unprepared when I open it and see my mom's face staring back at me.

"Let me talk to you."

"Okay."

Out in the hall, Mom's voice is low. "What you doing with that girl?"

"I don't know what—"

"Cut the shit, Calvin. I ask you what you doing with that girl."

"Nothing. It's a school project."

Mom glares at me. "What's this talk about other universes? And you're bringing in strays from outside?"

I consider for a moment what would happen if I tried to explain it to her, but I know she won't believe me, and this conversation we're having will get even worse. "It's just stories, Mom. A book I'm working on."

"This is the first I'm hearing about a book."

"I just started working on it."

"You're lying. That girl isn't talking about it like it's a book. She talking about it like it's real."

The hallway is dark, but I can still see her face clearly. There is anger, but also the same confusion I glimpsed when she was standing outside the door. She doesn't know what to make of everything, so she's made up a story in her own mind—one I'm sure I won't like. I wasn't sure how much she'd heard—apparently, the whole conversation.

"Mom," I say, "I don't know what you think you heard, but there's nothing going on here. We—"

"When you went out yesterday, I searched the room."

"What?"

She doesn't say more, but the silence tells me everything. She found my files. She's read some of them. I should have stopped Gina from bringing them with us.

"Mom, listen."

"You are putting nonsense in that little girl's head."

"I'm not—"

"You don't realize how much of an influence you are, Calvin. Cory used to look up to you just like Gina in there—hang on your every word."

It is finally happening, I think. I brace myself.

"You spent all that time in that apartment with him. He wouldn't listen to me. I talked and talked."

"He didn't listen to me either."

"But he *did* listen to you."

Never in my entire life did I simultaneously want so badly to reach into someone else's mind and run away at the same time. I'm grateful I don't have that power in my own universe. I don't think I'd be able to resist.

"There was nothing wrong with him. He was a good child."

"Gina is a good child too," I say. "She didn't deserve us abandoning her like that."

"You shut your mouth."

"Why? Because you don't like accepting blame?"

The slap comes quick, but the sound lingers, echoes off the walls. And then silence.

We stare at each other, astonished. Mom storms off, past me to her room, slamming the door. Thoughts are swirling and swirling, but it happened so fast—Mom not even there anymore—I'm already doubting that it happened at all. How much of that brief moment will be acknowledged tomorrow at breakfast? If I pretend it hasn't happened, will she also pretend?

I go back into the room.

Gina is still in the same spot. She watches me come in, close the door behind me again. She's heard everything; it's clear on her face.

"There's no armor big enough to save any of us," she says.

27

Cameron, on the eve of her death: "The goddess arrives through a break in reality. No, that's not right. It's as if the wall next to the sick child turned to liquid, ripples flowing out from the center, and then the goddess breached the surface of that ripple in reality, stepping out into the basement where we are."

Cameron doesn't register how everyone else reacts. The shock of the moment, her complete awe, eclipses any other thought or concern. For a moment, she even forgets about the child.

But when the goddess goes for the child, Cameron is jolted back to the reality of the situation.

Cameron: "It reaches down and touches the child. The child shivers but looks . . . *better.* I wish I could explain this."

"It makes sense," I say, recognizing the power of the being she is describing.

Jack is saying something, and Ace has stumbled back into

the doorway, terrified. Maybe he's worried his punishment has arrived, but the goddess isn't interested in anyone except the child.

The goddess reaches, from wherever she was, into the space between realities and pulls from that other place something very strange.

Cameron: "A black egg. No, not an egg, exactly, but something shaped like one, the color of void."

The goddess places the egg inside the child—right through the child's chest, using that same odd magic where the rules of solid matter do not apply. And the child changes, the blackness spreading outward, claiming everything. The transformation takes only moments: a sickly child oozing blood from its eyes, to a completely black shadow in the same shape as the child. Something else has changed too. It is obvious the power in the room has shifted. This new childlike being stands, and now the chains around the child's wrists are nothing more than a confusing impediment. Link by link, the metal chain shatters like glass.

The child has eyes only for the goddess, is not interested in anyone else in the room.

"You must stay here a while," the goddess says, "until the day the seer comes for you." And then the goddess is looking at Cameron. Cameron doesn't know how she knows this, but I understand because it has happened to me before. "Watch over them," the goddess says, and somehow Cameron understands that this child, this new being in the world, is a plurality of beings. More than one thing in the body of one thing, universes beyond her comprehension.

And then the goddess is gone.

Ace speaks first. "I'll help care for the creature."

Cameron looks his way, and if Ace was afraid, a wild curiosity has overcome some of that fear. How has she not noticed the insanity in his eyes before? She says, "You will not touch them. You will never see either of us again."

Ace is stunned, but he doesn't speak. And Jack, the man she has until this very moment decided to love, is both stunned and afraid. He will not allow this thing to live with them. He is unlike Ace, unlike Cameron—neither cruelty nor love will make him accept what now stands before him.

Cameron accepts this with the decision she has already made.

Cameron: "Why did I do it? Because I knew someone was suffering in that basement. I knew but didn't want to know, so I convinced myself I didn't. Nothing can right that. But I could do this one right thing. And I realized that these were not the people I wanted to spend the rest of my life knowing."

Cameron returns her attention to the child. They are standing there, waiting.

"Come with me," she says, and they ascend together from that terrible place.

Tanya calls out when I knock on her apartment door. "Come in."

Her living room is just as I remember. I glance at the couch where we made love, let my eyes wander past it.

"Sit wherever you like," Tanya yells from the kitchen.

I sit on the love seat, not the couch.

When Tanya comes in with two glasses, she stands there for a moment. The two glasses are filled near to the brim.

"Is that . . ."

"Guess."

"Passion and cran?"

"Thought I'd give you a taste of home."

Tanya sits on the couch, places the drinks on two coasters, and slides one to me.

"So," she says, "what's going on?"

I tell her about the fight with my mom, the part about Cory, and a little about my fear that I may also be a bad influence on my niece. The last part is hard to explain without going into the reasons I might think so. But Tanya understands enough of it without my needing to get into other elements that are harder to understand.

"In a way, I was glad to hear that you and your niece were getting close. It shows you want connection. It was almost enough to know that, even if it wasn't with me." She doesn't wait for me to respond. "Don't run away from her. Don't let how you've been in the past give you an excuse not to change. If you feel like you're being a bad influence, do something about it."

"You're right."

Tanya laughs. "Well, that was easy. I think your niece might be the one having an influence."

"I'd bet my life on it."

"I'm genuinely happy to hear that. When are you heading back home?"

"Day after tomorrow. Gina has one more university tour with her aunts."

"That's soon."

"I messed things up with you," I say.

Even with all her directness, she's surprised at mine. "We messed things up with each other. It's in the past now."

"You seeing someone?"

"Sure," she says.

"You think something could still happen between us?"

"Wow, you really are being more direct than usual."

I wait, not saying anything.

"Cal, you're very important to me. But you're not a serious person. Not in that way."

The sting of her words surprises me. I already knew Tanya

felt this way about me, and with good reason, but it still hits me square in the chest. Maybe I'm still raw from the argument with Mom. I look down at my hands.

"I'm not saying this to hurt you," Tanya adds, a note of remorse in her voice. "But I care about you, and I think it is important that I'm honest."

"I understand," I say. I look at the drink on the table in front of me. The ice has melted, fat dewdrops clinging to the glass. I keep my eyes on the glass, and suddenly, the words are coming out of me. "After Cory died . . . well, that's not true; it started happening before he died, and got worse after. Sometimes when I looked at him—this was when he was alive—I'd see an afterimage of him doing something else. I didn't know what it meant." I look at Tanya, and she is watching me, her expression a careful blankness. I go on. "But after he died, I started having these vivid dreams. I'd go to sleep and fall into a sea of colors, and I could pull myself down into places, the places inside the colors. I am doing a bad job of explaining . . . but in the dreams, I came to realize that these other places were other versions of this universe. Sometimes I'd see Cory in these other places, but I also saw a lot of other things. I started to write them down."

The words keep spilling out of me. I tell her about Gina reading the files, about my mom finding them. I don't tell her about the cat or Abyssia or the monsterverse. I have a sense that it may be a step too far, and I fear what might happen if I cross that line.

I say, "I've wanted to tell you the truth for a long time. I just didn't know how. And I don't expect you to believe me. I know you don't think much of me. And this isn't a justification either, to excuse how I've behaved. But it's the truth."

By this point, Tanya can no longer keep her face blank. Her concern for me is evident. But when she speaks, her words are carefully considered: "This is where you go off to in your head. These . . . other worlds?"

I nod. "Sometimes it feels like I've been sleeping for years, and when I wake up, my own life feels . . . unfamiliar, hazy, like . . . like . . ." I look at her, desperate. "A mirage. My head is full of these other places all the time, and they feel more real than my actual life."

"Oh," Tanya says. She puts a hand to one cheek and breaks eye contact with me. "Cal, I want to hear you."

"But I sound crazy."

"No," she says. "No. That's the problem. The way you're looking at me, I can tell you mean what you're saying. And you don't have that sleepwalking look you usually have. But, Cal . . . What you're saying can't be true. Have you seen someone about this?"

"What do you mean?"

"I don't know what I mean. A neurologist?"

I stand up. "I should go."

"Cal."

When I get to the door, I'm unsure what to do next. What I really want is to go back and sit down, try to convince her that this isn't just in my head. But at the same time, I know that's a mistake. What I've done is enough. "I care about you too," I say. "When I wake up most days, I think about you. I think what it might be like to have someone in my life who knows me."

Tanya's face is full of regret. I just don't know what she's regretting. Again, I wish for the power to read minds in this world. She stands up and then doesn't know what to do with herself.

The seconds stretch on. Finally, she says, "It means everything to me that you're telling me all this. I'm just worried about you."

I know. From her vantage, worry makes sense. But my own feeling is devastation. I want to reach for the fractal sea, but I'm awake. Still, I go to the place the power is, and I pull. Nothing happens. Having no other way out, I use the door instead.

29

It takes fifteen years for the seer to come for the child.

Cameron is no longer young, though still beautiful. In that time, Cameron's ward has not changed at all. The child does not eat, does not sleep. Instead, the child goes into a deep stillness, sometimes for months at a time, where they don't move or respond to outside stimuli. Cameron soon understands that watching over the child doesn't require her constant attention. She spends more and more time away from the apartment until, finally, she goes traveling for an entire year. When she returns, the child is in the same place she left it. It is difficult for her to sleep that night, and it takes several nights before she can close her eyes without her mind conjuring up the child strangling her in her sleep. But when she's there, and the child is awake, they spend hours together in comfortable silence.

Cameron herself has lived an eventful life. She has traveled across Europe and all three Americas. She has written poetry with the greatest poets of her time—at least, they consider themselves to be. She has become a painter of strange portraits. She has become an actor, a singer, and a lover of many people, some of whose faces she can barely remember and whose names she has forgotten. Jack is long dead, Ace only a memory, though she hears of him from time to time. He has not given up on his goals for greater power.

And then, late one night, Cameron finds the woman in the child's room. Another child is with her. It looks human enough but has bright, clear eyes under a mane of curls. Cameron feels seen by both the child and this woman—not just her physical body, but all the way down to her essence.

"Inness," the woman says, introducing herself. Her voice is flat, but her eyes are considering Cameron, weighing her.

"You've come for the child," Cameron says. There is no use postponing the inevitable.

The woman, Inness, says yes. The other child watches without a word.

Cameron's child hasn't spoken either. She has given the child a name, but she knows this is as useful as giving a name to a drop in the ocean. Over the years, they have become close, she and the beings in the child's body. Mostly in silence, but sometimes the child does speak to her, though its voice isn't always the same. The ones speaking to her aren't the child. The child is only silence, though the quality of that silence has changed over the years too. Where it was once a wound, the quiet has become something akin to peace. She is grateful the child is at peace, though she can't say she had anything to do with it.

"Well," Cameron says, "it was nice having you around for a while."

The voice that answers this time sounds incalculably old. "Thank you for taking care of us," the voice says out of the child's mouth.

Cameron suddenly feels dizzy. The realization that a god has just spoken to her from a place beyond the universe. She leans against the wall until the world rights itself.

"We'll be going now," Inness says in that same monotone. She nods to the child with the mane of curls and says, "You can do it now, Melku."

The child, who Cameron now knows is named Melku (and whom I've known for years now in a different time), utters a command that the room should open and release them. From the dark corners, ants come forth, meeting in an open space on the wall, next to the nameless child's bed. When they link in that perfect glowing circle I've now seen so many times, I am not surprised to see the hole open up within that circle, though the wall flickers in and out for a moment before fully committing to being a portal, and that does surprise me a little—a sign that Melku has not yet perfected the trick.

Inness takes the nameless child's hand. And Melku comes and stands beside her. They go through together, and the child— Cameron knows it is the child doing this—takes one more look back at her on the other side before the wall returns and the ants disperse.

I stay with Cameron, though I've told myself that I'll someday come back to this moment and go through that hole with them, see what's on the other side.

Cameron doesn't know I'm here, and I don't reveal myself. I just linger to see how she will handle this moment.

Her face is quiet, though her mind is a storm. She fixes the bed, straightens out the sheets, and leaves the room, closing the door behind her. Finally, she cries.

This rest stop in her life is over. *What now?* I consider with her.

I push ahead, the blur of time, of Cameron, moving forward to the moment of her death. Place and time and Cameron collapse into one another. And I, a harbinger, a barnacle attached to her mind, this spirit version of myself invisible.

And then we've arrived, together, at the end: Cameron in her hospital bed, Death finally ready to claim her.

I pick up where I left off. A final question before I unlatch myself from her life and return to the fractal sea.

"Would you do any of it differently?" I ask.

"Not a thing," she says.

I don't want to watch her die, so I push her back out into the stream of time without me. Her face, once animated, goes still as a painting, like everything else in the room.

I wait a moment in this pocket of frozen time and space, considering where I'll go next. Maybe forward in time to where the Zsouvox is now. Or check up on the wolves, or New Era, or Sondra and Matthew. Or step across to another timeline entirely, take a break in a quiet universe where monsters and magic are only stories. Or back to my mundane existence.

I reach for the fractal sea, but then I feel the incoming cold that I now recognize as the first sign of her coming. And suddenly, she is there watching me, two nebulae set where a pair of eyes should be, swirling slowly. It is the only thing I can look at to form a connection within the starlight and distant galaxies that make up Abyssia's body.

"So, you created the Zsouvox," I say.

She speaks, as always, inside my head. "In a way. To save

the child's life. It was the only thing I could do to make it a little right."

"Was what happened to the child your fault?"

"In a way." Her nebulae flash bright. "That's all I can say."

After several seconds, I ask, "How is it even possible to change a person by telling them a story?"

"It isn't, usually. Not in most other places in the vast everything." A pause, perhaps of contemplation. "The vast everything on *this* plane of existence."

"Pretend I'm a child," I say. "Tell me exactly what you mean."

"What you call magic, the gods call Creation. This multiverse has a special kind that allows for what you call choice, or nondeterminism."

Every word she says is slow, deliberately so, as if she were walking through a field where each word might explode.

"The universe has allowed a bit more of that creation to pool into this particular slice of reality. And so—"

"Humans may create monsters."

Her nebulae brighten again. "That's all I can say."

"Why did you come here?"

"To answer the questions I could."

"Why?"

The starlight inside the negative space of her body flashes for a moment. She doesn't speak.

"I'm sick of all of you. Tell me what you mean."

She still doesn't speak. Instead, she reaches out and touches me. I feel the cold before I feel myself slip down into some other place, a void black and endless. Out at the edges of my vision, I can see the shimmering of a trillion suns.

You'll forget, she is saying, thinking, through me. *You'll forget every single time. The answer isn't yours yet. By your concession, not mine.*

She spits me out again. As she does it, the world around both of us trembles, and something bright reaches out from a space in the air around us. I cannot adequately describe what I'm seeing. The brightness is like a hand, but not in any physical sense. My mind feels it as a hand, reaching up out of a space beneath my mind—beneath all minds my telepathy can reach—coalescing as the purest idea of a hand from every corner of reality.

And this brightness, this instance of true Creation, reaches into the room and grabs Abyssia by the neck and wrenches her out of the world.

WE ARE THE CRISIS

30

When Alex was in the field, she would go on long missions that occasionally went badly. There wasn't a clear moment when you knew you were burned. Dramatic confrontations were unusual—the stuff of fiction, really. Instead, if the marks were good at their job, they held their suspicion and waited. Once they knew for sure, they would set a trap. But suspicion has its tells: a sitting-up in the person's body, in the voice, the face. If the person was antagonistic before, they'd suddenly become nice. If they liked you, they leaned in closer, trying to see *your* tells, trying to find where the lie ended and the true you began. In the worst-case scenario, they took a mental inventory, kept you in play until they didn't need you anymore, and continued using you as a resource, with no change in their behavior at all. In short, they went undercover with you. Alex herself had successfully kept up the ruse of ignorance several times. Preemptively, she decided to believe that she had already been made in every assignment, even if she had no reason to think it. In her mind, every job was a game of undercover chicken. Never break cover. Never blink. Trust your instincts. Trust your luck.

In her opinion, nine-tenths of intelligence work was just that: luck. Anything and everything could go wrong—and often did, unexpectedly. But if an agent lived through it all—if, at the end of their career, they had their head and, one hoped, all their limbs—they would inevitably trace the path to their present and find all sorts of implausible coincidences and moments of chaotic fortune that would make most people want to believe in a god or some cosmic force that favored them specifically.

Alex was once on a mission in a place she wasn't supposed to be, where a bomb blew up right in front of her. A land mine that was untouched, or possibly disturbed by wind or a wisp of debris or some hapless critter nosing around the wrong bush. The mine blew up far enough away that she wasn't injured at all—only startled, with a slight ringing in her ears. Crazy. And during an undercover assignment, she got held up for a whole day and night in an abandoned building, waiting out the men who were chasing her in a bombed-out area of a city where she also wasn't supposed to be. She knew they could find her if they wanted to. She had bled all the way into the building and hid on the top floor, stuffed behind a stack of unused lumber quietly turning to mold and dust. She waited a long time for her death, but it never came. Eventually, she crawled out of her hiding place and went back out onto the street. The air smelled of fresh sick and every form of human waste. She walked right down the road, out in the open, and no one intercepted her. The men's hideout was another bombed-out building, its open facade tarped over to shield them from the rain. Only the building wasn't just missing part of its face anymore; it was rubble, all of it. When Alex got there in the dead of night, it was still smoking. She had not heard the bomb, or it had mixed with all the other terrible noises of that city. The relief was palpable, but she also had the thought that she had somehow caused their deaths, had been the one to tip the first domino. And more than that, she had caused the cascade of events that ultimately led her to infiltrate the group in the first place. And she didn't mean that she was a part of a system either, that she had blood on her hands because America had blood on its hands. This was true too, but not what she felt in that moment. The thought that came to her, standing on the road in a country she was not supposed to be in, doing things that she was not supposed to be doing, was that she, by her very existence, had caused the deaths of all these people. The bombed-out buildings, the whole city stinking of waste, the living things slowly dying behind all those slabs of cracked and crumbling concrete—they were all the price of her existence. It was she and no one else, an emergent calamity with her at the center—the butterfly that caused the hurricane, the finger tipping over the domino, the instrument of some deeper, darker thing, reaching up into the world. She had no reason to think this. Alex considered that she might have a fever along with the gash on her arm. But she knew somehow that she was right, or right enough—as right as she could be about her *wrongness*.

She kept on walking down that road and eventually found an American man who never gave her a name. He led her to a driver, who took her to the embassy, where a kind army nurse treated her wounds and gave her pills (perhaps for the fever), and she was out of that city by morning, having been thoroughly burned in that little pocket of the world. She tried another cover but was burned again within months on the assignment. And then again, on the next one, her luck and instincts saving her each time. She was a good agent. But sometimes you just know that your talents can't do a thing.

"You got the blight," her superior had said. "We all get it eventually, even if we never get completely burned. The blight finds you." It was superstitious nonsense, of course, but then she remembered what she had thought standing outside that building, all the men who were supposed to be chasing her inexplicably dead. Then she considered the silver lining. She could finally leave active fieldwork, maybe get behind a desk somewhere. Again, *luck*. Bad luck that was good luck.

Did she consider Mister? Of course. But she couldn't find any evidence to support his involvement in any of her misfortune. So she settled on the universe, the math underlying this complex simulation punching an escape for her, to do . . . what exactly? When the Order of the Zsouvox approached her, she decided that working for them was the *what*, and it was up to her to determine the *why*.

Alex spent the next few years developing a backstory for her identity as a disillusioned intelligence officer. A few essays in a few respectable newspapers, online magazines. A feature in *Slate* critical of the Afghanistan war. She amassed a Twitter following. And then she left Twitter to pursue activist work.

She came to New Era after the Emergence, early on, when they were still building and desperate for people—not for monsters but for human allies who could protect the monsters. She was the subject of a few meetings. Could she be trusted? Tez went to bat for her. Alex had told Tez about her mother ("she was a vampire") and why she had left the CIA ("because I couldn't convince myself that I was doing anything good or important anymore"). He seemed to believe her. She entertained the possibility that he didn't. And so, as always, Alex initiated a game of undercover chicken that she was determined to win at all costs.

BOSTON, MASSACHUSETTS

NOVEMBER 10, 2026

When Tez comes down from the community center and leans into Alex's driver's-side window and she senses it for the first time—those sharp eyes of his sending her spider senses tingling—Alex looks right back and pretends nothing has changed, because nothing has. If she's right, and he's somehow discovered the truth about her—or *a* truth about her that blows her cover wide open—Alex is not going to let on that she knows she's been made.

"Where you headed?" she asks casually.

"Home."

"Where's that this time?"

He makes a face. "*Home*-home."

Tez has had long-term relationships only with other men. Men allowed a bit more room for mess, he explained to her once. This didn't match Alex's experience of men, but she accepted that Tez knew another side to them that she had never had the pleasure of knowing.

"Or you can come home with me," Alex offers. And why did she say that? Could he read this as an overcompensation, as her leaning in? No matter. Soon as she sees the shock on his face, she decides that sex with an emotionally unavailable man-cat is something she actually wants.

"You don't want that," Tez says.

"Because you're a mess?"

"Because we have a good thing going. An uncomplicated good thing."

"And let me guess—I know too much about how you really are to have sex with you. You didn't strike me as that kind of person."

"What kind of person?"

"Precious."

Tez's smile is mischievous. "Okay. Your funeral."

They have sex with the lights on. Staring into each other's eyes the whole time, trying to solve the puzzle of each other. After, they lie together, Tez resting his head on her chest.

Alex considers that he's hiding his face from her, but she doesn't linger on the thought very long. Doesn't matter anyway. Suspicion or not, she's ready to shed more of her skin. She'll stay with the movement as long as he allows her to remain useful, make preparations to slip away at the right time. She has confidence in her instincts. She has even more confidence in her luck.

"You've seemed mostly okay after what happened with that Black Hand." Tez's statement is unexpected. It also isn't a question.

"I've seen worse things." A lie.

"Like what?"

"Like war. And all the terrible things in it."

Tez looks up at her. "It's not the same, but I spent some time in the Black Panthers. Lost a lot of friends. It felt a lot like war." He is remembering something terrible; the evidence is in his eyes. Alex doesn't fill the silence. "Some of them only got involved in the movement because of me."

"That's a terrible burden to carry."

"Yes." Then he asks, "How old do you think I am?"

Alex gives her honest guess, bolstered by hundreds of small observations she's made. "Sixty."

"Pretty good guess."

She isn't going to play this game on his terms. "How old were you when you were turned?"

Tez turns away from her again. "I was born a monster," he confesses.

He says it so quickly Alex feels a chill of alarm go through her. This is an intimate confession there's no going back from. If he knows who she is and is telling her this anyway . . . She suppresses her own paranoia, steadies her heart. She'll let him finish.

"My mother," he continues, "was *born* as well. A skinwalker, from an indigenous tribe in a corner of the Amazon. My father was turned. Old African magic. Got himself lost in a wild place and came back five days later with a scar across his chest, and the ability to slip in and out of animal form. He lived longer than anyone he ever knew. He was exiled from his village, returning every so often as a wanderer. No one recognized him, even though he recognized himself in their stories.

"When the slavers came, he let himself get caught. By that time, he was noticing the small signs of age. He was curious, wanted to see more of the world. I don't know if he understood what he was getting into. He survived the voyage across, settled in a plantation in Virginia. Stayed there for twenty years, learning and understanding the new world, gaining the trust of his slave master. As he left, he killed the white man who called him 'son.' To spare his fellow slaves, he made it look like an animal attack. He admitted that he'd had some affection for his master; he wasn't a terrible person in his everyday dealings. But he was a part of a system, my father said, 'and some things can't be forgiven.' He went south and kept going until he found a wild place to get lost in again. He met my mother there. They fell in love. When they left the jungle, they had two daughters and a son."

"Where are your sisters?"

"One is no longer in this world. The other went north and didn't come back. I went looking once." Tez sighs. "I left my mother and father and went as far as Chicago. Lived there for a long time. Then Detroit. Then here. Got myself mixed up in some activist organizations along the way. Walked away from two police raids. I was the only one each time. By the time I saw my parents again, they were old, and the world was different. They're both dead now. Neither of their magics granted immortality. Eventually, I'll die of old age too. Or in the coming conflict. Either way, I'll die having lost enough."

Alex rubs his back. "The ambivalence of a true revolutionary."

"No, I've just run away too many times. I'm simply choosing where to stand."

His words are romantic. Hearing it, Alex just feels sad. "Good that you know what you want."

"And what do you want?"

"I don't know. I am waiting for it to meet me."

Alex is still wondering how much time has passed from Tez's birth to this night, his head to her chest, her arm around his back. She can't imagine a life as long as she's now guessing his has been—hundreds of years, perhaps—or even fathom what she'd do with all that time. She can feel the old knife injury on cold nights, and her knees have begun to protest more than occasionally. She has a small scar on her ribs, the origin of which she honestly can't remember. What a life she has lived, unable to remember how she got her own scars. It would be nice not to have scars, to be young one's entire life, even if it should last only fifty years.

Tez is lying so still on her chest that she startles when he speaks.

"You know what's happening, don't you?" He doesn't wait for her to answer. "I am sure you do. The first time I saw you, I thought, *She has the eye for it; she can remake reality, knows the levers to pull.* Two kinds of people have the knack for this work: A person who has been a lot of places they shouldn't. And the sort of person who has lived a long time. Those two kinds of people are in this bed."

"Are you initiating me into a sex cult or something? Was this the price of entry?"

He laughs.

Alex laughs too. "In my experience, 'two kinds of people' arguments usually leave a lot of kinds out."

He's quiet for a moment. "Very soon I'll be asking you to follow me into a very different kind of life. Do you trust me enough to follow?"

"I don't trust people," Alex says. "But I can walk next to people I respect."

"Walk next to me, Alexandra."

She smiles, and it feels like something close to knowing. If she isn't careful, she'll lose track of herself in this bed. She makes herself stir, and they both sit up. They stare into each other's eyes, searching.

"Let me take you home," Alex says.

"All right."

They don't talk on the ride to Tez's co-op apartment.

Alex keeps the radio on. Pop songs and radio commercials keep their minds company.

As they arrive at the apartment building, Tez turns the radio down. "My mother's shifted form can only be inherited. Her form was bigger than my father's. I look more like her. But my father's magic can be passed through a scratch or bite. It only has to be deep enough to draw blood. I offered to turn someone once. In the end, he said no. I mourned his death long before I lost him. I didn't have to wait very long.

"That offer was out of passion. I'm applying cold reason here. And trust. You're strong. In ten years, you'll still be strong. In twenty, you'll be deadly. People will underestimate you, and they'll realize only too late what you are. In thirty years, you'll have to lean into the threat of violence more to compensate for your age. You'll have to carry yourself with it, and you'll be grateful when people don't push their luck. But in forty years, maybe sooner? You won't even have the threat. People won't understand your story just by looking at you. People won't see what you've carried. And you won't be able to show them."

"Getting old isn't a bad thing."

"It isn't for most people. You're not most people." Tez looks at her a while longer, reading her face. "Think about it."

Alex gives nothing away. "Good night." Once he is out of the car, she starts to drive home, her mind a nest of hornets.

She doesn't have time to reach a decision, because when Alex comes back to her apartment, Mister is there.

"We have twenty minutes," he says, as if this were a normal occurrence when, in fact, they haven't met like this in several months.

Alex shakes off the late-night chill. "Are you trying to blow my cover?" The question is a boundary, but she already knows that Mister won't see it.

He doesn't disappoint her. "I know when you're alone and when you're not."

Alex laughs to herself and sits at the kitchen table. He takes the seat across from her.

"Do I need to tell you to be careful?" he asks.

She grins at him. "You've never had to before. You don't have to now."

"That man is dangerous."

"*I'm* dangerous," Alex says.

Mister smiles warmly. "I know, daughter."

When Alex was a kid, Mister smiled a lot. He'd come over with his candy and his puzzles, smiling the entire time. The way his face moved was like a landscape painting, the edges blurred and dreamy. Alex used to think it was serene. She knows better now. He wears his smile like clothes. How she missed this in her youth, even after years of watching her real father, was a testament to Mister's skill at deception. Alex knows him well enough now, his calculating, unsmiling true self, to know that Mister's smiles are always attempts to manipulate her.

"If you know I'm dangerous, you don't need to worry," Alex says.

"I've studied Tezcat, the Wanderer. He is a different kind of dangerous."

"You're so direct tonight."

"Because you need to hear me."

Alex knows Mister is a vampire, knew it even before he told her. She recognizes the same predator in him as she did in her mother, and even though the Bone Witch buried her memories of her mother, she still recognized what he was. It was the only answer to all the things about him that didn't add up.

"My romantic life is private. But if you need reassurance, I'm really not Tez's type. We were just keeping each other company."

"Stay away from him."

"Why?"

"Your mission was to gather intel on New Era, figure out where their money is going. That's where your attention should be."

"Their money is going to community efforts."

"Not all of it."

Alex tries to read Mister, but, as always, his face settles into stillness. "What do you know? *How* do you know?"

"You're not the only one I've implanted." He puts up a hand to stop her from speaking. "We haven't figured out where the money is going, only that it is going somewhere. But there isn't enough time to find out. Two Black Hands have disappeared in recent weeks. Yes, I know about that. The city is simmering, daughter. Soon it will burn."

Alex didn't know about the second missing Black Hand. Tez has been busy. "You're being hyperbolic."

"I use my words precisely. Always."

"What does any of this have to do with Tez?"

Mister lets his exasperation show a little. "You already know the answer to that. Stay away from him."

"My mission was to stay *with* him. You were explicit. 'Befriend the leaders of New Era.'"

Mister doesn't respond.

Alex tries to wait him out. No use. She leans back in her seat and finally lets out a dramatic sigh. "Okay, fine."

"I mean it," he says. "You have a habit of pretending agree-ability."

"I said fine." Now he is being insistent? *What the hell is going on?*

"How are you doing otherwise? I know it has been a long assignment."

Alex laughs. "We're out of things to say, aren't we? Can't you call Smoke to pick you up early? Say some incantation. Flash a bat signal or something."

He furrows his brow deliberately. "You're angry with me."

"I'm just tired."

"You haven't been this petulant since you were a teenager."

"You've groomed me my entire life, covered up my parents' deaths, lied to me, trained me to be your little spook. I'm just tired of pretending this is a family. You're not my father. You're my handler. This"—she flicks her finger between them—"is a cover."

He looks away from her then, to a picture on the wall: a photo of Alex when she was in Afghanistan, standing with a group of soldiers, all of them in desert camo. It was part of her true story she used as cover. The life she'd left behind to be an activist against the state. He wasn't really looking at it, only pretending to look, to keep from looking at her.

Alex huffs. "Some part of you does care about me. And you've convinced yourself that some part of this is real because of it." She releases herself from the chain she's been holding herself with all her life. "I don't love you. And you don't really love me. I'm an obligation you took on because my parents died."

"Your mother isn't dead."

Alex reaches for a strong reply, but only one word slips out:

"Liar." Alex can hear how petulant she sounds, and feels shame for being so childish, and anger that he can make her feel shame.

"After she escaped, we found her. She'd killed three people. We had to cover up all the evidence, wiped the minds of witnesses. When one of us goes on a rampage, even a small one, we know the vampire is too dangerous to let free. I had to. And how could I tell you—"

"Stop."

"You were a young girl. You wanted a mother."

"I wanted parents who loved me. Like any child. I'm an adult now. What's your excuse for not telling me?"

"You'd want to see her. And she'd take advantage of it, use you to hurt me."

"Because you locked her up?"

"Because I changed her. It was part of the bargain to—"

"*Have* me."

He doesn't answer Alex's nonquestion. They understand each other. "You were special. I saw it in you. I have a sense for this. Picking the sort of people who could live among us unchanged. Do the work. And then, in the end, could control themselves with the power."

"Wait," Alex says. "What are you talking about?"

Mister moves only a little, but she sees the anticipation in him. This man, so old that he has learned to control his body entirely, is feeling an emotion strong enough to show.

No. "You can't."

"You might hate me," he says. "I can live with that. I've lived with worse. I've had to do so much to get here, close enough that I can change everything."

"Get out of my apartment."

"You're special."

"Get out!"

"You're more than a weapon, daughter."

"Shut up. Stay away from me."

The temperature in the room changes. "No, no, no." She stands up, looking around, readying herself. But Smoke is turning solid with his arms already around her, the edges of his skin dancing like stirred ash.

"You don't deserve this," Smoke whispers. "You an ungrateful child. I always known."

"You will not speak again," Mister says to Smoke.

She is frantic now, squirming in Smoke's grasp but unable to budge.

"You won't be a mistake," he says. "You're going to help me change everything."

"Get off! I do not consent!"

Mister frowns. "I expected you to handle this better."

Alex is kicking her legs out wildly. "You're a monster! You're a monster!"

He is quick. The memory of her mother, gliding across space. She knows it is an illusion, the magic bending her human perception to allow for impossible actions. Suddenly, he's close enough to whisper in her ear. "I was a monster before I ever was one. So are you."

She closes her eyes, leaves her body. She barely feels the teeth pierce her flesh.

31

NOVEMBER 12, 2026

"I want to thank you all for coming out," Ridley says. "What we're doing here is a trust exercise. We're hoping it can lead to solidarity. And healing."

A lot of people have shown up to the store's monster solidarity meeting, its first since Rebecca transformed in front of a different crowd of unsuspecting people. That last crowd didn't release video evidence of the change, but Ridley is sure they told others. He recognizes people from the cooperative movement in the crowd—various worker-owners and members of housing co-ops. There are also some store regulars. And then people none of them have seen before. Secretly, Ridley hopes that some of them might be monsters.

Family is also here. Not Ridley's—his relationship to his mother and father could best be described as estranged—but Manny is here, sitting in the back, and Laina's father is up front. Rebecca and Laina are both anxious but for different reasons.

Laina is also more than a little angry. She thought he had left the city. Had he come back? Was he here hovering around all this time?

"I'd like to ask all of you to put your phones away," Ridley says. "We'd like to share something with you."

Ridley looks to them both. Rebecca steps forward first, but then Laina puts out a hand. She begins to take off her clothes, her eyes on her father in the front row. She is happy when his face changes, from hope to discomfort to shame. She relishes the last part as she takes off the rest of her clothes, not the least bit self-conscious.

"This is what I am." She is looking at him as she says this, as she lets her whole body fall into the change. Wolf eyes replace her human ones, but not for a moment does she look away.

Her father looks away first, severely embarrassed. *Good.*

Even so, he doesn't move.

During all this, Ridley and Rebecca are watching Laina. They know her father had visited her, but now they know what he looks like. It is too late to unpack the moment privately.

Ridley pulls his attention back to the crowd, trying to read everyone's face. He can see fear, sure, but he is also seeing a leaning-in, an absolute presence. For them, he imagines, past and future have retreated, and there is just the moment, the change happening in front of them. He remembers what it was like to see the video for the first time. And then when he saw the change for the first time, Rebecca showing Laina and him what it would be like, who they would become if they chose to take that step. And at that time, he was also afraid. But then that cleared away, and he was struck by how beautiful it was, seeing it happen and then seeing the result.

Laina's wolf form is equally beautiful, gleaming gray-black fur and yellow shimmering eyes. Ridley can see that some people in the room are having a similar transcendent experience. He doesn't dare interrupt the moment with talking. He waits, lets their awe stretch on, and for the others struggling with fear, he gives them a moment to adjust to the thing before them.

He feels the room shift back to him, and then he speaks. "Solidarity is risk. We need your trust, and you need ours. I am hoping there are monsters in the room with us who may some-day feel comfortable sharing that part of themselves. But for now, we'll take the risk."

"And then what?" someone asks from the front. "We all risk, and then what do we do? I've been watching the news. I know what happens to monster supporters."

No one else speaks, but the room stirs. They all know about the couple who was murdered for just being suspected as allied with monsters. Ridley doesn't have a great answer for this. But he does have an answer to the bigger problem.

"There might come a time when monsters will need to go into hiding. True hiding. If that happens, we'll need allies who are willing to help us get what we need. It might be safer to build our own sanctuary communities. If that's the case, we'll need help there too."

"That doesn't answer the question," says another person from the crowd.

"It doesn't. Maybe we can build these sanctuaries together. But that is a lot to ask. I'm just saying, if we can trust each other in this moment, maybe we can come up with a plan that pro-tects all of us."

"I don't see how," says the same person as before.

Laina slowly moves toward this person. Seated in the front row next to her father, she fixes herself so that she's between them. The woman and her father both startle. Laina stops, puts her head down to the floor in a show of vulnerability.

Ridley knows this is something Laina would have done of her own volition, but they've discussed this, the need to be gentle with these new people.

"There's this idea of the intentional community. Co-op folks in the audience might know what I'm talking about. It is usually a single large property with a bunch of people living on it, often as a housing cooperative, but with a culture developed by those living there, a collectively decided way of life."

Ridley thought it all through after the altercation in the Boston Common, once he knew and everyone else knew that there really is no way to build a completely peaceful transition between the pre-monster and post-monster worlds. Ignoring the fact that monsters have always been here, he now knows they have secretly, quietly affected the human world, and that there is no way to convince anyone otherwise. Everyone knows this. Violence was present from the very beginning, and it will likely continue for a long time still. And whether by accident—like on that day with Sarah—or by intent, monsters, too, will be violent. Everyone, in their own minds, is fighting for their lives.

So, what to do about it? How do you fight against the inevitable, the conflict already happening? What's the point of drawing people to them if there is no way out of the coming war?

Ridley, Laina, and Rebecca discussed all this, and Ridley offered what he thought was the only solution: Solidarity first—that is, finding humans (only humans) who would ally themselves with monsters in large enough numbers as to be a shield, a defensive army. And then to find places to live together, work together, build together the world that they wanted. A world where monsters and humans might coexist.

It would be a long road from where they now were to that future. They would need resources and lots of people. In the interim, they would need something like the Black Panthers—a network of people willing to fight back for the cause, protect each other.

He had decided to do the demonstration at the chamber meeting to start. But he's at the moment now where he must say the soft part out loud.

"Here's the truth: This conflict *will* happen. Turns out, there's no way to avoid it. So we need to plan together smarter ways of defending ourselves. We'd like that to be a human and monster effort. We're not looking for fights, but we need to make sure we can do something when the fight comes to us."

And he sees what he was afraid he'd see. The room shifts so quickly.

"This sounds dangerous," says someone.

"It is already dangerous," says another.

Again, Ridley has no good reply. "This will only get worse, whether we organize or not."

"And what if our organizing gets a stronger response from the Black Hand?" asks a woman in the second row. "What if law enforcement responds?"

"Right now, the way things are emboldens terrorism. We need to put their perceived power in check by building our own power." Ridley looks around the room. "Look, I under-stand what we're asking here. We revealed what we are to share the risk. But you didn't know what we wanted to do until you came here. So, if you want to leave now, that's okay."

Ridley waits. A couple of seconds pass before two people in the front row stand to leave. Finally, Laina's father stands too. He doesn't look at her as he leaves, but she watches him go, and even in her wolf form Ridley and Rebecca can both see her satisfaction. They all hope this will be the end of it, and her father will never come back.

Another few gain the courage to stand, to walk away. Half the room empties. This is not good news, though it is expected. But then Manny gets up to leave.

"Wait," Rebecca calls out, but he ignores her. Grateful she is still in her human form, Rebecca runs to catch him on the street.

He's several feet away by the time she reaches the sidewalk outside the bookstore. She yells, "Now you know." When he turns, she lowers her voice, says, "I'm a monster. Mom is too." It takes her another moment to say the next part. "I turned her."

Manny laughs, which is the thing Rebecca least expects. "If I didn't show up tonight, were you ever going to tell me?" He doesn't dance around the question, just asks her, as though he's been saving it up. "Fucking hell, Bec. Did she ask you to do it? I'm assuming that all this monster solidarity shit isn't because you suddenly became a bleeding heart. You've put us in danger. Our entire family."

"Manny," Rebecca says.

"Save the '*Manny*.' Save the buying time to come up with a good lie. Just tell me all of it."

"All of it," Rebecca repeats. Under the streetlamp, she can see moths making circles in the light.

"Bec."

"I did it. She was sick."

"I knew she was sick; that's why I got suspicious. The doctors said it was 'miraculous.' Cancer doesn't just go away. And you didn't ask her if she wanted to be a monster, did you?"

"I didn't."

"Typical."

She reaches out to touch his shoulder, but he pulls away. "Manny."

"It is too late to fix this, Bec."

"I know. But I want to try. I need to do—" Something catches Rebecca's attention. She freezes. Across the street, coming down the sidewalk, are two men. In almost every way, they look normal, except for the black gloves.

And one of them is holding a bat.

Alex arrives a half hour after sunset at the community center, where she knows Tez will be. She ascends the stairs, passing what must be a member of the housing cooperative who lives above the community center. The building extends several floors, the center occupying only the first four. On the second and third floors are apartments that have been converted into offices for several of the many small co-op businesses in the building. She passes Vision Entertainment, a badly named media co-op that makes most of its money through advertisements and sponsorships on YouTube. The lights are still on and the door open, but inside is a solitary young woman, working on something at her desk, wedged against the only window in the large open space that would have been someone's living room in another time. One of those big five-gallon watercoolers stands not far from her desk, and Alex wonders how annoying it must be to have a workstation right next to where people congregate while avoiding their own work. Did this woman complain? Did she have a choice in her desk location? The woman spares a fleeting glance at Alex as she lingers in the doorway. Alex stays a while longer. From down the hall of the apartment-now-office, she can hear a woman's voice behind one of the closed doors. Her voice is lively, performative. "Some eagle-eyed viewers might have noticed the cross in the corner of Marshall's bedroom, dripping with blood. Or the glowing eyes peeking out from his closet in this shot."

Alex saw one of these rooms on a tour once, when she was only a few weeks into her job as a driver. Tez showed her each business, and she got to peek inside one of their makeshift studios—a green screen against one wall, a chair or two on the carpeting in front of that screen, and a busy array of lights and overhead microphones. She remembers that all the walls were covered in soundproofing foam. The tour guide said the foam was pretty effective at blocking sound. He demonstrated by having Tez stand inside and yell. Alex could hear him only faintly, standing just outside.

Now Alex can hear the woman inside that first room while standing in the doorway. The bright lights of the room sting her eyes. She has to blink away tears.

"You okay?" asks the woman, looking again at Alex.

Alex nods. She has the sudden and terrifying urge to walk up to this woman, touch her, bring her lips to her neck, and . . . *and*—

"Did you need something?"

"No, sorry." Alex's voice sounds strange, like a guitar string out of tune.

Deliberately, she steps away from the doorway. She passes a

few closed doors: a plumbing co-op, a private investigation firm, a website development collective. She can hear two people talking inside the last door. She can hear every word they are saying.

A thin man with a nose like a hawk's beak passes her, and she notes that she has seen him in the building before but has never been introduced. She stops to watch him walk to the stairs, thinking of Mister's other agents. The ones she didn't know about until two nights ago. The night she was turned.

The morning after, Alex woke up in her childhood bedroom at the Trapp mansion, the curtains drawn and shrouding the room in complete darkness. She could see the shadow of someone's feet outside her door. She knew it wasn't Mister. It wasn't Smoke either—a power like his kept him on the move. In the haze of those early moments, Alex tried to piece together the facts of her new situation and what she could do next. She knew, for one, that whoever was standing outside that door would not be able to stop her. But she would have to wait until sunset. But then that evening, Mister visited her room.

"How are you doing?"

Alex didn't answer. It was a calculation more than an attempt to freeze him out. If she gave him anything at all, he might change his approach, bind her so she couldn't escape.

"I trust you to do the right thing here," he said as if reading a part of her mind. "A vampire is vulnerable right after the change. The hunger is uncontrollable. I'll send someone up here to get you fed before sunrise, but you must stay here, where you can be monitored." He watched her closely as he said the final part: "You wouldn't want to risk killing some innocent person, would you?"

She kept silent but reassessed her situation. He didn't chain her up, but he did keep her in her room under supervision. He would feed her near sunrise, so her hunger wouldn't drive her outside, putting her in danger along with anyone she might encounter.

Did she feel the hunger he was describing? Nothing more than a dull ache. But she assumed that would change as soon as she was around a human. The thought made her angry that she was already thinking of other people as something different from her.

She made her plan. *Wait until an hour after he leaves. Incapacitate her guard. Slip out a window and start running. Pray she reaches shelter by sunrise.*

And it went just as she'd planned it: the guard easily incapacitated, Alex forcing open a window in one of the mansion's many unused rooms. From there, she ran through the night until she reached her car, then grabbed the spare key from under the right front tire and drove until she found a parking garage. It was sunrise by then, and she had to wait until sunset to complete her drive to the community center.

And now she is standing in front of Tez's office, unable to bring herself to turn the knob and walk in.

Inside, Tez and Kwame are talking.

"Yes, I know," Tez says. "They said they're almost ready. Don't look at me like that. I don't know why it can't happen now."

"Every day, more and more people are walking around with black gloves. There's no time for this secrecy bullshit. My family is in danger. You have to force them to tell you."

"You think I haven't tried that already? I'm doing everything I can; we just—Alex, I can smell you from here. Come in already."

Alex's steps are unsteady as she enters.

Tez's expression turns severe. "What happened? Where have you been?"

"It's not important. I need to tell you something."

"I already know."

"Not that. Well, more than that."

In the room, Kwame is sitting at the conference table, sheets of paper spread out in front of him. Watching her, Alex thinks, but he is overexposed in the light of the desk lamp beside him. Alex's eyes hurt looking into the light, so she looks away. The overhead lights are turned low, but she can feel the rays bouncing off the walls of her skull.

Tez is at his desk, sitting back in his office chair. "Well. Let's have it. This *more* you have to tell me."

Alex crosses the room to Tez but gets only halfway. She blinks away dizziness. "I think there's going to be an attack."

• • •

Sondra shouldn't have picked up the phone. "You want to go see her? Now? The hurricane is going to make landfall in hours."

"She should have someone with her."

Sondra looks at the time, looks out the window. The sky is gray with the coming storm. "All right, I'll come get you."

"Thank you."

"Ten minutes." Sondra grabs her keys and slips on her shoes.

The road is packed with other drivers trying to reach their own destinations, so although Sondra is speeding up the hill to her uncle's house, the ten minutes has stretched to twenty.

Her uncle is on the street to meet her.

"How long will it take to get over there?" he asks.

"We'll be fine," Sondra says. *Too long,* she thinks. Bordeaux is all the way on the west side of the island. It'll be at least a half hour given the last-minute traffic on the roads.

It takes longer—forty-five minutes to descend the narrow driveway to the Bordeaux compound.

"I didn't know this was here," her uncle says, "and I know where everything is on this island."

Sondra nods in agreement. Before she started visiting, Sondra didn't know it was there either.

There's a gate at the bottom of the stairs that opens when they approach.

"The witch is here," Sondra says. "The one I told you about who can heal you."

"Let's talk about it after I see my sister," her uncle says.

The door opens for them, no one there to greet them. But as they pass from the foyer to the expansive living room and then to the large kitchen, she sees Cassandra, the sight mage, sitting at the kitchen island.

"Good afternoon," her uncle says.

Cassandra tips her head to them, her eyes on Sondra. "Ask me a question," she says.

Not this bullshit again. Sondra ignores the seeress and leads her uncle away from the kitchen and down a too-long hallway with closed doors on each side. There's a stairwell that leads up and down to other places Sondra hasn't seen. Her mother's room is the last, by the stairs at the far end of the hall.

Sondra knocks, waits. She can feel her uncle's tension behind her.

"It's okay," she says to him softly. "She's been looking good lately. Talking like she used to."

Her uncle's tension eases a little.

The door opens, and her mother smiles up at Sondra. She steps minutely aside for her mother to see her uncle. Her mother's smile doesn't leave, but there's a stutter, a hitch in her expression, which falls away quickly.

"Bonnie," he says.

"Luke."

Her mother lets them in, and there's a long moment of all of them just standing there, looking at each other, waiting for something to happen. No one seems to know what it is they're expecting.

Her uncle breaks first, literally. Full sobs.

Sondra has never seen this before. She hasn't seen her uncle cry even a little.

"I'm sorry," he says. "I gave up on you."

Her mother steps closer. "It's all right. It's how we've been trained."

Sondra now understands what she means by this. How they've survived all this time through caution and, occasionally, killing the ones they love, to protect their secret.

Her mother comes to him. "You wouldn't have been able to find me."

"I tried."

"You could have searched for a hundred years."

She touches his arm, and he recoils. Then they fall into each other. The moment is so tender, so raw, that Sondra suddenly feels like an intruder.

As they hold each other, both in tears, Sondra steps out of the room.

Without thinking why, she heads back to the kitchen. But once she's there, she knows the reason.

"What is it?"

"Ask me a better question." Cassandra's eyes are fixed, unmoving.

"I don't know what to ask."

Cassandra doesn't speak, but can Sondra read some impatience there? The sight mage is . . . fidgeting. She never fidgets. Barely even moves unless she has to.

"Is something going to happen?"

"Yes."

"To me?"

"I have never answered that question."

"To . . ." Sondra doesn't have to finish the thought, the panic rising like bile in her throat. "If he comes out, tell my uncle I'll be back to get him later."

Cassandra nods slowly and doesn't say another word as Sondra runs out of the compound.

• • •

"Alex, tell me what's wrong with you."

"Are you listening to me?"

"Yes, you said you think there's going to be an attack. We'll deal with that after you tell me why you're swaying like that."

Alex is startled by light hitting the glass, the rumble of a bus passing on the road below. That's when she sees Dragon lying on the couch beneath the window, all his attention on her.

"Your organization has been infiltrated by another agent," she says. "I think they're Black Hand."

Tez acknowledges the information calmly. "Do you know who the other intruders might be?"

"No."

"So how do you know there's going to be an attack?"

"Because Black Hand is mobilizing."

"And how do you know that?"

Alex doesn't answer.

"Intel from the Cult of the Zsouvox?" Tez asks.

"You mean the *Order* of the Zsouvox?"

"Right." An expression crosses Tez's face. "Give me any information you have."

Alex hears footsteps down the hall, faint but getting closer. She remembers the people still working on this floor, so she disregards the sound but keeps an ear to what is going on outside.

She considers her words carefully. "It would be someone who joined recently. Or recent enough. Within the last year or so. Someone who keeps to theirself. Can you think of anyone like that?"

"At least five people. This sort of work, nonconformist, attracts all sorts. And folks come and go all the time. I'd need more than that."

Of course, she knows all this. It's what made the job easy. Radicals are distrustful of newcomers, but they are also hungry for newcomers. More activists for the cause. Radicals. She hasn't thought of them that way for a long time. Alex takes stock of that fact, how she has been subsumed by New Era's priorities, how she has become unaccustomed to questioning them. It is like her work in intelligence. She has fallen so deeply into their ideology that their imperatives have become her own. An organization has a way of subsuming everything into itself, contorting individualist views of the world. In intelligence, that process isn't particularly sneaky—patriotism is anything but subtle. Here it has happened subtly despite her shielding. She can't tell how much of it is her own feelings interceding—did she agree with these people?—and how much is about the comfort of being part of a group, especially one as earnest as this one, striving to find its place in the world. Tez is shrewd, calculating. But some of these people are naked in their faith in forging a better world, or at least a better corner of this one.

When she started working for the Order, it was with her eyes open, recognizing that she would be able to know the deeper machinations of this world only if she were willing to serve greater evils. And now she is betraying that larger goal for this lesser one. Was this organization—was Tez—even worth saving?

High beams flash again from outside the window, and she has to blink away the pain.

Dragon is leaning on the windowsill, observing everything with an expression Alex can't quite read—something like interest but with an edge of resolve. *That boy will be a problem someday,* Alex thinks. But it is even more unnerving that she can't tell who he'll be a problem for.

Again, there is another sound. This time, she knows what it is. The soft creak of a floorboard. Someone is slowly making their way to the end of the hall where they are.

Alex looks at the door, and when she looks back to Tez, he is looking too. That last footstep is closer. How did it get so close without her hearing it? She remembers something she learned during her training. Floorboards in the center of a room or hall are always weaker than the ones near the walls. If you need to make your way quietly through a building, the best strategy is to remove your shoes and hug the walls, moving slowly on the tips of your toes. At the time, she thought it was a great way to look suspicious if someone saw you, or get yourself killed. Most people's hearing isn't very good, and buildings make all sorts of noises. Simply being careful is just as effective and quicker. But here she is, listening with her enhanced hearing to subtle noises outside. And now she finally understands what that training exercise is for: hunting monsters.

Across from the bookstore, one of the men waves, the quirk of a grin illuminated by a streetlight overhead.

Rebecca grasps Manny by the arm. "We need to get back inside."

Manny tries to pull himself free. "I'm not going back in there. As far as I can tell, you're inviting more trouble. Why would you think—"

"Manny! Shut up and come with me!"

Alex signals silently to Tez, and he nods, bringing himself out of his chair.

Alex startles, realizing Dragon has moved from the windowsill. Sometime during the last few moments, he has gotten close to her.

Tez makes a motion with his hands. Keep talking, he is saying. Rushing to the door would be dangerous, so he quietly, cautiously inches toward the door.

"As far as I knew, I was the only person undercover with your organization. But they didn't share information with me, really. I found out a couple of nights ago that there were others."

"You're the daughter of a prominent Order member, or

else you wouldn't be standing here right now with the gift of immortality."

Tez is at the door now.

When Matthew hears the knock on the door, the storm is already wailing outside against the closed shutters. He's careful when he opens it, keeping a firm grip on the doorknob. The force on the other side pulls him forward. He thinks it is the wind at first until he sees the two masked men: one holding the door, the other standing with his back to the wind—a silhouette of a man pointing a gun at Matthew.

"Let's go inside," the man says.

Matthew does as they ask, and as he goes in ahead of them, he catches a glimpse of the sky, the greenish color, the clouds like teeth in some massive maw. God or some giant beast preparing to eat the world.

As he reaches for the knob, Tez lowers his voice, trying to throw off his position to whoever is outside. "What else can you tell me?"

He is very good at this—too good. She reminds herself, again, that this man has a history whose surface she has barely scratched.

He gestures for Alex to keep talking.

"I really don't know anything else. I did my job. I didn't ask questions."

"Why would you work for them?" This from Dragon, standing even closer to her now.

"I wanted to kill the spider at the center of the web. And I'd thought the best way to do it was to work for it." Alex is stunned silent by her own confession. Is it true? It feels so.

Tez urges her to continue, but she's lost the ability to speak.

"Who did you work for in the Order?" Kwame asks. The overhead light is still obscuring his face, but it is more than obvious that he's angry with her.

"My adopted father, Valter Trapp."

"What?" Dragon looks around frantically. "Does Smoke know I'm here?"

Alex is confused but shakes her head. "I don't know. How do you know about Smoke?"

"They kept me in the basement," Dragon says.

"Get away from the windows." Rebecca shuts the door to the bookstore, locking it behind her.

"What's going on?" Ridley asks.

"Several Black Hand are outside the bookshop," Rebecca says.

From where he's standing, Ridley can see some of them under the streetlights across the street.

"What are they doing?" Ridley asks.

"Let us out of here," says someone else.

"Hold on," Ridley says. It occurs to Ridley that the Black Hand are waiting for reinforcements to arrive so they can attack the store. He can see that a few of them have unlit Molotov cocktails in their hands, and the realization hits him like ice down his spine.

"They're going to burn the store down."

A chorus of terrified chatter.

Ridley tries to think through their options. Could they go out the fire exit? No, the Black Hand likely has the exits blocked. That's probably why they are waiting for backup. Could they call the police? But then, he knows they won't come. Some of the local officers are definitely Black Hand. They already know about this.

No good options. But if they don't do something, they will all be trapped in the store when it starts to burn.

Rebecca says aloud what Ridley is thinking in his head.

"We have to attack."

Alex blinks in surprise at Dragon. "I'm sorry. I really didn't know . . ." Dragon was likely there after she left. For as long as she could remember, she was trying to get out of that house. But she had been home many times over the years. How could she not have known? "Where did they keep you?"

"In the cells with the others," Dragon says.

"There were others?"

Dragon's tone is terse, unyielding. "You wanted to kill the spider at the center of the web. It was right beneath your feet."

Tez is looking at Alex, staring into her eyes. She tries to imagine how she must look to him, the shock on her face. In his expression isn't judgment, but something more complicated. She wishes she could have access to his mind. What is hiding behind those eyes?

The sound of footsteps, retreating quickly.

Tez turns away from her. His hand is on the knob, and so he turns it and flings the door open. Tez makes to lunge, but then stops short. His body tenses, shudders. And then Alex hears the click.

The door, the walls, the man, *ripple*, the room awash in dazzling light.

32

"Get behind us," Ridley tells the group, starting to strip off his clothes, the vulnerability at being naked in front of strangers countered by the adrenaline starting to course through him. "Once we're out and keeping the Black Hand busy, the rest of you can escape."

Laina is already in wolf form, so when Rebecca has stripped, Ridley opens the door. Just as he does, they both shift and, joining Laina, they burst out into the night.

The Black Hands respond in alarm. One of them shakes off his shock and tries to light his Molotov cocktail. Rebecca goes for him, taking him by the arm and dragging him away from the rest of the Black Hand. The others try to respond, but Ridley is on them too. And Laina, her wolf massive—a blur of fur and teeth and streaking eyes.

She heads first to the several Black Hand under the streetlight, aiming herself at the man holding the gun. By how he is carrying himself, she knows he is the one in charge.

They've all shifted their attention to her, some of them instinctively scattering. The leader yells orders, trying to distract them from their fear. He points his gun down at Laina, but suddenly Ridley is out from behind her and whipping around to pin the Hands in from the left side. Rebecca surges forth, jumping up and over Laina, for a moment looking as if she has taken flight.

The leader with the gun looks up but hesitates. When he finally fires his weapon, Ridley is there just in time, clenching his teeth around the man's arm. The bullet is diverted, hitting a streetlight nearby, that part of the street going dark. Laina changes course and goes for a Black Hand at the leader's side. The human side of herself stiffens, even as her wolf leans into instinct, tearing through the man like a hot knife through butter. The young man, barely into adulthood, is left bleeding from his side, holding his shredded flesh together with his torn clothes. Another Hand tries to shoot Laina, but she rams into his legs, flipping him onto his back. The sound as he hits pavement is percussive, like a mallet hitting a bass drum. He sucks in a breath of pain and surprise. She turns, bites down on his arm, and drags him away into the dark beyond the streetlights.

Rebecca pounces on a man—she is grateful these are all men—and goes for the head. She bites down hard and releases. She leaves him rolling on the ground, screaming in agony. All she needs to do—all *they* need to do—is incapacitate all these people.

But their luck cannot last.

They all see it happen—the moment a Hand leans out from behind a parked car and shoots Ridley in the side, Ridley whining from the shock of pain. Laina releases the man she's caught—alive but gravely damaged. She launches onto the roof of the car, the metal buckling under her weight, and lands on the gunman, biting down on his shoulder. There's a snap of bone breaking under the pressure. He is too debilitated to scream. Realizing what she has done, she releases him.

The rest of the Black Hand are now dispersed, impossible to attack all at once. Rebecca watches one of them throw a Molotov cocktail through the window of the store before running off. The flames catch fast, but luckily everyone inside has already escaped. Rebecca and Laina go to Ridley. Laina licks his wound, and he whines. She soothes him with the voice of her wolf—a low, ghostly keening. Ridley's eyes look to her and then to the bookstore, and she knows what he is feeling even if he can't speak. Rebecca understands too. This is Ridley's life's work, and soon there will be nothing left of it.

None of them see when the reinforcements first arrive, noticing only when one of them throws another firebomb through the broken window of the store. Many from this group have weapons: bats and sticks, machetes, and two with assault rifles. The wolves are together now, having lost the element of surprise. And with the store in flames and Ridley wounded, they have to make a stand where they are, no matter the result. Laina stands up, steps between Ridley and the men. Rebecca growls like a cornered predator, ready to kill anything that gets close. And suddenly, Manny is there, standing next to his sister. She looks up at him, trying to communicate her horror with her eyes. Rebecca thought—had hoped—the threat of violence would scare her brother away. But now she knows that was wishful thinking. Her brother isn't the sort of person who would be useful in a street brawl. But he isn't the sort who would run either, especially with family in danger. Nothing he could do up until this point. Nothing he can do now. Except die with them.

The sick feeling in Rebecca's gut, the utter hopelessness, the rekindled trauma of watching Sarah die, glues her to the spot. The Black Hand are too far away to reach. Is it worth an attempt? She would be leaving her brother unprotected. Rebecca tries to move in front of her brother, but he won't let her. He's looking down at her with a ferociously protective expression. Manny was always like this—unselfish when she couldn't be anything but the opposite. And now she must be responsible for his death.

More Black Hand come from every direction. They won't be able to fight through all these people. All three wolves stay where they are.

A Black Hand points his rifle.

• • •

For a moment, Alex doesn't know where she is. She can't hear anything, and her ears are raw from the pain. Her senses are going haywire. So many of her perceptions are new and hypersensitive, the overload shutting down her brain, keeping her from grasping a bigger picture. She is pretty sure her eardrums have burst. Her skin feels silky-numb. She can feel, faintly, the blood running down the side of her face and down her neck. She opens her eyes, but what she sees doesn't make sense. She *can* see, but everything is blurred, like a watercolor painting. She is surrounded by flickering lights, but they are all outside some veil that blurs the surroundings into a suggestion of shapes, everything tinged green. It occurs to her that if the world is outside this veil, she is somehow within it. The veil is like creased paper, the creases in a predictable hexagonal pattern like honey-comb but as if the patterns were pressed onto a thin membrane of skin. Next to her, something is breathing, slow and labored. No, not next to her. Around her.

Once Alex is aware of the creature, she can finally see one large eye staring back at her, bright and deep, reflecting the circle of fire beyond the veil. But before she can process what's happening, the eye shifts away from her, and a massive, clawed hand quickly grips her around her right shoulder. She feels the violent pull before her feet leave the ground; bits of rubble fly past her, and then she is out of the burning building, hover-ing above the street below. Dragon's wings are flapping slowly, parachuting them down to the street. Alex can't see the large eye anymore. Instead, just the boy, sporting the three-taloned hand that holds her, and the too-large wings keeping them aloft.

Dragon drops her as soon as he gets close enough to the ground, and then he folds into himself, falling next to her, stumbling only a little. He looks around, taking stock of his surroundings. Alex is still too disoriented to fall back into her training. She tries pulling herself to her feet but can't. Absently, Dragon reaches out a hand and pulls her up.

"Tez?" Alex asks.

She can't hear a thing but sees Dragon shake his head. "Kwame is gone too." Anguish creases the boy's face, but the moment is interrupted by someone screaming. Dragon pulls Alex by the hand into an alleyway. From there, they watch the ball of flames that was the community center. The explosion has chewed a chunk out of the corner of the building. The confer-ence room has collapsed, along with much of the second and third floors. The rest of the building has caught fire. People are rushing outside. But there are some people above the explosion who are trying to leap from the windows. Alex looks away as one man makes the jump.

On the street, people are everywhere. Some stand in the alleyways or on sidewalks watching the fire. No one wants to get close. They are sensing another kind of heat. This fire is the epicenter of something more, the oracle of future danger ringing its bell.

Some of these people work in the community center and have managed an escape in the important moments just after the explosion, when people can still get out. Those lucky ones—and *lucky* is a simple word that tells nothing of the pain and trauma they will feel later when the shock wears off—watch the devastation in stunned relief. And guilt. Not everyone has made it out.

So far, there is no echo of sirens blaring through the city. The police response is unusually slow. Several blocks away from the community center, from Alex and Dragon, two officers in plain clothes stand on the sidewalks and watch members of the Black Hand smash cars with baseball bats. One wears a pin: the name of a woman killed three years ago, crushed under the weight of Sarah's paws. He won't participate, he tells himself, and up until this point he has considered the possibility that he might intervene. But he won't; he cannot intervene. He knows what the monsters can do, knows they have to kill all of them to be safe.

It is cold out, a gentle snow starting to fall on cars, buildings, black gloves.

• • •

Sondra is there as the storm comes inland. The wind is so strong that the rain falls near-horizontal, fine pinpricks wetting her face and clothes. The wind is already lifting debris, whipping bits of trash and palm fiber through the air. The trees overhead bend in on themselves. Leaves are plucked from their branches and whisked up into the gray-green sky. Sondra holds herself tight and moves with her knees bent, trying to keep herself on the ground. Could the storm actually pick her up? Certainly not in her woo-woo form, but as a person? Very likely.

She descends the stairs, crosses the porch to the door, and opens it with the key already clutched in her hand. She can smell them before she sees them, mixed in with Matthew's sweat. She sees Matthew first, sitting on the living-room couch, hunched in on himself. She keeps her eyes on Matthew as she rushes to him, using her other senses to place the two men. One is leaning against a cupboard in the kitchen, the other standing in the dining room, gun pointed at her.

She reaches Matthew and stoops to one knee. "You okay?"

"They say they're here for you."

Sondra has a moment of relief then. She can take care of herself better than Matthew can, especially right now, in the midst of a storm.

"All right," she says to the two men, "what do you want?"

"Capture or death, whichever come easiest," says the bigger one. His voice is like sandpaper. "Capture better for our plans."

Only at that moment does she finally look at them with her eyes. They're both masked, which isn't a surprise, but they also are both wearing a glove on their right hand. The Black Hand? Here? These men are definitely local. She figured the human-supremacist group had made it to the island, but this is the first time she's seen anyone wearing a black glove.

"Capture is fine with me," she says. She'll wait until she's outside with them in the storm.

"No," Matthew says. One word, but the force of the word, the absence of fear, makes Sondra look to him again. "I've been having a dream," he says, and he is nodding as if that were sufficient explanation. To the two men, he says, "I'm not letting you take her."

Neither man speaks. But the one in the dining room shifts his body, moving his weight over to the other side, and shrugs. He re-aims his gun. And even though Sondra is sitting right next to him—and even though time slows in that moment, and Sondra tries to move between the man and the love of her life—the bullet seems to curve around her and into Matthew's head.

Sondra watches the life leave Matthew. Too quickly for his shock to fade to anything else. Not even time for a last word.

"Baby," she says, but it is already too late.

"Now, where were we?"

It isn't a decision. Sondra is falling, was falling from the moment the bullet left the chamber. The tile beneath her cracks under her new weight. She looks at them, the blood burning in her face, her pupils fiery gold. She should have come in like this. She should have trusted the part of herself that is useful.

The man who killed her husband understands. And the other one, also armed, stops leaning and pulls his gun from his waistband.

Sondra flips the living-room table with one hand, and it goes spinning into the first man. A bullet ricochets off the walls. He doesn't see her change, but the other one does, and he lets out an involuntary yelp of surprise.

In a storm, a woo-woo can change its size as well as its mass.

The tiles continue to crack beneath her, protesting her increased weight. The shreds of her clothing fall away. The regret is fire in Sondra's lungs, steaming from her nostrils as she charges forward. Everything folds around her as she cuts through the standing bar, the furniture, anything in her way. This isn't—could never be—an equal fight. The woo-woo punches through the man who killed the love of her life. His body stretches around the point of impact, and suddenly, terribly, he is everywhere all at once. Bits of him paint the walls. He is dead in a fraction of a second.

The other has time to fire once more. Sondra lets the bullet cut through her without slowing. She is there before he can get out another shot. She bites down on his entire head, rips it from his body, spits out the crushed remains.

This isn't enough. Unsatisfied, she goes for the cabinets and the fridge and the stove, turning everything into splinters and crumpled metal. Then she returns to the second man, but there isn't enough of him to quell her rage. Her animal mind thinks to go from house to house until she is satisfied, and not even that chilling thought brings her back to herself. No, it is Matthew who finally wakes Sondra's sane mind. During the violence, he has slid to the floor, the couch broken behind him. Besides the bullet to the head, he is whole and seems almost peaceful, but she remembers he is dead, and he is hers, and this is enough to allow her to crawl back down into herself.

The shift back stings, but it is fast. She crawls to him and puts her arms around Matthew, holds him there.

Outside, the hurricane continues uninterrupted. The force of the wind pushes through tiny creases and gaps in the house, playing against the architecture like an instrument. The sound of it is like a sustained scream. When Sondra was young, she used to think it sounded like an angry spirit. Now she can hear the note of something else, and it revises all her memories at once. All hurricanes are grieving ghosts.

There is nowhere else for her rage to go, so she transmutes it into despair. Her cries mix with the grieving spirit outside her door, and they form a harmony too painful to listen to.

I know she can't see me or hear me, but I stay anyway so that she isn't alone.

33

How long is she sitting there with Matthew's body? Feels like hours, though it might be only minutes. Nothing to do and nowhere to go.

Sondra's eyes are closed, focused inward on Matthew, trying to plead life back into his cooling flesh.

The miracle doesn't come, but something else does. The sound of tiny insect legs on the wall behind her. She opens her eyes when the abdomens of the machine ants start to glow, and the portal opens.

Laina sees it first, the ants forming the portal around them, and then, just as a barrage of automatic gunfire erupts, they fall down through the hole in the world.

Alex and Dragon are walking down the street to find Alex's car, Alex in a smudged white T-shirt and jeans, Dragon in an

WE ARE THE CRISIS   305

overlong coat and nothing else. The car is only a few blocks
away from the community center, but they walk slowly, trying
to appear calm and purposeful as Black Hand and civilians—
impossible to differentiate now—break store windows and loot
the interiors. Somehow the attack has fueled a riot, or perhaps
it was already happening before the explosion. Alex isn't sure.
Dragon's mind is elsewhere. He is thinking about Tez and
Kwame. He is thinking about the Wallaces. He is thinking
about Smoke, expecting him to appear any second. If he was
so close all this time, why didn't he find Dragon? The hex that
Damsel cast on Dragon not only obscured his appearance but
also dampened people's memory of him when they weren't in
his presence. The effect seemed less effective as people got to
know him. The Wallaces remembered him. Tez remembered
him. It seems to Dragon that the price of remembering him
is death. He looks at Alex, her eyes unfocused, ears bleeding,
and decides that even though he is angry with her for being
a spy, even though she is the daughter of the man who kept
him underground for all those years, he's going to protect her
anyway. He is going to make sure she doesn't die for remembering him.

They turn a corner and see the car parked there. Alex sees
that someone has broken the windows, punched one of the tires,
scratched and dented the exterior. A light snow dusting the roof
and no doubt blanketing the leather seats. *Damn it.* They won't
be able to get out of here in that wreck.

While Alex's attention is on the car, Dragon's is on the crowd
directly across from it. All of them are wearing gloves. And one
of them Dragon recognizes. His mind skips back to the checkout aisle at the bulk store, the man's creepy smile. He's wearing

it now as he lifts a gloved hand in their direction. They are close enough that Dragon can hear the man say, "Over there."

Dragon has bees in his ears. He can feel something in him shifting. What is it? How does he still not know himself, his own feelings? How is he still so unsure?

Alex doesn't hear the man's words, but as the man and his gang approach, she finally registers the threat. Still unsteady on her feet, Alex lumbers ahead to meet them. There is no exchange of words. When Alex meets the group, she swings at the first person, and it connects with such violence that the man is dead before he hits the ground. It isn't the man Dragon knows. That man has recalculated, has stepped back from the fight. Alex is dancing drunkenly amid the crowd, smashing one person and then another, graceful even while struggling not to topple over from the momentum of her punches. She is pummeling one man, and then she kicks another into a parked car. He slides down to the pavement as the car alarm blares into the night. She grabs another and, instead of hitting him, sinks her teeth into his neck. She releases him, the blood bright on her mouth and her shirt.

One of the stores on that side of the street is on fire, and the brightness of the flames distracts her for a moment. That's all it takes. Suddenly, Alex is hemmed in on all sides by assailants. She is swinging wildly. Pipes and bats and knives fall in on her until Dragon can't see where she is. He wants to help, but he is frozen, afraid of himself.

The man reaches him. "Were you the one who found them?" he asks. "Little monster boy."

Dragon steps back. He understands everything then: the long line from the checkout to here, and the space between, when this man killed the family Dragon was beginning to love.

"What kind of monster are you?" the man asks.

Dragon is dangerous. He is truly understanding this about himself, grasping the whole of the understanding—and, worse, accepting it.

"You're about to find out," Dragon says. He opens his mouth, too wide, and screams out a steady torrent of flame. The man catches, his whole body in flames, screaming and stumbling blindly. Dragon screams fire at the man until he stops moving, until he is nothing but charred remains. He turns and screams at the crowd, and they catch like a little forest of matchsticks. They scatter, their screams mixing with the sizzle and pop of their own bodies burning.

Alex is on the ground. One of her arms is twisted at a strange angle, but she gets up, untouched by fire. She walks through the flailing Black Hands to Dragon.

"My God," she says.

Dragon is crying. Because even though he wanted to do this, he already knows that he has lost something in himself that he can never get back.

"It's okay," Alex says. "Come here." And she hugs Dragon to her with her uninjured arm. "You're going to be okay now."

Alex is bleeding on Dragon, but he doesn't mind. And they are there for a little while before Alex says, "What the hell is that?"

In front of them on the street, the ants have already completed the circle before them. No, not a circle—a rectangle, like a doorway. Their abdomens start to glow, and the portal opens. The light slow-falls through the portal into the place below. Dragon can see some of what lies within that doorway in the street. The snow is a little heavier now, falling through to this other place with its walls and warm yellow light. And safety.

"Escape," Dragon says.

"What?" Alex is still having trouble hearing. Dragon's words come to her as a garble, as if she has cotton in her ears.

"Escape!" Dragon yells.

Alex is blinking at him. She's heard him this time; she just doesn't understand.

No one is on the street. They've been scared off by the violence that just happened, but Dragon spares a moment to wonder what anyone else might think, seeing this particularly strange bit of magic.

No time to linger. They should take this exit while it lasts. Dragon grabs Alex's hand. She protests, but he shifts one of his arms to provide extra strength as he hoists her up. With one leap, he's up in the air and falling down into the portal, Alex yelping in surprise. As they fall through, there's a moment when they stop. It's like those cartoons that Smoke let Dragon watch sometimes—the luckless coyote running off the edge of a cliff. The portal closes just as gravity rights itself. Alex has a sense of vertigo as they fall onto their backs.

It takes a moment for Dragon to understand what has happened. What he thought was the floor is actually a wall, the gravity of this place ninety degrees out of phase with where they just were. Dragon knows the term *out of phase* only because of his tutor. Who could have guessed it would come to be useful in this particular way?

Alex doesn't understand what has happened. She is still trying to process the fact that they've jumped through a portal. Who or what has the technology to manipulate matter? The thought is terrifying to her—even more terrifying than what might be beyond the door she can now see.

It's Dragon who gets up first, who trusts this new place enough to see what is behind the door. He expects someone will be there, but when he opens the door, what he finds is an expansive high-ceilinged room, and over a dozen people staring back at him. Dragon steps out, and Alex reluctantly follows.

They are the last to enter this place. The barn is large and welcoming—long tables in rows to one side, and an open kitchen in the far back on the other side. Before them is an open space surrounded on three sides by couches where the many (mostly) strangers are seated. It is a lot to take in, all the more so because of where Dragon and Alex have just been: from a horrific scene of burning buildings (and people) to this cozy . . . what? Dragon has no referent for this, but Alex thinks *recreation center.* A meeting place, but where? For who? For these people, obviously, but who are these people?

A list of those present:

1. Ridley, Laina, and Rebecca, and several other wolves from Rebecca's old pack. Ridley appears to be injured, a bloody swath of gauze wrapped around his midsection.

2. Several complete strangers, monsters from other places and unknown to any of the Boston contingent.

3. A woman covered in a large blanket. Dragon recognizes her. He tries to make eye contact, and her eyes do look in his direction, though he can tell she isn't staring at him, but merely *through* him. He feels a sadness he doesn't know what to do about. Vaguely, he understands that something is

wrong with Sondra, but the look on her face isn't anything he recognizes. It's as if she has been hollowed out from the inside.

4. In the kitchen in the back, a man with one hand, the limb missing up to the forearm, wrinkled dark flesh at the end of the limb—an old burn scar. (Dragon sees him and experiences a complicated series of emotions. The man recognizes him too. His expression is less ambiguous. Harry does not like seeing Dragon here.)

5. Someone Alex recognizes from many years ago, from before she started at the CIA.

"It has been a long time," says Georgie. "My aunt told me you reached out."

"I did," Alex says. "What the hell is this place?"

"Moon," says someone neither of them knows. Dragon and Alex both stare at him. "Sorry, lots of introductions to be made. I'm Connor. I was just explaining the situation to the other arrivals. Now, where was I? Right. Let me begin again with the strangest thing: how you were transported here. Well, we all came here that way. I try not to think about it too much, or it hurts my brain. I was one of the first to arrive. When I got here, the ants told me to make myself at home. Yeah, I can't explain that part either. But they also told me that this place is a haven, that there are several more in North America, and dozens all over the world. This one is called Moon. Collectively, they are called the Commonwealth.

"That was then. Now newcomers hear it from us. We've been getting a lot of arrivals today. I believe I've said all this at least four times already."

Dragon and Alex both stare.

"Yeah, I know," Connor says. "It's a lot."

Ridley, Rebecca, and Laina are faring better. They still have the shell-shocked look of people who have survived a near brush with death, but beneath that, slowly coming to the surface, is relief and wide-eyed curiosity. Here they have found safety, and several questions that need answers. Manny, for his part, looks as if he wants to jump out of his skin. And no wonder—these people around him are not his people. They're all monsters. He may be okay with being around his sister—he knew her when she wasn't a werewolf—but he doesn't know any of these other . . . creatures.

"Moon is an intentional community," Georgie says. "A big one, the size of a town. Actually, it is a rebuilt township. Until just a few years ago, it was a ghost town—one of several that were acquired to create monster settlements. The ants explained this to us. Apparently, they built the town too; 'they' meaning the ants—assume I'm always talking about the ants."

Dragon is paying only partial attention. He keeps looking at Sondra, trying to find the woman he remembers. At the moment, she has become a little more animated. She appears to be sniffing the air, her eyes moving around the barn.

"How many people are here?" Ridley asks.

"Where are we?" Rebecca asks.

Connor shrugs. "We haven't been allowed to leave. This place is a secret."

Rebecca doesn't ask the obvious follow-up question: Why does it have to be secret? She knows why; they all know. What happened tonight will happen in other places, sooner or later. No, sooner. What's happening in Boston is going to happen everywhere. Instead, Rebecca asks, "How are you getting supplies?"

"Maybe we should table some of this talk," Georgie says. "Some of you are distressed and—"

"That's the weird part," Connor says, animated. "Little robots come through the portals. They look like boxes on wheels. And, get this, they ask us what we want. They bring our requests the next time they come. I asked for a box of painting brushes some weeks back, and they brought it back with them."

Ridley is experiencing déjà vu. It isn't the same barn the SEN Collective was attacked in, or the same people standing around them. But it is close enough.

"Well, I can tell you one thing you don't know," Ridley says. "The person who controls the ants is a tech mage. Their name is Melku, and they are a member of a secret monster society."

If the previous information caused a stir, Ridley's revelation is like an asteroid breaking through the atmosphere.

"Hold on," Connor says. "You'll have to unpack that for us."

"That's just about the extent of what I know. Well, I also know there's an opposing secret society called the Order of the—"

"Did you *really* think you could hide from me?" Sondra says. She doesn't say the words loudly, but everyone's attention shifts her way.

"I can smell you no matter what that witch does to you." And then suddenly, she is yelling, "Where are you going? Don't you dare!"

Sondra is up. She flings off her blanket, unabashed at her nakedness. "Goddamn you," she says, running toward the door that has just opened, the door Dragon and Alex entered through.

Her voice carries ahead of her: "Why didn't you save him? Why didn't you get there sooner? Answer me!"

Sondra can't cover the distance, but I can. I pull myself toward the doorway—as easy as any action I can do within the fractal sea—and I'm through the door just in time to see the portal open. Sonya is invisible, but I can feel the static of her voided mind right in front of me. I follow her through, Sondra's frustrated yell coming up behind us.

But still not quickly enough. The portal closes.

This other place is familiar. We are back in Melku's apartment in Somerville. Sonya walks down the bare hallway, past empty rooms, making her way through the living room. She is there and isn't, the very slight sound of footsteps, and a faint buzzing where her mind should be. No thoughts, only clear direction. Sonya has something to do.

Outside the apartment building, Sonya leaps into the air. In the chaos outside, no one sees the stray flash of fire. She is a fireball burning across heaven. And then maybe someone looks up curiously and wonders what she is, perhaps asking themselves if an asteroid would be the worst thing right now, given everything that has happened already. Get it all over with, this endless march toward ever greater calamities.

But soon she is high enough that no one would wonder. She is more there now, a halo of fire around a body still not there, hurtling through the sky.

She lands on a quiet road. It is still snowing, the fluffy flakes collecting on naked tree limbs. She walks along the road, fresh footprints appearing magically in the snow. Along the lonely stretch of road are four other houses. One has a single light on inside. These houses are not quaint. They are monsters themselves. Only significant wealth could afford them—the sort of money that leaves a trail of victims elsewhere.

Onward she goes, to the biggest house at the end of the road. Several minutes searching for an open window. One on the third floor yields to her prodding. She slips in.

Through a room with sheets over the furniture. Down an empty hall. Inside the manor, the rooms lie dark and unused. Most of the rooms Sonya passes are open, catching faint moonlight on the right side of the hall, the left side eating the remaining light in thick shadow. Down two flights of stairs until she is at ground level again. Two staircases wrapping around an archway that leads deeper into the house. A chandelier like a swollen uvula hanging from the ceiling. A short walk. A door opening down into a dark, swirling stairwell. A giant hall. And another stairwell, leading deeper down into the darkness.

There is life elsewhere in the house, but most of the place has been left alone, most of the staff gone on to more useful jobs. The manor, as it was known by the staff—or the Trapp Compound, as it is called by the Order of the Zsouvox, now the Cult of the Zsouvox—has stopped entertaining visitors since its last recruits, those poor souls who followed clues only to stumble into a spider's web during the early months of the Emergence. The staff, for the most part, have been let go. Those up above left with a good spot on their résumé, and stories of strange visitors that they never saw leave, a mysterious boy sitting in the sunroom, his smiling face always in a sunbeam, or the sense that the house is bottomless—a mouth that, if you weren't careful, might swallow you and you would fall down, down, down forever. The staff below are gone too, leaving with gaps in their memory, the meat above their wrists scooped out by "the forgetment." They would reach for memories to tell friends or family, and they would be unable to say a word about what their jobs were like or where they went on those nights when they returned inexplicably different. They don't remember the forgetment, but some of them do dream on occasion: the one perfect bite from their arm, and the fish tank the forgetment was held in turning an impossible bright red with their blood, the glowing eye of the eel staring up at them. They dream of their tongue sticking to the roof of their mouth, the taste of metal and lit matches.

Before, a servant of the house had to open the doors that led to the below. A master key was required. Now everything is open, and the house lies silent to the ear.

It isn't long before Sonya reaches the dungeon, which opens up to a row of cells—metal bars on either side of her, monsters lying in the shadows behind them. A dozen minds down here in dreams or looped thoughts, or near madness.

Cautiously now, Sonya walks along the uncaged center of this terrible dungeon. The smell of human waste reeking from each cage of misery. Two humans are among the monsters, but their minds are so frayed they could barely be called that anymore. One of the cells is open, and Sonya becomes activated by some unnamed urgency.

More monsters and more humans lie dormant in their barred cages. Some are sleeping, and as Sonya passes, those monsters don't stir, or else turn their face to the wall of their cell, instinctively hiding from the phantom presence making her way down the row. Others lie or sit on their mattresses, which are wedged up in a corner of their enclosure, right on the grimy floor. Flush toilets on the other side of these small rooms do little against the smell of biological waste. The ones who are awake, leaning against walls or lying on their cots, their eyes open and fixed on the ceiling, stir even less than the sleepers. They've gotten used to emptying themselves. There is only so long one can exist in such a place, letting their mind feed on their memories or their despair or their rage. Those things feed you only until they don't anymore. The empty comes eventually, and by the time it comes, there is nothing to do but embrace it.

At the end of the row, one of the two cells is lit. Sonya stops there and looks inside. Unlike the other cells, this one is furnished with a small couch and carpet. And lamps in each corner of the room, and a small enclosure where the toilet would be in the other cells. The woman, sitting in a chair beside a dresser with its own lamp, is inspecting her neck, where a line of neat stitching binds pale flesh. Her spiky hair is different now, pressed down and wet, a bathrobe around her body, one pale leg revealed all the way to the upper thigh.

She frowns at her stitching, passes her hand along the braided threads over and over. The light from her lamp spreads into the adjacent cell. It isn't clear when Sonya looks, but after a minute she opens the adjacent cell, breaking the lock easily.

The vampire turns her attention to the opened cell, watching with interest. A subtle smile visits her face and is gone.

In the dark is an animal. It is lanky, with matted fur, though it looks better than it did in the forest outside the Pennsylvania diner. Fresh wounds on its skin are sewn up and seem to be healing. It is quiet, but as Sonya enters, it starts sniffing the air and whining.

Sonya has not noticed that the floor of the animal's cell is covered in sand. She has been caught up in the moment, her footsteps drawing closer to the animal.

She speaks, not loudly. "Papa?"

The entire dungeon erupts in sobs, yelling, and deranged laughter. Someone is smacking something against their bars, and the wet, fleshy sound of it carries above all the noise.

Sonya steps forward once more. The animal whines loudly.

Behind her, black ash takes form. Lawrence, the creature trapped in animal form, keens desperately. Sonya understands too late, reacts too late—Smoke's arms are already around her, turning solid just as they wrap around her invisible body.

"Got you," Smoke says. And just as she yells out, they are both gone, Smoke's body returning to dust and then nothing.

The woman stands and glides to the bars of her cell. "Don't worry, *Papa*," she says. "I'm sure they'll take good care of her."

Lawrence, the woo-woo and the man trapped inside him, cries.

Beyond that dungeon is another dungeon with even stranger creatures: a frail witch, a woman with veined wings and claws for hands, a sleeping giant. And then stairs that lead up again into a large space, like the hall from before, but furnished with centuries-old paintings and ceremonial relics on altars, platforms along every wall, with a center pulpit that sits deep into the floor.

But in the front of the room, the platform is different. On a golden seat sits a child, or something in the shape of a child.

Three others are present, in the midst of a serious conversation.

"Why not end it now?" Twenty-Nine asks. He is the same pale man from years before, the gray hair at his temples styled two hundred years out of date. Before, he had a quiet, powerful voice, but in this context, speaking to this being before him, he chooses his words carefully, a tremor of fear betraying him as he speaks.

"I don't require your advice on what speed we should take," says the thing in the shape of a child. The Zsouvox, or one of them at least. Eyes the color of eggshell peer at Twenty-Nine. "Everything in its time."

"Our enemies are gaining in power."

"We have no enemies on this plane of existence."

"You should not scare him," says the third occupant of the room—a woman with gold knee-high boots and a burgundy cape that reaches down to her thighs. Her hair is braided back in a single plait.

"He is a believer," the Zsouvox says in a mocking tone.

Twenty-Nine keeps his face even, but his hands give him away. He is terrified and confused.

The caped woman moves, but Twenty-Nine's eyes do not follow. Where she once stood, Smoke appears, quiet and expressionless.

"Where is she?" Twenty-Nine asks.

"Fourteen talking to her," Smoke says. He looks mildly annoyed, but it blends well with his usual expression. No one seems to register it. There is the familiar buzz of static. All these minds are closed. Except for Twenty-Nine, but he is not worth my attention.

I stay in the dark hallway just to be safe. People with closed minds have noticed me before.

"Everything must align," the Zsouvox says. "Asha needs to crawl out of whatever hole she is in. And if I can obliterate Abyssia while I'm at it, I'll have the whole set. The Universe will be the final challenge. Once I'm whole, I can leave this black prison."

"The Universe," Twenty-Nine repeats. Almost a question,

but he doesn't know how to make the question useful. He stands there, stupefied.

"Yes," the Zsouvox says. "There is a thing below the world; did you not consider the thing that *is* the world?"

"And the thing above," says the woman.

The Zsouvox nods. "Many things."

The woman lets her eyes slowly drift over to the dark hallway where I'm standing. I go still out of hope that she hasn't seen me, but reach for the fractal sea all the same.

The woman lifts her hand—a lazy action. But everything that isn't me or her freezes in place. Even the Zsouvox stops moving.

This is my power. My mind empties of all thought. On instinct, I reach to stop time, and find the place that the power resides empty, spent.

"Progenitor," she says. "What a beautiful young man you were."

"What?" I let go of my hold on the fractal sea, or something pulls it free of me.

She floats over to me in that special way, folding space around her until the distance between us is gone. "A dangerous place for you to be. Every day, the Zsouvox gets stronger. This"—she gestures around them—"*trick* won't last forever."

"Do you have a contract?" I ask. It is the only thing I can think to ask.

"Your power," she says. "It has a gap. You can't see ahead in this universe, can you? If that's the case, there's not much I can tell you."

I shudder at her reply. She is right. This is the one universe besides my own where the future is blocked to me.

"You told me once that I would someday . . . that we would meet outside the stream of time," the caped woman says. "Is this the moment, Progenitor?"

She is smiling at me, and it is with a familiar warmth that terrifies me even more. I say nothing, trying to hide my emotions.

"Well, you can't answer me, can you? My past. Your future."

I don't reach for the sea; the waking world rushes up to meet me. I fall down into it, and a roiling ocean of galaxies and time takes me under.

35

When I return to my world, it is 10:00 p.m., though it has felt like an eternity since I fell asleep. In reality, it's been only four hours. I go out into the living room, and Brian is on the couch, watching TV.

"You've been in there a while," he says. "And don't take this the wrong way, but you look like shit. You okay, dude?"

No, I am not okay, but there's no way to explain my particular state of not-okayness to Brian. "You want to go out to Red Hook?" I ask.

He laughs, then sees I'm serious. "We about to party like schoolkids?"

"Just want to get out of the house. And Red Hook is bound to have some shit going on."

Nothing is, in fact, going on in Red Hook, but we find a bar up a flight of stairs with a pool table and a friendly bartender. Only five people are there when we arrive, and within an hour that number goes up and down until it lands back at the same value.

Brian and I are playing pool. Two women come over to the table and ask to play, and so we go a couple of rounds with them. The balls crash against each other, still audible as music blares from speakers mounted near the ceiling. From the open porch of the bar, noise travels up from the street below. A couple fighting. Why couldn't he leave things alone? Why couldn't she defend him?

At first I think I'm the only one hearing it, but one of the women says, "I don't know why people stay together if they don't like each other."

I think to say that they probably do like each other, just not at the moment. But the tone of the man's voice stops me from committing to the words.

"I don't know," Brian says. He has an easy shot lined up: five ball to three, corner pocket. "Aren't relationships about working through shit?" The three ball makes a satisfying sound as it falls into the pocket. Brian lines up another shot.

We're all watching, our pool cues serving as support beams in that classic pose, fingers clasped around the smooth wood.

The woman—Tracy?—has let go of the pretense for the discussion. "Relationships are a waste of time. Better just to hook up and keep it moving." She looks at me.

It has been a while since anyone even appeared interested in my direction, so I'm not sure if that's what is happening. "So, you like things casual?" I ask. The words sound false in my mouth.

"For now," she says. "If I'm ready for something serious, I'll go with it. But better to be with someone I actually like. Most of the time. And never dislike so much that I sound like those two down there."

I'm taking her in for the first time. She's in her thirties, I think. And she looks together. But she also looks tired in the way of someone who has been running a long time from something she hasn't acknowledged to herself. I try to imagine what I look like to her. Perhaps she sees in me some part of herself. What a romantic thought to have in a nearly empty bar.

"Nothing is perfect," I say. "I think fighting is how you find out if it's worth sticking around." I am not sure I believe this. It feels as though I'm just saying the words. It may be the passion of the couple below that has struck me, to feel so strongly about anything—even a thing that makes other people think you're being foolish.

Tracy—or maybe it's Lacey; I'm starting to doubt myself—watches me for a moment, and her lips curl ever so slightly. I can't tell if she thinks I'm silly or if I've just sealed the deal. Brian misses, and she runs the table—four balls and then the eight ball. She was good before, but getting better and better as she plays. Some people play pool better the drunker they get. I'm not that kind of person.

Brian gets a call and steps out onto the balcony, and when he returns, he leans in close to me as I'm lining up for the break.

"I'm going to head out. You okay to get home?"

"Wait, what?"

"Eve is down by Duffy's. I'm going to go home with her."

Had he told me about this woman before? He must have seen my incredulous expression, because he says, "Jesus, Cal. Do you listen to anything I tell you?"

"Hold up," I say. "Eve that graduated from high school two years after us? *That* Eve?"

He's smiling a little, but he's also shaking his head. "Where do you go?" he asks. "In that head of yours." He says to the two women, "It has been lovely to meet you two." He says to me, "Don't drink too much." And then he goes to the bartender to pay his tab.

In the minutes he is doing this, you can see that the other woman is a little disappointed. They whisper to each other, their voices inaudible under the music.

Tracy-Lacey looks at me, sees me looking at her looking at me. "Hey," she says. "We're going to head out too."

As all this happens, I break, managing to get zero balls into pockets.

She doesn't say anything after that, waiting for my response.

It feels as if I've shown up to a test I haven't studied for. "Okay," I say. "Was nice meeting you both."

She shakes her head. I've clearly said the wrong thing. "Sure," she says. I watch them go to the bartender to pay their tab, and it's as if time has skipped. Brian isn't there; somehow he slipped away without my noticing.

I spend a minute or two knocking random balls into pockets. It is easier when you don't have to follow the rules.

"You ready to square up?" the bartender says as I approach the bar.

"Can I have a Heineken?" I ask.

Only two people are in the bar now: me and an older white gentleman who has seen too many days in bars.

Wordlessly, the bartender passes me a Heineken.

I drink at the bar, looking at the muted television screen. *The Fresh Prince of Bel-Air* is playing. I've seen the episode before. I'm back in my apartment with Cory. He comes out of the bedroom and gets a glass of water from the fridge. In my memory, he is shirtless. But gone are the boxer days, when he was all muscle. Now he's skin and bones.

"You don't get tired of watching *Fresh Prince*," he says to me. Not a question.

I shrug. "Come watch with me."

"Nah, I good." He finishes his water in one gulp.

"Rinse that out," I say.

He chupses his teeth and places the glass in the sink, watching me the whole time.

It is one of those moments that I could have challenged him, confronted him the way Mom said I should have. But I don't want to upset the uneasy peace between us.

"You don't listen to nobody, huh?" I say with faux lightness in my voice. "Big man."

He laughs and goes back to his room.

It was just a cup in the sink. I left cups in the sink all the time. But was he trying to provoke me into a confrontation? He did a lot of little things back then. If I were firmer . . .

Some sort of embarrassment makes me finish my beer quickly, pay my tab, and leave the bar.

On the stairs, I am struck with a bout of vertigo, or more accurately, a sort of twinning effect I experienced during the early months of my power. A shadow of another self.

I start to drive home, winding along dimly lit streets. I have to blink away sleep twice. Am I really sleeping if I spend all my time dream-walking through other universes? Do I ever dream my own dreams? There is a cost to the way I've been living, I'm sure. A gradual untethering from my own reality, until . . . until—

327 WE ARE THE CRISIS

Some sensation catches me by the neck, and by instinct I look over to the passenger seat. There she is—the woman from before in her maroon cape and gold boots.

"You're slipping," she says, concern in her voice.

I look through the glass beyond her, and I can see that the world outside has stopped, though the blur of movement remains. The scene outside the car swirls like ink in water. I try to unstop time but find I can't.

"I initiated Stillness," she says, her voice bright as if she were talking to a child. "You can't undo it. You're not as strong as I am. Not right now, anyway."

I don't need to ask what she wants. She tells me.

"You know, I've been to a thousand worlds like yours. The quiet ones. And I mean quiet in the sense that nothing truly weird is happening here or will happen for a long time. Eventually, all realities get a little weird. You know what I've learned from all my travels? That there's always a level above, another stage with another cast of characters. Infinite ascension. We all are a little paranoid because of it: you, me, every living-thinking being. Our uncertainty makes us act like children—even the gods."

"You're going to tell me I'm playing a dangerous game, sticking my nose where I don't belong."

"Am I a hypocrite?" She laughs. There is a warmth to her expression that makes me want to trust her, but I don't. "I am going to tell you something you've probably heard before. The answers are not satisfying. But you'll have to seek them out anyway."

"You've definitely signed a contract," I say. "I recognize the condescension and the riddles. I'll tell you something too. I'm not in the mood for whatever this is."

"*Whatever this is*," the woman repeats, "is the destruction of this entire multiverse—and, eventually, everything else."

Her words can't fit in my head. "And you know this how?"

The woman smiles at me. "A historian is a witness to all time in all places—the ensoulers and the ensouled. If that sounds crazy, it won't forever."

"Always riddles with you people."

"Soon it will make *too much* sense," she says. "I can't stop what is about to happen. You shouldn't have driven home in this state. But I can promise you this: What you wish for, you will receive. And then you'll sound just like me. That is the price of knowledge."

On the way out of Red Hook, there's a very sharp bend in the road that has caused more than its share of accidents. Drive too fast or don't pay enough attention, and you're likely to reach that bend and be helpless to correct yourself. Had I passed it already? The fact that I am too tired, too buzzed, too bone-deep weary to remember . . . Comprehension hits me at once. Before I can respond, she unstops time. And it is already too late to do anything. As the car hurtles toward the bend, I remember Gina, and she is saying those words again to me, then and now.

There is no armor strong enough to save you. Nowhere—

ACKNOWLEDGMENTS

Here we are again.

A big thank-you to my usual conspirators:

My editor, Michael Carr, for saving my life this time around. For opening my manuscript and not running for the hills. Would not have made it if not for your careful eye and extreme patience.

Ananda Finwall, my copyeditor, who not only had my back on the line edits but reminded me of things I'd said in *No Gods, No Monsters* that I'd inexplicably forgotten.

My former agent, Nell Pierce, and my current agent, Kim-Mei Kirtland. Both wonderful people and incredibly generous with their time and guidance.

My Blackstone family, who has grown over the years, and who has continued to support me and give me grace when I've needed it. Especially this time around. Boy, were they patient.

Kathryn G. English, for designing another incredible cover. I mean, look at it.

My crew at Many Worlds, particularly Josh Eure, M. Darusha Wehm, Craig Lincoln, and Ben Murphy. For being supportive and for giving me time when I needed to finish this book. We got some work of our own ahead of us, but I'm grateful for the ride so far.

My Cambridge Friends writing group. For listening to me panic for two years straight. Somehow you remained compassionate, which got me through a few hard times.

My fellow Cryptids from the Clock Tower. For continuing to be early and enthusiastic readers of my work. And for just being awesome weirdos and kindred spirits.

I didn't interview many people this time around, but I did read a lot of books. The big ones:

Life Undercover: Coming of Age in the CIA by Amaryllis Fox, which helped me fill out so much of Alexandra Trapp's background.

Wormwood Star: The Magickal Life of Marjorie Cameron by Spencer Kansa. I took major liberties with Cameron's life, which are entirely on me, but this book was a foundation.

The Assassination of Fred Hampton: How the FBI and the Chicago Police Murdered a Black Panther by Jeffrey Haas and *Black against Empire: The History and Politics of the Black Panther Party* by Joshua Bloom and Waldo E. Martin Jr. These books were a huge help with filling in Tez, the Wanderer's background details—I wish more could've made it into this book—as well as offered inspiration for developing New Era's food program. If you know, you know.

The work of Jessica Gordon Nembhard, which continues to be an inspiration. *Collective Courage: A History of African American Cooperative Economic Thought and Practice* is a must-have for any person's library.

More people to thank for being who they are:

The members of Grassroots Economic Organizing.

My La Roche Writers' Center crew.

My friends at the North Island Workshop.

My friends, students, and colleagues at North Carolina State University.

All my people at Clarion West (Team Arsenic for life!).

All my writing friends and peers who have encouraged me over these years. And the genre and literary organizations that poured love on *No Gods, No Monsters*. My gratitude is endless.

My mother, sister, brother, and my whole extended family. For being the first to believe in me and for continuing to hype me up every chance they get. Mom, I love you.

My best friend, Elliot. We've had some tough times these past few years, but we continue to be in each other's corner. I am so proud of him (my boy is putting out work!). I'm so grateful for all our conversations about movies, TV shows, and writing.

All my friends for their support and guidance, but most of all for their love.

To anyone I might've missed or can't mention by name (I'm thinking of my therapist in particular).

To my new and returning readers. This one was a long time coming. Thank you for your patience and enthusiasm. I hope this one is less confusing (things are coming together, promise!).

My wife, *Doctor* Anju. For her heart, her laugh, her incredible mind. For telling me to stop confusing readers when I needed to hear it. For being my home, my rock, my biggest supporter. But also for saying, "Oh, that's cool," when I come to her with my latest "exciting news." With you, it is impossible to get a big-big head. Without you, none of this would be possible.